Secrets
of Castle Creet

MEAGAN HOLLINGSWORTH

Copyright © 2022 Meagan Hollingsworth
All rights reserved
First Edition

Fulton Books
Meadville, PA

Published by Fulton Books 2022

ISBN 979-8-88505-379-2 (paperback)
ISBN 979-8-88505-380-8 (digital)

Printed in the United States of America

It was beautiful, partially hidden behind the draping green willow trees. Ivy had begun to slowly climb up the sides of the solid gray brick. There was a small stone and wooden well standing in the front and a marvelous stone path that led all the way to the front door. There were three glass pane windows to the right and one large one above the door, giving the old place a face and identity. It was old but didn't show its age. There were nicely placed stones encompassing the outer sides of the castle, building and building into the sky. The structure, the backbone of the building, was still standing perfectly. It was beautifully made up and arranged just enough to picture what it once was. A closer glance revealed a sign hanging off to the right of the red wooden door, "Castle Creet."

The sound of birds chirping in the background gave a sense of life upon the area, and wild lilies grew in the deepness of the woods close by. Somewhere in the distance, the sound of a small stream could be heard. The wind blew softly, and the clean, fresh scent of the open air was pleasant to inhale.

Part 1

Chapter 1

"I've been dying for an international vacation," said Carla as she was running the treadmill at her local gym just down the street from her house in Boise, Idaho.

She wore AirPods in her ears and wasn't worried about anyone around her hearing her conversation or observing her workout that afternoon.

"I just feel tired of the same old same. I need a bigger getaway." She breathed out and took a deep breath in, looking at the time on her treadmill. There were five minutes left of this exhausting run. She had always had a love-hate relationship with running. Sometimes it was her escape, and sometimes it was just work. Today, it was the latter.

"Yes, I know. I just got back from New York… I want something overseas. Somewhere people go and always come back, talking about how it was the trip of a lifetime," she huffed.

Carla had just gotten back from visiting her brother in New York City. A short trip. Just long enough to catch up with him and his family and see her new niece, born three weeks earlier. It was a nice trip and a good visit, but it was not the vacation she was yearning for.

Carla had never traveled outside America and had never had the desire until recently. She always felt as if there was enough to explore around here that would keep her occupied for her life. She had always wanted to see the Grand Canyon, Mount Rushmore, Yosemite, and Yellowstone, but at this particular time, it was like those places weren't enough. She wanted to learn new cultures and

3

lifestyles. She wanted to go exploring across the oceans, across different countries. Where? She didn't know yet.

Interestingly enough, even though Carla had never wanted to travel outside her own country, she had always kept her passport current. Whether she used it or not, she wanted one just to say she did. It made her feel sophisticated and professional. Perhaps she would need it one day if she ever needed to flee the country in a hurry.

"Nate won't care. He'll probably want to go," Carla said as she hit the Stop button on the treadmill. Her feet started slowing, and she was finally able to step off. She walked over and grabbed her towel while she downed a quick sip of water.

"No, I feel like he is so back and forth. He can't make up his mind, and it drives me crazy. Even last night, he said he wanted to read a new book but couldn't decide among the three he had picked out from the library. I said the one on the right looked good. Of course he still couldn't decide… Maybe I just need a girl's vacation. What do you have going on in the next couple weeks? Want to take a trip?" Carla said to her friend on the phone.

"Okay, I'll see you in a few minutes. I'm going to go shower." She shut off her phone and pulled out her AirPods, tossing them on top of her backpack near the locker she had picked that day.

Carla had made up her mind that she and her best friend, Adria, were going to take a trip. They could both use a break. She from her boyfriend, Nate, and Adria because she had lost her husband last year in a motorcycle accident. She would meet Adria at work in a few minutes, and they could discuss places they would like to visit.

Carla finished her shower, put on some cute, casual clothes and headed to the coffee shop she and Adria opened together three years ago, High Desert Coffee. Carla must have arrived just minutes after Adria because the door to her Honda Civic was still open in the parking lot.

Carla ran over to grab the rest of the coffee house merchandise out of Adria's car and gave the door a quick booty bump, shutting it behind her. She walked up to the coffee house door and gave it a light tap with her foot. Marcus came over quickly and opened the door for her.

Marcus was the first employee they hired to work at the coffeehouse. He was a twenty-one-year-old hard worker who was attending college at Boise State. He had gained the title of manager only one month after working there. Both Carla and Adria had been impressed with his timeliness, professionalism, and work ethic. Plus, his personality was friendly and inviting toward the customers and the other employees. He had been thrilled and accepted the position immediately.

"Thanks," Carla said as she hauled the big box up onto the counter.

"No problem. What should I do with this box?" Marcus asked, walking over and picking it up himself.

"Will you run it to my office desk?" Carla asked. "I'll put it away in a few minutes."

"I got you," Marcus said.

"Have you seen Adria?" Carla asked.

"Yeah, I think she is already back there," Marcus said, nodding toward the hallway where their office was located at the back.

Carla followed behind him and opened the door so he could place the box on her desk. Adria was on the phone and held her finger to her lips, so they both knew to be quiet.

"Must be important," Carla whispered to Marcus. "Fifteen minutes to open, Marcus. Make sure the first customer of the day gets his drink for free." She winked as she closed the door behind him, and he made his way back out to the main lobby.

Carla crossed over the new glamorous gold, tan, and white rug they had just ordered. Admiring it, she thought, *What a great find it has been.* And for Amazon, it was the perfect price and went pretty well in their newly renovated office. She sat down at her desk opposite Adria and tried to listen in on the end of her conversation.

A few minutes later, Adria hung up the phone and plopped down into her own swivel chair. She hung her head in her hands.

Silent for a few seconds, Carla drew in a heavy breath and asked, "Was it Carter's parents?"

Adria raised her head. Tears filled her eyes. "It's been a year. I miss him terribly, but every time his parents call to invite me to a family gathering, it just brings up so many emotions. I need to let him go, and the only way to do that is to let his family go too. I can't keep going over there like he is still with me."

Carla scooted closer to her friend and placed her arm around her shoulders. She remained quiet and let her friend feel her support and love.

"I don't want to forget him. I just need to be able to move forward," Adria said.

Carla and Adria had been friends since the seventh grade. Adria was the newbie who had just moved from California. Carla had been the one to make her feel welcomed. It was an instant friendship from the first "hi" at the cafeteria lunch table.

Carla had been there through everything that Adria went through and vice versa. They had been there to always offer support to each other, for the first boyfriends, the first breakups, high school graduation, college, Adria's wedding, and a horrible miscarriage. And Carter's death.

Adria too was there when Carla called her the morning after a drunken one night stand, the night Brian, her ex-boyfriend, slapped her across the face and everything in between. These two friends were inseparable. They were the sisters that neither of them had.

The clock struck 8:00 a.m. Adria sucked in a deep breath, stood up, straightened out her skirt, and said in a quiet yet confident voice, "Let's get to work."

Carla, always trying to make the mood lighter, said, "I know what would make you feel better...a trip. A getaway, a vacation. Somewhere far away."

"Like the one we were talking about, oh, I don't know...an hour ago?" Adria said, catching on. She tilted her head and raised one eyebrow.

"That's the one," Carla said, pointing her index finger at her friend. "It's like you can read my mind."

They both giggled and got busy pulling out High Desert Coffee shirts and other merchandise from their previous order. They needed to be sized, priced, and labeled before heading to the shelves in the front of the store.

After a few moments of silence, Carla asked Adria where she would want to go on this grand vacation she was concocting for them.

"I'm not sure," said Adria. "I don't think I can be too picky about this lovely vacation you are laying out for me. What about Hawaii?"

Carla wasn't sure. She had already been to Hawaii, and not that it wasn't beautiful, but Carla wanted something more. "How about Paris?" she almost shouted. "We could go to the Eiffel Tower. I've always wanted to climb all the way to the top."

"That would be fun, but we wouldn't be able to understand anyone. Do you speak French?"

Adria made a good point. Maybe they should visit somewhere they could understand the locals. It would also make it easier when checking into hotels, asking for directions, and ordering food.

"I'm going to think on it more tonight, and I'm sure I'll be picking your brain with more places tomorrow," Carla said as she stood up and grabbed a handful of shirts to be taken to the front. "Do you want a coffee while I'm going out there? I want to grab something before our zoom call with Mr. Carlson."

"Oh, shoot, I forgot about that," said Adria. "What time is that again?"

"Ten o'clock. I'm hoping they have everything in stock we need to order this time. Our milk and syrups are running low," Carla said as she opened the office door.

"Will you just grab me an Americano?" called Adria as Carla was halfway up the hallway. Carla nodded to acknowledge that she had heard Adria's order.

*****

Carla made a few greetings to the customers sitting in the shop. She asked Mrs. Kelly how her day was going and asked Mr. Andrews if his dog was feeling better. Carla really felt like this coffee shop had become her second home, and she loved seeing new faces and meeting new people.

She loved everything about being here. The people, the laughter, the coffee smell, the way they had decorated it just three short years ago, and she loved that it belonged to her. It was something she created that had become her own.

It had always been a dream for Carla to own her own business. When she graduated from Treasure Valley Community College, she knew she wanted something that was upbeat, and she wanted to provide something that everyone loved. Those who didn't love coffee could choose between the teas, Italian sodas, and pastries that the shop provided. Besides just the menu, she wanted it to be a place where people could come and feel comfortable, a family place.

The idea had come to her one day while she was running on the treadmill, like a lightbulb that pops into most people's heads when they have just come up with the best idea of the twenty-first century. She knew she couldn't do it alone, and she knew she didn't want to do it alone. She had to bring it up to her best friend.

It took Adria a long while to agree. Adria was more reserved and had more questions and concerns. "This is Boise we are talking about. It's overpopulated with coffee shops. Everywhere you look, there is one. Drive two more miles and there is another one."

Carla could see her friend's point but insisted their coffee shop would be one of a kind. They offered free drinks for birthdays and punch cards for their loyal customers, but they also gave back to local charities and did clothing and food drives.

They both had saved up a little money, and after having a meeting with their bank, they were approved for a loan. They had decided to give it a whirl. They purchased an old, rundown building close enough to campus that they could employ college students and grab their attention when they needed a midday pick-me-up. They also wanted to provide a separate room so their more corporate customers would have a place to hold meetings.

They decorated with modern bar seating and eight concrete tables with steel chairs. There were pops of yellow colors and a small gold couch in the corner, just big enough to hold a cute couple or a small group of friends.

One thing Carla was persistent on was having a wall garden. She loved greenery and wanted a little bit of outside to be captured inside. There were succulents and ferns covering the floor-to-ceiling display and a small rock fountain sitting at the base of the wall. Everyone marveled at it anytime they walked by.

Carla loved to sit and watch the customers' expressions and wide-eyed grins as they saw it for the first time too. It was right inside, just as you opened the front door. It was definitely built to give a great first impression.

*****

The two were luckily able to grab everything they needed on this order with Mr. Carlson. They made sure this time it was set up as a continuous order every week. They needed to make sure it was available every time when they placed their coffee supply order.

As they were ending their phone call with Mr. Carlson, Carla's phone rang in her pocket. She looked at the screen to see that it was her boyfriend, Nate. She didn't know if she wanted to talk to him. Their fights lately had really been getting on her nerves, and she couldn't shake the feeling that this relationship might not be working.

Before she could talk herself out of answering, she pushed the green button and said, "Hello."

"Hello," she said again. Ugh, another reason to be annoyed with him. It was a butt dial.

"I don't know if this is going to work," Carla said to Adria.

There was a pause of Adria just looking at her, a "trying to figure out what she was talking about" look. But before Adria could say anything, Carla changed the subject.

"I'm going to go down the road and grab some Pita Pit. Is there anything you want for lunch?" she asked.

"I packed my own salad but thanks," Adria said as she pushed in their filing cabinet drawer and headed back to her desk.

"Hey, didn't your brother visit Dublin, Ireland?" she said as she sat back down at her desk.

"He lived there for a year while he went to school. Why? What are you thinking?" Carla said with a curious look on her face.

"Maybe we could go there. I have very distant family there. It wouldn't be a totally random place, and your brother could give us some insight on places to stay and visit," replied Adria. Just then, she heard a voice in the back of her mind, like someone was saying, "Go."

Thinking to herself that it might not be a bad idea, Carla replied, "I'll ask him what he thinks when I get home this evening… I'll be back in a few minutes. Are you sure you don't want anything?"

Adria nodded and dug out her notes from their Zoom call earlier.

On Carla's way to Pita Pit, she realized it really was the perfect place to visit. Adria had distant relatives, Carla's brother had firsthand insight, and they could learn so much history while being there.

It was almost as if her mind was made up before she could make the call to her brother.

*****

That night, Carla hit the dial button on her phone to call her brother, Jacob. *What would he think if I wanted to visit Dublin, a place I had no interest in visiting while he was actually living there?* she thought as she counted how many rings.

It rang only a few times, and then her brother answered on the other line.

When Carla had finished telling him what had been going on with Nate, her conversation with Adria, and the need to get out of dodge, it was silent for a few moments before he finally spoke.

"I understand where you are coming from, but if it's that big of a deal, then why don't you just break it off with Nate?" Jacob asked.

"Because I don't know if that's really what I want to do. I'm confused," Carla replied. "I do love him. We've been together for almost two years. We live together. We have a life together. I just figured I could use some time to really think about where this is going."

"So Dublin, huh?" He changed the subject. "Couldn't come visit me while I was actually living there, but now, you want to grow up and go check out the world," he said sarcastically.

Carla cleared her throat. "Excuse me, in case you've forgotten, I am thirty-two years old. I would say I'm pretty grown up. I'm just ready to check out a new adventure. You know, like you were when you randomly decided to go to school in a different country," she teased.

"Okay, well, if that is what you want, I will get you the number of my friend, Miriam. She owns a little Airbnb, and you could see if she has availability when you want to go," he said. "When *do* you want to go?"

"As soon as possible," she basically shouted.

"Well, I will text her number to you when we get off the phone, and you can give her a call. Oh, and just so you know, there is a seven-hour time difference, so please make sure you don't call her right now. I'm sure she wouldn't have a place for you to stay if you woke her up at two o'clock in the morning." He laughed, and they said their goodbyes ending the phone call.

Carla calculated that if she called this "friend" in the morning, it would be around the time she would be getting off work, Dublin time. Carla just had to remember to actually make the call.

She was so excited she could barely sleep that night. *This is going to be the best adventure. Random and out of the blue for sure, but maybe this is exactly what I need to get my mind off the present,* she thought.

When would she tell Nate?

Chapter 2

The alarm clock started ringing at 6:30 a.m., that automatic jingle that annoyingly gets stuck in your head. Carla rolled over to hit Snooze and tucked her head under her pillow, pulling both ends down over her ears. She couldn't stand waking up to alarm clocks. It shook her, scared her, and always made her instantly mad for a few minutes. She could hear the shower water running and knew that Nate was already up and getting ready.

Nate was a pediatrician, one of the things about him she'd fallen in love with. He loved kids. He wanted to help kids. He wanted to have kids. But being a pediatrician always kept him busy, and it had left little time for them to be able to discuss any of that or any of their future plans they might have. *One of the reasons*, she thought, *this might not be working*.

Nate and Carla had met at a local grocery store, one of those that you would call a *meet-cute*. They both reached for the same package of double-stuffed Oreos at the same time. It had been the last package on the shelf. They gently touched hands, but she had pulled away suddenly. He apologized but took the Oreos anyway and turned to put them in his cart.

She had been shocked and was thinking how extremely rude and ungentlemanly this man was. She was about to open her mouth to say something when he turned back with a big smile on his face and said, "Just kidding." He started to chuckle, and he reached over to put the Oreos in her own basket.

She remembered thinking he had a cute laugh. In turn, she had started to laugh too. She told him she was making Oreo truffles, and the recipe specifically called for double stuffed. The regular Oreos simply would not do. Their conversation continued for a few minutes, and the attraction began to grow. He had asked if she wanted to go for coffee. Normally, she would have said no, but something had changed her mind. And that had been the start of it.

Carla and Nate dated for six months and eventually decided to move in together. They had fallen for each other fast, and after just a few dates, Nate had said, "I love you." She felt the same, and they agreed they were both ready for the next step in their lives. They, after all, knew they wanted to get married.

It was just recently that Carla had been having second thoughts.

*****

Carla walked into the back of the office of High Desert Coffee and found Adria in a downward dog yoga position. Her thin pink mat was laid out across the rug they had recently purchased.

"Do I need to ask?" Carla said with a slight laugh.

"I didn't have time to do my yoga this morning, and I thought this would be the perfect place to get it in before the doors open," replied Adria with an upside-down smile.

"Got ya. Well, you almost finished?" Carla asked. "I've got some news about our trip."

"Shoot," said Adria, "I'm listening."

"Well, I talked to my brother last night, and he gave me the information of one of his friends in Dublin. She owns an Airbnb. I want to call this morning if you're really up for this," said Carla.

"Yeah. I'm all in. Let's do it," she said as she flipped over and sat in crisscross applesauce.

"Ahh, this is going to be so exciting," said Carla excitedly. "What do you think it's going to be like? What are we going to do? Where do we want to visit first? I definitely want to visit some old antique stores. Can you imagine what it would be like to bring home some antiques from the Irish culture and history?"

The questions just kept coming until finally Adria butted in, "Have you told Nate yet?"

Carla stood there with a blank face.

"I will take that as a no," Adria said. "What do you think he will say? This is going to be so out of the blue for you to just spring on him. Have you guys talked about how you've been feeling lately?"

"I can't talk to him about my feelings right now. He has been so busy with training the residents he has at the clinic. It's like everything I say goes in one ear and out the other. I doubt he'll even miss me," Carla said.

"Well, I don't think that's true or fair," exclaimed Adria. "He loves you."

"He has an odd way of showing it," Carla said, rolling her eyes.

"Even so, you have to talk to him about it sometime," Adria said, trying to be encouraging.

"I will… I'll call him when he is on his lunch break. I guess my call to Miriam will have to wait until I get this conversation over with Nate," said Carla.

"Don't you think that's a better idea anyway? I mean you can't just disappear and not say anything to him," Adria explained.

"Why not?" Carla said sarcastically. Adria gave her a look.

"Okay, you're right." Carla was trying not to get impatient. She started digging through her purse and realized her cell phone was not in there. She walked over to her computer bag, opening the top, and saw that it was not there either. "Well, I guess I need to run home. I forgot my phone. I'll be back in twenty minutes."

"Would you mind stopping at the post office and grabbing some stamps?" Adria asked. "I thought I just bought some, but I can't find them anywhere."

"Okay, then I'll be back in thirty-five minutes," Carla said as she headed out the door.

*****

Carla was waiting in the line at the post office, seven people ahead of her, all with a package under their arms. She wondered if it would have been better to just grab some stamps at the local grocery store.

Her phone rang, and she looked up at the screen. It was Nate. *Great time to call*, she thought, *but not exactly the greatest place to have this conversation. I'll have to call him back,* and she pushed the End button.

Her phone buzzed as a text came in from Nate. "Call me," it read.

Another buzz. "Where are you?" It was from Adria.

Good grief, thought Carla. *This day is getting busy.*

Carla hit Adria's text and replied, "I'm still at the post office. This place is crazy busy."

She backed out of her messages and went to reply to Nate, but her fingers could not put words together. She left the text alone and put her phone in the back pocket of her pants.

She walked up to the counter, finally her turn to grab a simple book of stamps. "Can I grab two books of stamps, please?" she said.

The worker behind the desk gave her what she needed. She paid for the stamps and grabbed them from the counter before walking out of the post office. She held the door for an elderly lady and waited until she was inside before she let go of the door and walked off toward her car.

"You'll have fun in Ireland," someone whispered from behind.

She turned around quickly, but no one was there. She looked right, left, and did a quick turn around a circle. There was no one even close to her. Carla was completely freaked out. The hair on the back of her neck stood up, and goosebumps covered her body. She hesitantly continued on to her car, and she sat there for a few minutes. *Who had said that?* she thought. *And where did they disappear to so quickly?*

Carla put her car in reverse, checked her mirrors and backed out of her parking place. She drove off and headed back to the coffee house, eager to tell Adria what had just happened.

She walked quickly past the front doors and went straight toward the back office. She practically blurted it out as soon as she entered the office door: "You won't believe what happened to me."

Adria stared at Carla waiting for her to continue.

"I was walking out of the post office, and someone behind told me I'll have a fun trip to Ireland. When I turned around, there was no one there. I have goosebumps just thinking about it again." She rolled up her sleeve and showed off the hair standing straight up on her arm.

"I got in my car and waited a few minutes to see if anyone would appear, but I didn't see anyone," Carla said.

"That is super weird," said Adria. "Did you recognize the voice?"

"It caught me so off guard," Carla said. "I didn't even have time to think about it. It was female, small, childish even—that's all I can remember."

"Well, obviously someone was pulling a prank on you. It's the only logical thing," Adria said as she moved over to show Carla something from her phone.

"Obviously, but I did not appreciate it, and no one even knows about this trip yet except us and my brother." Carla shook her feelings and decided to forget about it for now.

"What's that?" she asked.

Adria held up a picture. "My mom sent it to me last night. Isn't it beautiful? Which leads me to telling you that my mom knows about our trip too. I told her last night that we wanted to get away and take a break. She sent this to me this morning."

"Is that in Ireland?" Carla asked. Then she thought to herself, *Would Adria's mom play a trick on me like that?*

"It sure is. My great-great-great-grandmother lived there. My mom said this is where she lived when they got married," Adria explained, "and before you say anything about my mom, she is out of town for the day, so there is no way it could have been her at the post office."

"It's a castle?" Carla said, questioning her. "Your family used to live in a castle?"

"I thought it would be a fun place to visit when we are there. My mom said it has been abandoned for years. I'll have to do some more research on it when I get home tonight," said Adria.

"Why didn't you tell me this earlier? A freaking castle, your family lived in a castle." Carla couldn't get over it.

"I didn't even know they lived in a castle," Adria said.

"Well, I love it. Just another reason why Ireland was an excellent choice," Carla replied.

*****

"Nate, Adria and I have decided to take a trip in a couple weeks." Carla set her lemonade down on the kitchen table. "I think now would be a good time for us to think about our relationship. I think a trip would be good for me," she said as they were eating dinner together that night.

Nate sat for a moment in silence before he answered, "If that is what you think you need... I know things haven't been perfect for us. And I know my work is keeping me busy. Maybe you should go."

"I think this is exactly what I need. Then maybe I will have some answers about us," Carla said to Nate while looking down at her dinner plate. The Chinese food sat there getting cold while Carla poked and prodded at it.

"Carla, this might be coming at the perfect time," Nate interrupted her silent thoughts.

"What do you mean?" she said.

"I've been asked to speak at a pediatrics event overseas in two weeks. I wasn't going to accept it until I spoke to you, but now that you may be gone, I might as well take the opportunity," Nate said cautiously.

"Oh," was all Carla could muster.

Another opportunity Nate was going to take that would keep them away from each other. Apparently, Carla guessed she should feel content that he at least wasn't going to accept it until they talked it through, which usually meant he would take it anyway. If she hadn't been sure before, she was even more convinced that now was the perfect time to get away. Maybe things were just taking a certain path to show them they weren't right for each other like they had originally thought.

"I'll call the office and let them know I will be accepting the invitation. They will be paying for everything, so there won't be anything to worry about financially," Nate said. "What about your coffee shop?"

"Adria had a conversation with Marcus after work today to see if he'd like to tackle a little more for a couple weeks. She just texted and said he was happy and excited to take on more responsibility."

"Well, that's good news. You won't have to worry about it while you vacation," Nate replied.

"Yeah, it's in good hands with Marcus. I guess I'll start making arrangements in the morning. Jacob gave me the number of a friend in Dublin so we could stay at her Airbnb. I'll text you the number in case you need to get hold of me for any reason."

"Dublin?" Nate asked, almost spitting out his drink of Pepsi.

"Yes, Dublin. I'm not going to plan something small. I want to get out of this house, this town, this country," Carla started defensively. "Why can't…why shouldn't I go to Dublin?" she stuttered, not really looking for an answer.

"The convention I was asked to speak at is in Dublin," Nate said, not sure what else to add.

"Well, what are the odds?" Carla said sarcastically as she got up and took her food and glass over to sink. "What are the dates again?"

"I leave in two weeks, on Friday. Have you guys picked your dates yet?" Nate asked.

"I have to call Jacob's friend, so I guess it will be when she has availability. What was her name again?" She was asking herself as if to remember. "Um, Miriam, I think. I just sent you the number."

*****

Later before hopping into bed, Carla had a lot going through her mind. First, the creepy voice she heard earlier at the post office telling her she'd have a fun trip then turning to find no one standing there. And secondly, what were the odds that she was taking a trip to Dublin and that was exactly the same place Nate was going? What was life trying to tell her?

Carla read into things…a lot. She overthought; she obsessed over conversations and situations. She questioned everything. Her mind was racing. She couldn't shake the weird feeling and emotions bubbling up inside her. Was it adrenaline? Was it excitement? Was it doubt?

She decided to grab her journal and write down a few things before going to bed. She had always been a night owl, and staying up late was her alone time. A time for her to think and not be interrupted by Nate, phone calls, or anything about the coffee shop.

Dear Journal,

I'm so mixed with emotions. I'm so excited to go to Dublin, but now Nate is going too. I thought this trip would be about getting away and thinking about us. Thinking about our relationship and if this is going to work out. Now it's as if he's intruding on our trip even though the likelihood of me seeing him is slim. Ugh, why is this eating at me?

Adria's mom sent her a picture of an old family castle. She said she was going to look it up when she got home and see if she could find anything out about it. I hope she does. It looks intriguing. And I love what the history of this is and could be.

This will be the perfect place to visit and learn about. I wonder if...

Her thoughts were interrupted by a buzz from her phone, a text alert. She grabbed her phone and saw it was from Adria.

"There is a spooky story about the castle. It's called Castle Creet but was shut down due to a murder/suicide incident inside the castle," the text from Adria said.

Another text from Adria: "I've asked my mom to come up with family names and history. We may be on our way to solving a mystery. What an adventure this will be."

Carla could picture Adria clear as day excited and giddy with the thoughts of this thrilling vacation—now turning into a murder/mystery. It sent chills up Carla's spine. She decided that she would reply to the texts in the morning, and she went to climb into her comfy, warm bed.

Sleep would not come. She tossed and turned for several minutes, fluffed pillows, rearranged her positions, and then finally gave up. Lying on her side facing opposite Nate, she tried to will herself to sleep.

A few moments later, Nate placed his arm around Carla's waist, pulling her closer to him.

"Can't sleep?" he asked.

"Nope," Carla replied.

"I know things aren't perfect. But I want you to know that I love you," he whispered.

There were those words. Those soft-spoken words. The words that always made her go weak in the knees. The words that the first time Nate had said them to her, she had known she loved him too. Carla felt small butterflies fluttering inside her stomach. She closed her eyes as he continued to run his fingertips up and down her side.

He slowly slid his hand up the inside of Carla's shirt, stroking the top of her breasts. He pulled her shoulder toward him, rolling her to face him as he kissed her lips tenderly. Wrapping his arms around her and pulling her against him, he deepened his kiss.

Carla could not resist and let out a small moan. She couldn't help it. She loved his soft touch. She kissed him back, giving in to their passion. She wrapped her arms around him, continuing what he started.

That night they forgot their troubles, forgot the worries of their relationship. That night, they loved each other.

*****

Carla woke up to the sun, peeking through the curtains and shining in her eyes. She almost panicked before she remembered it was Wednesday, her day off. She rolled over rubbing her eyes and willing herself to fully wake. She needed to get up and make a cup of coffee. It always made her feel better when she had her morning coffee.

She pulled the blankets back and put her feet to the floor. Stretching out the morning stiffness, she stepped into her slippers and reached over to check her phone. On her nightstand was a small, yellow sticky note from Nate that read, "I loved last night. I love you."

She wrapped her robe around her body and headed for the kitchen. *Ugh, why? Why do I do this to myself? I let myself go. I give in too easily. Now he won't forget about it, and I won't hear the end of it,* she thought to herself out loud.

Carla punched the coffeepot back into the holder and hit the On button. Flipping through her text messages, she decided to reply to Adria's text from the night before.

"Looks like an adventure indeed. Did you get any sleep last night?" Carla knew the answer, but thought she would ask anyways.

"Good morning, sleepyhead. Glad you are finally awake. And no, my answer is no. I did not sleep last night. Too excited," came the text from Adria.

"I'm going to call Miriam in a few minutes. I'll let you know what she says," Carla texted back and set her phone down while she grabbed a coffee mug from the side cabinet. The smell of coffee was already making her feel better. She poured the black coffee into her cup and added a little cream.

Walking over to the window, she took a sip of coffee, letting the first of the creamy liquid seep into the very bones of her body. She closed her eyes and tried to forget last night.

Halfway through her cup, she began to think about all the things she needed to get done today. She and Adria would have to dust off their passports, buy plane tickets, gather money for their stay, and find food and transport.

Carla's mind wandered. *I'll finally get to use that passport of mine,* she thought. After a few minutes, she decided now would be a good time to call Miriam.

The phone rang three, four, five times before someone finally answered. The young woman had an Irish accent, and it almost threw her off before she remembered whom she was calling.

"Hello," came from the other end of the call.

"H-hi, is this Miriam?" Carla said. She didn't know why she was nervous.

"It is. Who is this?" Miriam asked.

"My name is Carla Murphey. I'm the sister of Jacob Murphey."

When there was no reply, she went on, "I don't know if you remember him, but he gave me your number and said that you owned an Airbnb that might be available for me and a friend to stay." It was a semi question and she was hoping Miriam would reply with good news.

"Aye, I remember Jacob fondly. And I do have an Airbnb. When are you wanting it for?" Miriam asked.

Miriam had a nice, soft voice. Her accent made her sound especially lovely. Carla could imagine her being very friendly. "I was hoping in a couple weeks you would have something available."

"Let me check." Carla could hear papers rustling in the background. "I have availability in two weeks come Saturday," said Miriam.

"Anything will work. Thank you," Carla said. "Do you have it available for a two-week stay?"

"Aye, I do but just shy of one day. Will that work?" Miriam had asked.

"That will work," Carla said.

"I'll write you down on the schedule," Miriam replied.

"Also, I was wondering if I could bother you with a question? Do you know anything about Castle Creet?" Carla had asked sheepishly.

"I have heard of it. But I don't know much. It's very old. I can see what I can find out and I can get back to you?" Miriam was asking.

"I would really appreciate it. I'm so glad you had availability with such short notice," replied Carla. "Do you need anything to secure my spot?"

"I'm glad too. If you can fax me a photo copy of your driver's license, that will do for now," Miriam finished, giving her the number to fax it to.

"Perfect. I will get that to you as soon as I can. Thank you so much," Carla said.

"I will talk to you later, and tell that brother of yours I said hi," Miriam said as she hung up the phone.

Carla didn't put down her phone but entered a text to Adria: "Get your passport ready, we're going to Ireland."

Chapter 3

It was Saturday afternoon, and Adria was headed to Carla's house. Adria's mother had been able to find out more information about her family ancestry. She had researched Adria's great-great-great-grandmother's name and a few little details about the castle known to them as Castle Creet. Adria had Irish heritage on her father's side, so it didn't take too long for her mother to get together some information for the two of them to go through.

Adria was getting excited to visit a new country. She had been to Mexico before, but she had never crossed an ocean. She was determined not to be nervous or anxious about the trip.

Besides, she was too consumed with all the information her mother had given her. She was excited to dig into the paper folder as soon as she arrived at Carla's for the evening.

Adria pulled up to Carla's little bungalow, rolled up her window, and grabbed her purse, folder, and keys. As she walked up the pathway, she saw that Carla had already opened the door for her.

"Hello?" Adria said as she knocked on the open door and walked right in.

"I'm in the kitchen. Do you want coffee or tea?" Carla replied from the next room over.

"I think we are going to need coffee for this," Adria exclaimed.

Carla walked out of the kitchen with two coffee mugs a few moments later. "Should we sit here at the coffee table, or would the dining table be better?"

"Maybe the dining table," Adria said, thinking. "I've got quite a few pages we can lay out."

They scooped up their things and made their way to the next room. Sitting next to each other, one at each corner, Adria began to pull some pages out of the folder her mother had provided.

"This is my great-great-great-grandmother, Mary Williams Gallagher," Adria said as she pulled out a black-and-white picture of a very beautiful young girl. "She had three brothers and one sister. She was somewhere in the middle. We haven't been able to narrow that down." On the back of the portrait, the year was smudged, but they thought they could make out *1884*.

"Do we know how old she is here?" Carla asked.

"I think my mother said she had to be around fourteen or fifteen," Adria was trying to remember. "What else do we know?" Carla could barely contain her excitement.

Adria pulled out another piece of paper that looked like an Irish marriage certificate.

She handed it to Carla. "She was married when she was seventeen to Henry Gallagher in 1887."

Adria pulled out another picture of both of them together. "They were a very handsome couple," she said. "They look so happy."

Mary was wearing what looked like a long, white dress with lace detail around the collar and hemline. It had longer, three quarter-length sleeves. She held a small, quaint bouquet of flowers in one hand and a small handheld fan in the other. She had a medium-sized brooch just at her collar.

Adria imagined the most beautiful colors of reds, whites, and blues circling around the gem. She wished that she could have seen the picture in color.

Henry was wearing slacks and an unbuttoned jacket. He stood half a foot taller than Mary, and her fingers were wrapped around the inside of his elbow. At first glance, neither of them wore a smile, but if you looked closer, it was almost as if you could see the softest smile from Mary.

"Look at this." Carla said abruptly. "She died in 1908. She was only thirty-eight when she died from unforeseen, unfortunate circumstances… She was close to our age."

Carla had a twinge of upsetting emotions rise in her body. The word *unforeseen* stuck in her head. It made her mind start wondering, *Aren't all deaths unforeseen, and did Mary's death have to with the murder/suicide at Castle Creet?*

"Adria, do you think she was murdered?" Carla said slowly as if reading Adria's mind.

Adria turned to her friend and gave her a slight shrug, trying to brush it off and place her mind elsewhere.

*****

The girls spent the afternoon unpacking the folder and reading everything over multiple times.

Carla would pull something out and show Adria. They would talk about it for a few minutes before one of them would find something else and they would start chatting about that.

Carla thought it was time they made an itinerary for their trip.

She pulled out a paper and jotted down a few notes. "Do we want to rent a car?"

"Yeah, I don't want to be waiting on someone every time we want to go somewhere," Adria responded.

"And you will be okay with driving on the opposite side of the car, on the opposite side of the road?" Carla said smiling, but she already knew what her answer would be.

"Oh, right. Well, maybe we will just find transportation while we are there," Adria finally said.

Carla pulled out her phone from the back pocket of her jeans and jotted something in the search bar. "Number one form of transportation in Dublin is buses. That should be fairly easy. Also, I'll call my bank and see about converting some of our money to euros," Carla said, getting up to go in the other room. She felt brilliant for having remembered about needing a different currency.

"Good thinking," Adria chimed in.

After a few minutes, Carla walked back in the room. "It shouldn't be a problem. I will go into the bank tomorrow to talk to someone, and it should only take one to three days to get it back, so that worked out wonderfully," she smiled.

Adria had grabbed her computer from her bag and had it sitting on the kitchen table. "I found flights last night. I wanted to run them by you before purchasing."

"All right, let's see what you got," Carla said. "Whew, I didn't realize that the travel was eighteen hours and thirty minutes, but I guess that makes sense, and this flight has two stops."

"Yep, that's what we are signing up for, but this one puts us there in the morning," she said, pointing to the computer screen. "So we have the whole day to do whatever we want, and hopefully, we can sleep on the plane."

"Sounds good to me. You should book them," Carla said.

After most of the planning had been done the girls decided to order take out and watch a movie. Rock, paper, scissors, best two out of three decides the winner. Adria won, so she got to pick the movie. She was feeling like something comical and picked *Jumanji: Welcome to the Jungle*.

The girls filled their tummies with Mexican, cracked open a bottle of wine, and giggled the night away.

*****

The next couple of days rolled on like normal. Get up, work out, head to work, go home, etc. Carla and Adria couldn't stop talking about their trip like giddy little schoolgirls.

It was a normal Tuesday morning when Adria danced her way into the coffee shop office.

"Why are you looking so chipper?" Carla said, not knowing if she really wanted to know the answer.

"My mom found a letter yesterday. Guess who wrote it?" Adria wanted Carla to know but had just enough patience to wait for her to guess a couple times.

"A relative? Carter?" Carla said, treading lightly.

"It is written by none other than the famous Mary Williams Gallagher."

Carla shoved papers out of the way and practically stumbled as she got up to go Adria's desk. "Show me, show me."

Adria handed the letter to Carla, and she started reading out loud.

> Dear Mother,
>
> My heart has broken into pieces. I feel as if I will never be whole again. The walls inside this place Henry still calls home are starting to suffocate me. Every time I am near him and that room, I feel so heavy. How did this happen? This is not a home. It's a dungeon. It's a reminder every day of what happened to my sweet Amelia.
>
> I want to come home. I don't want to live this life with him anymore. How do I keep going? Oh, Mother, please send for me. Until I see you again, keep this safe. The room is locked. Henry is making me send away the key. I will never enter again. No one will.
>
> Mary

"Look, Adria, there is an old weathered outline of something at the bottom of the page. What do you think it is?" Carla questioned.

"It's looks like a ring," Adria added.

"No, there are two of them. They look like they could be touching." *The room is locked,* Carla read again. "A key, it's a key. I bet you anything. That has to be what it was. She talks about it in her letter."

"My heart is skipping, Carla. I've never been this into my family heritage, but now all I want to know is what happened to the women of my past. How many more days until we leave?"

"Ten"—Carla added up on her fingers—"and it can't come soon enough." She was just as excited as Adria, and it wasn't even her family. She almost felt like she was in the middle of some television show solving a mystery or crime.

Adria called her mother to tell her the news that they think there was a key that went with the letter. She wanted to see if her mother knew anything about it or where it could be. Probably long gone, she knew, but it was worth a shot, and maybe her mother could look for it.

*****

Carla and Adria pulled up into a parking space at the mall. They had decided it was time to do a little shopping for their trip. They would need warmer clothes and a good rain jacket.

"These rain boots are super cute," Adria said as she looked them over, checking the size and the foot padding. She slipped them inside their cart.

"Do you need a new suitcase?" Carla called out from around the corner. "These ones are on sale."

"I have one from my last trip, but you should get one." Adria came around the corner. "That one is cute, and red is your favorite color. You shouldn't lose that at any airport."

"Right you are," Carla said in her best Irish accent.

She grabbed the red, slightly textured suitcase off the shelf and begin examining it. It was large and hard plastic on the outside, which she liked. She thought that plastic would hold up better and not get ripped or caught on anything. Plus she could clean it easier than a fabric suitcase.

She began rolling it around the store while she looked for warm socks, a cross-body bag, and some warmer clothes. "I'm going to look in the sock section," she told Adria as she rolled the suitcase in that direction.

"Grab me a longer pair if you find some. They'll go with my rain boots," Adria said.

Adria had found three neutral-colored sweaters and a bright-green microfiber plastic raincoat. She began searching around the store to see if there was another one, perhaps in a different color, she could grab for Carla. The inside didn't seem too warm, but she was hoping it would keep them dry and they could just layer up.

While walking up another aisle, Carla found some wool-lined leggings she thought would be perfect for whatever Irish weather they encountered. And they were black, so they would go with anything. She also spotted a cute jacket on the other side of the aisle. She walked around to the corner to take a look at it. It wasn't her favorite color, but she thought it would do the trick if she could just get it out of her head that she might look like Christmas decorations standing next to her new suitcase.

She grabbed the raincoat and slid the hanger under her arm. Her hands were getting full with the socks, leggings, and luggage she was lugging around. She went to find Adria to unload her items into the cart.

"Look what I found," Carla said, walking up behind Adria.

Adria caught her breath, and with a slight jump, she turned to see Carla standing there, holding the exact same rain jacket Adria had picked out. "Well," she said, grabbing hers out of the cart, "maybe we spend too much time together because I picked out the same one."

Both girls chuckled and added them back to the cart. "If we don't already act like twins, people may think we are when they see us walking side by side in these," Carla joked. "You don't care that I get the same color?"

"Not at all," Adria responded. "I'm surprised you want it. Green isn't your favorite color."

"No, but I think it will do the trick," Carla said and then saw something out of the corner of her eye that caught her attention. She moved a few feet down the aisle, walking away from Adria. Carla grabbed the cute vest from the rack and held it up, sizing it up to her body. She needed to find a mirror to see if she liked the way it looked. She was just about to take a step around the corner when she felt someone grab her wrist. She turned. "What do you think of this?" she asked, expecting to see Adria behind her.

When she turned, no one was there…again.

Adria had moved to a different aisle several rows down from Carla.

She went white as a ghost. This was the second time within a matter of days something strange like this had happened to her. She searched the store, her eyes darting to anything that may have been close to her or looked like it could have brushed up against her wrist. She was searching for something that wasn't there. She was trying to understand these precarious moments that were happening to her.

Just then Adria walked over, noticing something was wrong with Carla. "Are you okay?"

"I d-d-don't know," Carla whispered. "Someone just grabbed my wrist."

"Who? We need to tell a store manager," Adria said, immediately taking off to find someone who worked for the store.

"Adria," Carla called out, "they grabbed my wrist, but when I turned around, no one was there."

"What do you mean?" Adria questioned her.

"It was plain as day that I felt someone grab me. I thought it was you, but when I turned around, no one was there. No one was even close to me."

"It must have been a shirt or something rubbing up against you," Adria added.

"I don't think so. I felt the fingers wrapping around my wrist. It happened so fast, just like the incident at the post office," Carla responded.

Carla was not a superstition person, and she had never really believed in ghosts. Yes, she had seen those shows on television, and she watched them mostly for a good fright, but she wasn't sure how she felt about all of it. Some shows had made her laugh, making her feel like it was just really good acting.

Right now, she was beginning to question everything.

Carla and Adria decided to check out and head back to Carla's house. They continued to talk about it in the car. Adria kept asking Carla questions about what she thought it was or if she was going to pass if off as nothing. They decided to put it past them…for now and if Carla could shake it.

Chapter 4

"Yes, I've got everything I need," Carla heard Nate say as she and Adria were entering their little house.

"Yes and my passport. I'm telling you there is nothing to worry about. I'm more than prepared," Nate said to the person opposite the cell phone.

"Okay, I will talk to you later." And he hung up the phone and placed it on the side table next to the brown leather couch he was sitting on. "How was your shopping trip ladies?" he asked both of them, truly curious if they had found what they were looking for.

"I think we got what we were looking for," said Adria.

"And more," added Carla, not just talking about the items they had purchased.

"Well, I'm glad," Nate said genuinely. "I figured since we are leaving the same day, we could Uber to the airport together…unless you would rather not?" He looked back and forth between the two.

"That will work. I was really hoping we wouldn't have to leave a car there," Adria replied. If Carla had given Adria the wide-eyed, raised-eyebrow look, Adria missed it.

"Well, I'm going to get my things home, and I might even start laying some things aside that I know I will want to pack," Adria said as she picked up her shopping bag and backpack purse. "Do you think this backpack counts as a purse or my carry-on?"

"I think purse. You have your wallet and cell phone in there, and the stuff you would put in a carry-on wouldn't fit anyways," Carla answered her question.

Nate nodded. "Agree."

"Okay, see you tomorrow?" Carla asked Adria.

"Yes, but this weekend, I'm going to my mother's to search the attic and see if I can find anything else," Adria said.

"Sounds like a plan," Carla replied.

*****

"I have to head back to the office in a few minutes," Nate said to Carla. "Should I pick something up for dinner? I'll be back around six o'clock."

"No, I pulled out some ground beef. I'm going to make spaghetti," Carla said.

"Perfect. I'll be back in a few hours. Nate said and brushed a kiss atop Carla's hair as he walked toward the front door.

Shivers ran up Carla's spine. *Why does he have to do that?* she thought.

Carla walked into the bedroom she shared with Nate. She was going to leave her purchased items in the corner so she would know where they were when she was ready to pack them. She sat down on the green, purple, and black comforter they had bought when they first moved in together. She let out a heavy sigh and lay back on the bed with her hands behind her head.

In her head, she knew Nate could provide everything she needed from a physical relationship. He knew just how to get to her. Soft touches, light kisses, his hand on the small of her back. Her love language was definitely physical touch. He was the perfect boyfriend in that aspect, but it was emotionally and mentally that she felt something was lacking. Or did she? Was it all in her head? She felt so confused.

The other night popped back into her head. The night they shared their bodies with each other. She had enjoyed it. She felt comfortable lying in his arms and falling asleep to Nate rubbing the back of her neck and playing with her hair. It was one of her favorite things Nate could do for her.

Why was she so upset the morning after? She knew he wouldn't be able to stop thinking about it and he would bring it up for days. But he hadn't. Was he starting to not feel anything for her?

A slight panic rose in her throat. Was Nate losing his feelings for her? Carla hadn't thought about the possibility of Nate not wanting her before, only her feelings of not knowing if she wanted him.

She lay on the bed, thinking for a few minutes as her eyes slowly closed shut. She could feel her feelings floating away as she drifted off.

*****

Carla woke up to the sound of her front door opening. She would know that sound anywhere. Their screen door had a small hitch on the top clasp of the door. It would let out a small *pop pop pop* like the sound of child playing with a BB gun. She knew because her younger cousins used to play with BB guns all the time when they were at their grandparents' house together.

A small panic hit Carla's chest, and for a split second, she remembered what had happened at the mall earlier. Had someone followed her home? She couldn't have been asleep long. They had waited for Nate to leave, and now they were breaking in.

She jumped up and headed to her bedroom door. Her back against the wall, she peered out and saw Nate setting down a grocery bag.

"Hey," he said with that slight sideways grin.

"Hi," she said, letting out her breath and coming out into the living room.

"Are you okay?" Nate asked, clearly noticing something was wrong.

"No, no. I had fallen asleep, and I didn't realize it was so late. I wasn't sure who was coming in the front door," said Carla.

"Were you expecting someone else?" Nate said with a slight chuckle.

"No, I just wasn't expecting you home and I guess I woke up too abruptly," she explained. "I got French bread. I thought we could have it with dinner," Nate added.

Carla looked into the kitchen. "I haven't even started dinner. Good thing spaghetti doesn't take too long to make."

"I'll help," Nate said.

"Nate, it's okay. I'm awake now, and I can get it going," she said, slightly frustrated.

"Carla, I was thinking," Nate said cautiously, "since we are going to be in the same country and town, do you want to get together one night? I don't want to intrude on your space, but I'd love to take you out."

What was he doing? Carla thought. She can't even remember the last time he wanted to take her on date. "Nate, I...don't know. I don't want the hype of being somewhere new to lighten the mood of the way things have been going lately."

"But the other night, Carla," he said, giving her a pleading look, "I thought…"

There it was. He was bringing it up. She knew he would. She just didn't realize it would take him this long. So predictable. He always thought he knew what she was thinking or feeling. She admitted that sometimes he did, but things had been changing between them.

"Nate, it was a moment of passion," Carla said, trying not to snap.

"Forget I mentioned it. I did say I didn't want to intrude on your space, and I meant it. I love you, Carla," he whispered as he left the room. "I'm going to get changed."

Carla instantly felt bad. She felt like she was leading Nate on. They were dating, but they both knew there were problems. Maybe she was leading him on. She just didn't know what she wanted to do with their relationship or with him. She did love him. She just didn't know if he was providing her the stability she was looking for.

She had been so sure about Nate when they moved in together. Maybe this time, living together hadn't given her clarity she needed. After all this time, why was she still feeling this way toward him?

He interrupted her thoughts when he came back in the kitchen. "Are you sure you don't want help?" he asked.

"I've got it handled," she said. "It's almost ready anyway. Just waiting on the noodles to finish boiling."

An hour passed, and they were both clearing the table from their meal. "Want to watch a show tonight?" Nate asked her.

"I thought you would want to prepare for your presentation," said Carla.

"I'm almost done, I think… I've been working on it at lunchtime," said Nate.

"Okay, sure. Pick something out, and I'll go slip into some sweats." Carla finished loading the dish washer and clicked the On button before she walked down the hallway.

They cozied in for the night and watched an episode of *When Calls the Heart*. There was no more talk about the relationship or the trip, and Carla was glad they could just sit and not think about anything.

*****

The next few days went on routinely. Monday came and went. Tuesday came and went. Now it was the Wednesday before their trip, just two days until they would leave.

Wednesday was normally their day off, but Adria and Carla decided to work that day to make sure everything with High Desert Coffee was in order before they left.

Marcus had a few questions, but Adria and Carla had already written out a list of responsibilities that needed to get done. Included on the list was making sure he ordered the appropriate amount of supplies on Monday's call order.

"We will have our phones on us. So if you have any other questions, you can always call us," Adria said.

"Do try to remember there is seven hours' difference, so if you need anything when you get off at five o'clock, don't call us because it will be midnight," Carla added smiling.

"Got it," Marcus said, replying with his own confident smile.

They headed back to their office to wrap up some last-minute details while Marcus got back to work at the counter.

"Oh, here," Carla said. "I ordered this for you. I think these might come in handy." She handed Adria her power converter.

"I didn't even think of these. Good thing you are on top of it," Adria said, paying her friend a compliment.

"Well, I thought we might want to charge our phones and do our hair," Carla added with a laugh. "Hey, I've been meaning to ask you if you found anything out about if there was a key in the letter? Didn't you say you were going to sort through your parents' attic?"

"Yeah, nothing came of it. Mom said I could call my grandmother, but I don't know how she would feel about all the questions," said Adria.

"Did your grandmother grow up in Ireland?" Carla asked. "Maybe you should call her. She might be able to give us some advice getting adjusted when we get there."

"No… I mean yes… She still lives there," Adria added quietly.

"And you're just now bringing this up?" Carla said softly, hitting the side of Adria's shoulder.

"I didn't really think anything of it until recently. I mean it's not like I'm close with her, and she is ninety years old or something like that," Adria added.

"That's not that old," Carla laughed. "Can she talk? Is she coherent? She hasn't lost her marbles, has she?"

Here come the questions, Adria thought. "As far as I know everything is fine with her, and she is healthy as a horse."

"Then you are calling her," Carla demanded, not giving Adria much of an option.

"No! Maybe I could ask my mother to do it," Adria thought out loud.

"Okay, call your mother," Carla said, hurriedly handing Adria her cell phone and set it on top of the desk. "Here, I'll dial her number."

"No, Carla. I don't…" Adria started.

"It's ringing. No turning back," Carla said.

"There is if I just hang up," Adria was saying as her mother answered on the other end.

Carla sat back in her chair and let Adria ask the questions to her mother.

"Hi, Mom…would you mind calling Roisina and asking her if she knows any…"—Adria was thinking what it was exactly they wanted from her grandmother—"good places to eat?" she finished.

Carla gave Adria a funny look. Adria just shrugged.

Carla could imagine the conversation. Adria's mother was questioning her daughter, trying to figure out more about why she was really calling.

Adria was rolling her eyes, and Carla knew they hadn't gotten very far.

"Yes, I know that, but you've said she is still very healthy. Carla and I thought we could use her help," Adria was saying to her mother, finally admitting the real reason for calling.

"You would? Oh, you're the best. Thanks, Mom." Adria hung up the phone. "Bye."

"You realize you just hung up and then said bye?" Carla said, laughing.

"Oh, ha. Oops," Adria responded.

"Well, what did she say?" Carla waited.

"She said she would call tomorrow and get back to me later."

Finishing out their day at the coffee shop, they both headed home for the evening.

"I've got lots of packing to do. See you tomorrow," Carla said when she rolled down the window of her car. "And let me know what your mom says tomorrow."

Adria waved and she sat down in the driver's seat of her little Honda.

*****

Carla could hear her phone ringing from the shower. She wondered whom that could be. She couldn't recall the exact time, but she was pretty sure it was after ten. She let it go to voicemail, but a few minutes later, it was ringing again. She quickly finished her shower and hopped out to grab her towel.

She was drying off when her phone buzzed. It was a text message.

"Call me!" it read from Adria.

Carla needed to finish drying off and get dressed in her night shirt. *Ugh*, she thought as she looked in the mirror, mascara running down the sides of her cheeks. She pulled out the drawer to her makeup cabinet and grabbed her makeup removing wipes. She quickly wiped each eye to get the old makeup off and grabbed her tube of moisturizer and blotted a few dots around her face. She grabbed her phone off the counter and hit FaceTime to call Adria.

Adria answered on the first ring. "You will not believe what my mother did." Carla didn't say anything but waited for Adria to continue.

"She set up a day for me to meet with my grandmother, one day next week," Adria said, the words spilling out as fast as she could spit them.

"Actually, that's a good idea," Carla said. She could feel Adria glaring at her from the other side of the phone.

"Think about it. We want more information about your family history. We want to visit the castle where one of your distant grandmothers lived, and we want to find out what happened with this murder/suicide information we have. Don't you think this would be the perfect resource?" Carla questioned Adria.

"I don't know my grandmother, Carla. She isn't a relative to me. She is a stranger," Adria added.

"Then think of it like talking to a professor or librarian or a historian," Carla said.

"Oh, fine! I can see I'm not going to get any sympathy from you." Adria spouted. "This is turning into more of an investigation and not a vacation."

Carla was stunned. "I thought you were excited to find out about your heritage and family history?"

A few moments of silence passed. Adria could see that she was out of turn. "I'm sorry," she said quietly. "I didn't mean to come down on you. I just didn't think this would turn into a meeting with a family member I have never met before."

"Listen," Carla began, "does she live in Dublin?"

"No, my mother said she lives close to Bray Harbour, which I think is south of Dublin. I'll have to look it up and make sure I heard her right," said Adria.

"It will be an adventure. That's what we wanted. It'll be fun," Carla tried to convince Adria. "I'm going to head to bed. One more day." She then hung up their FaceTime call.

*****

It was Thursday before they were to leave. Last-minute details were being wrapped up by the girls. Adria sent Carla a checklist. "Make sure you have these things," she said in the email. Passport, airline tickets, phone charger, and euros were among the more important things. Toothbrush, swimsuit, and lotion were among the smaller needed necessities.

Carla sent Adria a text. "Swimsuit?" she said. "It's only supposed to be in the fifties while we are there."

"You never know," Adria responded quickly.

Carla decided to head to the store to grab some snacks for the car ride and plane trip. She knew this was going to be a very long eighteen hours, and she wanted to make sure she had enough things to keep her busy and energized. She walked up and down a few aisles, snatching a magazine and flipping through it quickly. She noticed a page on antiques. It was a no-brainer; she was getting it, and she placed it in her shopping basket. She found a toothbrush holder that she couldn't find the other day at Target and threw that in the basket as well. She grabbed a pack of gum, trail mix, and her favorite snack, apple chips.

Carla sent a quick text to Nate: "Need anything while I'm at the store?"

"I don't think so… I'm leaving in a couple hours," Nate replied.

"What? How? Why?" was all Carla could reply in the text.

"They got me on an earlier flight so that I would have more time to prepare my speech. I didn't really have a say in the matter," came his reply.

"Okay, well, that's unexpected. I'll be home in a few minutes," said Carla.

Carla had around a ten-minute drive from the store to their home. She thought about how this would change her and Adria's plan too. She could ask Adria to stay the night so they wouldn't have to do extra driving in the morning, and they would need to book their own uber without Nate. Their uber would probably be cheaper since they wouldn't have to get an SUV.

She pulled into the driveway as Nate was setting his suitcase just outside the front door. "I grabbed you some jerky," she said to Nate.

"Ah, my favorite. Thanks. This will be perfect for the long flight," responded Nate.

"I know how awful it is to travel on an empty stomach," said Carla.

Nate didn't mention that food was included in his trip. That meant meals on the plane ride. He had already pre-ordered grilled chicken, mashed potatoes, and a side salad.

He didn't always love airline food, but he knew he would need the energy for his trip. His first stop was in Fort Worth, Texas. He would then switch planes and arrive around nine o'clock in Philadelphia, Pennsylvania. The longest part of his journey would be to Dublin with a six-and-a-half-hour flight over the Atlantic Ocean. He would arrive around 4:00 a.m.

That would give Nate enough time to catch his ride to his hotel and the rest of the morning to sleep and prepare for his speech, which would be the following morning. Nate had meetings Monday through Thursday of his trip and a training the next Friday.

Nate would take the next three days after his meetings to sightsee a few places, including, the Little Museum of Dublin, the Rock of Cashel, and Blarney Castle. If there was time, he'd love to take a hiking adventure and see more of the coastline.

Nate laid it all out for Carla, handing her his itinerary. He let her know he would be home in thirteen days.

"If you change your mind about having a day together, just let me know," said Nate. "Dublin would be romantic and maybe just what we need." He rubbed his hand down the side of Carla's arm, stopping to grab her hand and willing her to look at him.

Carla kept her head down. "Enjoy your time, Nate," she replied but not to his statement. She didn't want to give Nate false hope, and she didn't know if Nate was part of her trip. He wasn't supposed to be, so why would she change that now?

Carla heard a car door shut and stepped away quickly to break the connection between their hands.

"That must be your ride," she said.

"Yep, that's the make and model of the Uber." Nate popped his head out the door and held out his finger as to give the driver an "I'll be out in a second." "Look, Carla, I love you. That will never change. If you feel like I've been distant or haven't been there for you lately, I ask your forgiveness."

"This is a horrible time to have a conversation about it, Nate." Carla spewed at him, half-mad that he was saying it and yet feeling a slight tinge of hope.

"I know… I know. And it's my fault. Carla, let me be better. Give me time to be better," Nate said, partly pleading with her.

"Your car is waiting," she replied.

"I love you, Carla Leann Murphey," said Nate as he reached for her in a small embrace. He wrapped his arms around her, feeling her body tighten for a few seconds. He waited for her to lean into him.

She extended her arms around Nate's back and returned the hug. She was surprised by her feelings just then. She felt warm and comfortable and…safe.

Nate was a bigger build and a good eight inches taller than her. He had always made Carla feel like her protector. It was just another one of the many reasons she had fallen for him in the first place.

Nate released Carla and took a few steps to the front door. "Be safe on your trip, Carla. I'll be waiting for you when you come home."

Nate grabbed his suitcase and headed down the front steps to his uber.

Carla just stood there. Why couldn't she say the words she knew Nate wanted to hear? "I love you," she whispered. Why didn't she just say them to Nate while he was right there?

Chapter 5

Carla walked back into the kitchen to grab her phone, which she thought was still in her purse. And that's exactly where she found it.

She sent out a text to Adria: "Nate left early. His flight got changed to this evening." She hit Send.

She then punched out another text: "Want to just stay the night here so you don't have to drive over in the morning?"

Adria responded a few minutes later: "That sounds good. I'm finishing up dinner with a friend and then I'll head your way."

"Dinner? Friend? Who?" Carla texted back.

Adria knew Carla would be the one to blast out all the questions. Adria decided not to respond right away. It was a longer conversation, and she would rather just tell Carla in person.

Five minutes later… "Who are you having dinner with?" Carla persisted with more questions. A couple more minutes. "Adria Marie Layne, you tell me right now!

"Daniel Tanner." Adria sent the text and then put her phone away in her purse.

Buzz, buzz, buzz. Adria counted three, four, five text messages. *I'm going to hear it when I get to Carla's. I'll tell her about it when I get there*, she thought.

Carla was beginning to get frustrated that Adria wasn't texting her back. She wanted to know about this Daniel guy and why this was the first she was hearing about this date because that is surely what it was. She pulled out her laptop and googled Daniel Tanner. Scrolling through the pages, she found a couple pictures of different people. *Well, that's normal*, she was thinking.

Multiple people have the same name, but which one was this Daniel Tanner?

She opened a new tab and clicked Facebook. She typed out Daniel Tanner in the search box, but before hitting Enter, she thought that maybe he was Adria's friend on Facebook. She could go to her page and search her friends. She clicked Adria's name when it popped up and then typed in Daniel's name again. There he was. She clicked on his profile… Private. She clicked on his profile picture to make it bigger. It was a faraway picture of him on some mountain. She couldn't make out his face, and it was bugging her. Nosy as she is, it was killing her that she couldn't see anything. She clicked his other pictures to see if anything else popped up. There was a picture of a little girl with a dog, another picture of him with a dirt bike, and a photo of a landscape.

Carla thought the little girl was adorable, and she loved yellow labs. It was about all she could think since she didn't know much about this guy.

"Be there in a few minutes," read a text from Adria. "Stopping by my house to get my stuff first."

"It's about time," Carla said to herself.

*****

Adria got in her Honda and started on her way to Carla's house. "It's not a big deal. There is nothing to this. It was just a get-together. Two friends catching up. And it was just dinner," she said to herself.

She didn't know what this was. Did she want it to be something? She thought about what she would tell Carla, and Adria knew she would be smothered with question after question. She better prepare herself. Her brain made a mental list:

1. No, this was not a date.
2. Yes, he was nice to her.
3. He reintroduced himself to her in the lobby at the coffee shop
4. Yes, he did have a daughter

Do I like him? She thought to herself? She knew the question was going to come from Carla. Adria continued driving, trying to answer the question for herself. She didn't know. It would be nice to see him again. That is, if he ever asks.

Before she knew it, she was pulling up to Carla's house. It was one of those out-of-body experiences when you're in the car thinking about something but can't actually remember how you got from point A to point B. "Well, here goes nothing."

Adria decided to grab her luggage now and not have to haul it out of her car in the morning or later that night. She swung her carry-on over her shoulder and grabbed her laptop from the front seat. She planned on putting it in her suitcase so she could take it with her on the trip.

She finished grabbing the rest of her things before Carla ran out to greet her. "Well, hi, stranger," Adria said.

"Hi, yourself," Carla responded.

"Stop," Adria instantly started. "Don't be upset with me. It was sudden and last minute."

"Whatever are you talking about?" Carla said sarcastically.

Carla grabbed Adria's suitcase and began rolling it to the front steps. "I'm not mad. I'm just curious about everything and wondering why you didn't mention it to me."

"I didn't mention it because I thought it would never happen. And like I said it was so last minute. He came into the coffee shop and recognized me right away. He asked if he could call sometime and maybe do coffee," Adria began.

"And…" Carla was ushering her to continue.

"Well, he didn't call. I ordered take out from that place on West Broad Street and went to pick it up. He was there too. He asked if I would sit with him, and I didn't want to be rude, so I said yes. That's it. End of story," Adria responded.

"Not end of story. Not really even a beginning. Who is he?" Carla said.

"He's a guy I met at the gym a couple months ago. We started talking about what high schools we were from, and he went to the same high school as Nate. I think he said he knows him," said Adria.

"Hmm," Carla said, thinking, "so you went on a date. Do you like him?"

"I wouldn't really consider that a date, and I don't know. He's nice," Adria was explaining.

"Do you want to see him again?" Carla asked.

"I don't know. I'm not going to say yes, and I'm not going to say no." Adria was trying to get out of the conversation.

Carla, of course, would not let Adria, and they spent the next thirty minutes talking about this guy named Daniel Tanner. Carla explained that she had searched him online. Adria confirmed that he did have a daughter, but Carla wanted to know more. She thought about texting Nate but thought she better not. He was on his flight and was probably sleeping or catching up on some paperwork.

The two decided to call it a night since they had to be at the airport at 5:00 a.m. Carla told Adria she could sleep in the bed Carla shared with Nate and that she would sleep on Nate's side. But Adria decided against it and took the couch.

Carla washed her face and pulled her hair up in a bun. She added some night cream and then put her glasses on and headed to the kitchen. She grabbed a bottle of water from the counter, and as she was walking through the living room, she said one last comment to Adria: "He's cute. I think you should see him again."

"Good night, Carla," Adria said, and she settled down into her makeshift bed.

*****

Four in the morning came early. Both girls were awake and trying to get ready. They couldn't wait for their adventure to begin. Adria was up before her alarm clock, going through her things one last time. *Passport, check. Airline tickets are on my phone. Check.* So many things running through her head. She grabbed her carry-on and went to the bathroom to wash her face, put on a dab of makeup, and brush her teeth. She threw her hair up in a messy bun as Carla was walking in behind her, still half-asleep but dressed in her travel sweats.

Carla was not a morning person, and Adria was. "Good morning," Adria said.

Carla didn't say anything or smile. She nodded and turned the hot water on in the shower. Carla knew the only way she could fully wake up was to take a shower in the morning. It usually washed away her sleepiness, and she liked feeling fresh when she got out. Adria grabbed her stuff and headed back to the living room so Carla could have the bathroom to herself.

Adria looked at the clock. "We have twenty-five minutes until the Uber is here," she yelled at Carla in the other room.

Carla stuck her hand out the bathroom door and gave her a thumbs-up. *The one thing you need to remember about Carla was that she doesn't like to think, walk, or talk until she is fully awake. A coffee in hand is even better,* thought Adria.

Adria went to the kitchen and brewed a pot of coffee. She waited while it trickled into the pot and filled the room with the most delicious coffee bean smell. When it was done, she poured herself a cup and began drinking it. She was eager to get this journey started. Once she was ready, she hated waiting around.

Adria went back into the living to put away the blankets and pillows she had used the night before. She picked up the phone to check the time again, and she noticed she had missed a text from the night before.

It was a text from Carter's dad. She hadn't heard from him in a few weeks, and she was hoping things were trailing off. This trip was supposed to be about letting Carter go, letting his family go, and moving on. How was she supposed to do that if Carter's family kept bugging her?

> We want you to know we love you and will always think of you like family. Your mom told us about your trip. Carter would have loved Ireland. Have fun, sweetie. We're praying for you.—Mike

Tears welled up in Adria's eyes, and she turned her head to see Carla standing at the end of the hallway.

"Why does this have to be so hard?" she asked Carla as a tear slipped down her cheek.

"Was it Carter's mom?" Carla asked curiously as she came and sat next to her friend on the couch.

"His dad. He barely ever texts me." Adria held the text up to Carla so she could read it for herself.

"You know, I don't think they'll be upset for you to move on. They just consider you a daughter and want you to know that." Carla was trying to be comforting.

"How can I move on if they won't let me?" Adria said, wiping tears that were now flowing down her face.

"I don't know. Maybe that has to do more with you," said Carla. "You finding a middle ground with letting go of Carter and being okay with his family still being your friends."

"I just don't know how I'm supposed to do that," Adria said.

Just then, they saw headlights flash through the front window. Carla stood up and went to grab her belongings from the bedroom. When she came back in the living room, Adria was up and ready like the moments before had not just happened.

"You ready?" Adria said. She had made it up in her mind not to let this ruin their trip. They both headed for the front door.

*****

The car ride to the airport was cold. The Uber driver apologized over and over again for not having heat in his car. He told them it went out a couple days ago, and with his other job, he hadn't had the time to get it fixed yet. He offered them a complimentary blanket, but they both declined.

It was also quiet. The driver kept to himself, and neither Carla nor Adria said anything. They both seemed to be staring out the windows, thinking.

Carla was thinking about their trip: the things she wanted to discover, going to see Adria's grandmother, Castle Creet, Mary Gallagher, the key. It was all coming to her like it was something she could reach out and grab. It felt so close.

Adria was thinking about Carter and then Daniel and then Carter and then his family. She was feeling dizzy and needed a drink of water stat. She decided the moment she got to the airport, all thoughts of anything from home would be out the window, including Daniel. She didn't know why she was thinking of him in the first place.

Their flight would be similar to Nate's except they would land in Chicago first and then Philadelphia and then make their way to Dublin.

The driver pulled up next to drop off, and the girls grabbed their luggage out of the trunk. They tipped the man. Even though it was a freezing cold ride, he was still nice. They walked up to the line at American Airlines and hoped they wouldn't have to wait too long.

After they got their boarding passes and checked their suitcases, they made their way to security. Another line. This one was longer than before as was to be expected.

"When we get through security, let's get a Bloody Mary," Carla said. She had never gotten a drink before takeoff, and she decided to let this be a vacation of firsts.

"I like the sound of that. I could use a little pick-me-up before this long trip," Adria said.

Security check took longer than they were expecting. Going through every traveler's ticket, ID, and then going through the metal detector took time. Coats off, electronics in the bin, shoes off, belts off—the list went on and on. The guard at the front of the metal detector was yelling on repeat so everyone could hear. Carla had to be scanned twice, and Adria got called back because the alarm of the metal detector went off.

Of course, leave it to Adria to get called back. *She must have left her belt on*, Carla was thinking.

Later, the security guard checking with Adria asked, "Do you have anything in your pockets? Did you put your cell phone in the bin? Are you wearing a belt?"

She padded at her body, hitting her pockets in the front and back. She felt her belt she had kept on when pulling on her jeans that morning. It was left in the buckle loops from the last wear, and she decided to keep it on while getting dressed. She slid it off and put it in the bin. She walked through the detector again, this time giving a sideways smile to the guard. "Sorry," she said when she reached the other side.

"Happens all the time, ma'am," he replied.

Adria grabbed her items out of the bin and headed for Carla, who was already put back together and ready to walk to their terminal.

"I see the bar," she said.

They sat down and enjoyed their drinks before heading to a seat at their terminal, and they waited for their plane to arrive.

*****

The announcements had come over the intercom to let families with children board the plane first. They waited until they heard their seat numbers and walked up to get in line. It wasn't long before they were sitting as comfortably as they could be in the airplane seats. Carla next to the window and Adria in the center seat.

Carla pulled out her phone to turn it on airplane mode and noticed a text from Nate. She hadn't been on her phone all day, leaving it tucked away and out of sight. It was from a couple of hours ago. *I made it safely. Have a good trip.*

"That was nice," Adria said, seeing the text since she was sitting so closely next to her.

"He's been really different lately. You know, he apologized the other day. He said he knew he wasn't giving me the attention I deserved and he wanted to be better." Carla turned slightly to Adria.

"Really? Do you believe him?" Adria questioned.

"I don't know," Carla responded to her. "I think I want to, but I just don't know."

They talked a little while longer about Nate. They wanted to remember to ask him how he knew Daniel, and then they talked about Daniel. Adria had told him they were going on a two-week trip, but she was secretly hoping he would text her.

*****

Daniel Tanner was tall. At six foot two, he was the tallest man Adria had ever been interested in.

She was only five foot four. He had dark skin, dark hair, and dark brown eyes. He had an athletic build and probably played football or soccer. Adria had to stop denying that she was into him.

Carla had put in her AirPods, put on a random podcast, and closed her eyes. She leaned her head up against the airplane window and tried to fall asleep.

It gave Adria plenty of time to think about this Daniel Tanner. He was a high school math teacher, and he was crazy about it and his students. Adria could tell he loved what he did by the way he talked about it the other night at dinner.

She began to think about his daughter. Her name was Sophie. There had to be a story there, but he didn't get into it. Probably a good thing since this was a first "get-together." Adria couldn't bring herself to say date because she didn't even know if that's what it was. He had pulled out his phone and showed her a picture. Sophie had dark olive skin like him, but from what Adria could tell, Sophie had bright blue eyes. *She is gorgeous,* Adria thought.

Adria began to wonder about Sophie's mom and why it hadn't worked out with Daniel. Why hadn't they been able to make it work in the long run or had there even been a committed relationship? For all Adria knew, this could have been a one-time thing. She began to think about how hard it would be to be a single mom and how hard it must be for Daniel, only getting to see his daughter every other weekend.

The more she thought about Daniel, the more curious she was about his life. She was confused about her feelings, but she was also open to exploring them. *I have to move on,* she thought.

And that's exactly what she was going to do. It's not going to be easy, but she could do it. *For a better me. It's what Carter would want,* she thought.

She decided that when their plane landed in Dublin, she would send a text to Daniel. She didn't know what she was going to say. But she had an eighteen-hour series of flights to think about it.

She closed her eyes and tried to get some sleep.

Chapter 6

"My granddaughter is coming to visit me," said Roisina.

"That will be nice," said Laura, the caretaker to Roisina O'Brien. "Is this her first visit?"

"Aye. She has never been here before. I doubt she even knew I existed until the other day when I talked to my daughter-in-law," Roisina was saying.

"I'm sure you will have a lot to talk about," said Laura, being hopeful. She pulled out the plastic bag from the trash can and replaced it with a new one.

"Before you leave deary, will you grab a box of family heirlooms out of the top of my closet? She comes seeking family history, and whatever I have will be in there," Roisina claimed.

"Of course." Laura had already started grabbing it before she finished her sentence. "When do you expect your granddaughter?"

"She should be coming on Monday," said Roisina.

"That will be a great something to look forward too," Laura said as she handed Roisina the box of old photo albums, loose pictures, and papers.

*****

Adria and Carla had a short layover in Philadelphia, so they decided it would be a good time to refuel. They didn't order food on the airplane and decided one of the airport restaurants would be a good place for dinner. Carla found a little Mexican place and ordered some street tacos. Adria found Subway and ordered the Chicken Bacon Ranch Sandwich.

Both girls met back at their terminal and sat down to eat their dinner together. "Only one more flight left," said Carla.

"You never realize how exhausting traveling is, and the time difference is really going to give us jet lag," Adria said. "We're going to need the whole day just to sleep."

"Did you sleep at all on the plane?" Carla asked.

"No, I think I may have drifted off, but the turbulence startled me awake," said Adria. "Have you finished reading your magazine?"

"No, I saved the antique article for this part of the journey. You can read it when I'm done," Carla replied.

"I brought a book, but I was getting motion sickness, so I don't know if I can read a magazine either," Adria was saying. "I might just listen to a couple podcasts."

"You can borrow my iPad and watch the documentaries I downloaded if you want," Carla said, holding the electronic device out to her.

"I might if I don't get motion sick again. Thanks for the offer," Adria said.

The intercom interrupted their thoughts as it called for the first passengers to start loading onto the plane. "Welcome to America Airlines…"

Carla and Adria finished their food. Carla threw away their garbage away, while Adria ran to the bathroom. When she returned, it was time for them to get in line and start the next leg of their journey.

"Dublin, here we come," Adria said.

*****

Daniel Tanner was grading papers at his desk on Friday after school. He had a couple of students in his classroom catching up on school work they had missed the day before.

Daniel couldn't stop thinking about the dinner he had with Adria just the night before. It wasn't exactly the kind of date he was expecting, but it was more time that he got to spend with her. He was so glad he ran into her at the coffee shop and had been meaning to call her, but time had got away from him. He had been going to that coffee shop for a long time and had no idea she was a partial owner. He'd have to make his stops more frequent.

He was excited about whatever *this* was. It has been a long time since he had dated anyone. His ex-wife, Lacey, was his last relationship, and that clearly did not work out. It had ended two years ago, but he didn't want to think about Lacey right now. Daniel was interested in Adria Layne.

They met a few months ago when they were both working out at the same gym. She was running on a treadmill, and he was lifting weights a couple of rows over. He noticed her almost as soon as he arrived, thinking about how beautiful she was even with all the sweat.

He could see her mouthing the song of whatever was playing in her AirPods, and he could almost make out a few miniature dance moves. She would quickly grab the handrails as if to stop herself from tripping over her own feet. They made eye contact a couple times, and he gave her a sweaty wave and smile.

One time, when they were both there, Adria had hopped off after about a twenty-minute run. She walked over to him, asking to see if he could help her get the leg press ready so she could use it. He walked around to help her and tripped over a flap of gym mat that had been raised up. He bumped into her while trying to grab at anything to stop himself from falling on his face. She, in turn, stumbled over her own feet hitting her head on the top of the equipment.

He landed on his knees but shot up, quickly going to her. He apologized again and again and offered to get her an ice pack. She waved him off, saying she just needed to sit down for a second. When she pulled her hand away from her head, she had a small cut above her left eyebrow close to the hairline.

"Oh, shit," he had said. She was bleeding. He went and grabbed a couple tissues from the counter a few feet away, and he apologized several more times.

She insisted she was fine, but if she had been completely honest, it had made her a bit dizzy. She decided to call off the rest of her workout and head home. He asked her if he could walk her to the car, and she allowed him to.

Daniel had felt so awful the rest of the day and couldn't get her or what he accidentally had done to her out of his head. He needed to remember to get her name the next time he saw her.

They had seen each other several more times throughout the next weeks at the gym, and they found out each other's names. But other than that they had only exchanged a few "hellos" and "see ya laters."

He was so glad he found her at the coffee shop, and now that they had had dinner together, he was very certain that he wanted to see her again.

He knew she was on a vacation and wondered if it would be okay to call her. Okay, maybe not call; maybe he could send a text. He wouldn't do it right away, he'd wait a few days and let her get settled into her hotel or wherever she was staying.

It popped into Daniel's head that she had mentioned she knew Nate Duncan. He hadn't spoken to Nate in a while but maybe he would know more about Adria's life, including the area of her love life. Maybe he would give Nate a call and see if he wanted to catch up and grab a beer.

*****

Carla and Adria were walking down the Dublin Airport hallway, anxious to get to the luggage claim and grab their suitcases. "We better have both suitcases, or you'll be sharing all your clothes with me," Adria joked.

"I will not," laughed Carla. "Miriam said she would pick us up in a few minutes. Let's grab our stuff and head that way." She pointed out to the sidewalk curb.

They continued to walk up to the baggage carousel and waited for their suitcases. Carla's bright-red suitcase hit the conveyor belt and slowly moved toward them. And right behind it was Adria's navy suitcase. Both girls pulled up the handle to their suitcase and took off to the door, dragging the large luggage behind them.

Miriam was waiting for them just a few cars down.

"Hi, I'm Carla. It's so nice to finally meet you and thank you so much for picking us up. We really appreciate it."

"My pleasure," Miriam responded. "And you must be Adria?" She shook Carla's hand and then Adria's. "Let me help you get your luggage in the car."

Suitcases were loaded. The trunk was shut. Adria pulled her carry-on off her shoulder and took the little backpack purse off so she could climb in the back seat. Carla went over to the right side of the car to get in the passenger seat, not knowing Miriam was headed that way to get in the driver's seat. They bumped into each other as Miriam went to pull open the door.

"Oops," Carla said as she saw the steering wheel just inside the car door, "I guess I've got some things to get used to."

All three ladies burst into a fit of laughter.

They all got comfortable with their seat belts on and took off merging out into traffic.

"Would you like to go straight to the cottage, or would you like to stop at the store to grab some things you might need?" Miriam asked.

"I think we're ready to head to the cottage if that's all right?" said Carla. "We're very tired from the trip and would love to lay down and unwind a bit."

"Of course. We'll be there in about twenty five minutes," Miriam replied.

"You didn't say we were staying in a cottage," Adria chimed in.

"I swear I told you," said Carla.

"I hope it's comfortable for you. It was passed down to me when my parents died." Miriam said. "When my husband, Craig, and I got married, I didn't know if I should keep it or sell it. He convinced me to keep it, and now we rent it out as an Airbnb."

"You seem to keep pretty busy with renting it out?" Carla asked.

"It has been nice to have the extra income, and I'll be able to be a stay at home more when our little one comes in about two months…or less," Miriam said.

"Congratulations," Adria said.

Carla snuck a peek back at Adria to see if there was any hint of sadness. Adria had suffered a miscarriage when she was married to Carter. It had broken her, and she still blamed herself for the accident of falling down the stairs. Three weeks later at their ultrasound, the baby no longer had a heartbeat. Adria had only been twelve weeks along.

Adria had always wanted to be a mother. When she and Carter were married, it was all she could talk about. She wanted to be a stay-at-home mom, the cool mom, the soccer mom, and for now, she had lost out on that chance.

Carla got to thinking about Daniel, and maybe he would be the new Mr. Right. She decided she was going to text Nate when they got to the cottage. She would find out anything she could about Daniel Tanner.

"Are you hungry?" Miriam interrupted Carla's thoughts. "My husband and I have a full crock pot this evening, and you are more than welcome to come to dinner... It's stew."

"Thank you," Carla replied, "but we have reservations at Numero 6 for tonight."

"Their Seafood Platter is delicious. Or the Gnocchi Bolognese is good too," Miriam was telling them. "They also have burgers and chicken wings if that is more suited to your taste buds."

"Oh good, you've heard of it," Adria said. "Are we staying close to it? That all sounds so yummy."

"Oh my, yes," Miriam said. "It's quite literally down the road and around the corner. Maybe two or three miles. You two could take the bikes provided in the cottage shed."

"Oh that's great," Carla said. "I'd love to as long as it's not raining."

"And it shouldn't be too cold for you," said Miriam. "What time is your reservation?"

"Six o'clock," both Carla and Adria said at the same time.

"Perfect. You'll have time to make it back just before dark," Miriam added.

The rest of the trip was spent taking in Ireland. There was beautiful green landscape surrounding them. They past a sign saying

River Liffey and Lucan House, and they watched as the buildings in the city slowly turned into a charming, picturesque countryside.

Miriam pulled into the long driveway close to River Liffey. It was landscaped with rose bushes all along each side of the gravel road. There was a small pond on the right hand side with a walking path weaving in and out of the bushes. There was also a path that lead into the shrubs behind the small shed. On the left, there was a flower garden with a few benches and beautiful views overlooking the green fields.

A minute's drive and they were pulling up to the front of the cottage. It was a white stone, one-story traditional structure. It had a green wooden door in the center and two medium-sized, twelve-paned windows on each side. There was a stone path that lead to the front door, and flower boxes hung under each window. A few birdhouses hung from the nearby trees and a small fountain sat in the front yard. The house's yard was lined with short hedges instead of a white picket fence like Adria had imagined. The hedges stood just one foot off the ground so everything around the home could still be visible.

"This is the most beautiful cottage I have ever seen," Carla said. "It's so well-kept."

"Thank you," Miriam said proudly.

Adria and Carla grabbed their bags from the car while Miriam walked up the path to open the door. She handed them the keys. "It's all yours," she said.

"Thank you so much," Carla replied, taking the keys from her.

"Make yourself at home," Miriam said and headed out to let them get settled.

*****

After things had been put away and they had chosen who would sleep where, Adria called her mother to let her know they had made it, and Carla send a text to Nate just so he wouldn't be worried.

The two decided to take it easy and relax on the light blue couch in the living room. It was covered with pretty white pillows and a soft fleece blanket.

Ding. Adria's phone had received a text message alert. She picked it up and flipped it over. "Hey. It's Daniel. Just wanted to see how your trip was going."

"Who is it?" asked Carla.

"It's Daniel," replied Adria.

Carla perked up and switched her feet so her body position was facing Adria. Carla waited for Adria to continue.

"He just asked how the trip was going is all," Adria said, giving Carla a look.

Adria typed out a text: "We just got here, LOL. It's been a long journey and we are just resting."

"That's great," his text replied. "I was thinking about our conversation and how you said you knew Nate Duncan. I was wondering if you had his number?"

Adria was taken aback. It was not the text she was expecting to get. "Sure, let me grab it for you."

"What does he want?" Carla asked.

"He just wanted Nate's number. I guess he wants to catch up with him," Adria said back to Carla.

"Nate's number? Interesting. I'll have to ask Nate later if Daniel ends up calling him. Are you okay?" Carla wanted to make sure her friend wasn't disappointed.

"Yeah." Before Adria could say anything else, another text from Daniel appeared: "Thanks. Was just thinking I could grab a beer and catch up with him."

"You know he is in Dublin, right?" Adria sent back.

Daniel responded: "Oh, no I didn't. I guess that won't work. I'll call and see if he has plans when he returns."

"Wait is he with you guys?" came another text from Daniel.

"No he had a business trip," replied Adria.

"I see… Do you have plans when you return?" Daniel asked, slipping the text in there nonchalantly.

Carla could see Adria's eyes light up and she knew she had received "the" text message she had been anticipating.

"I think he wants to get together when I get home," Adria said to Carla. "What do I say? I don't want to sound too forward."

"Just act casual."

"Just the usual and work," Adria said back to Daniel.

Daniel's text came back: "Maybe instead of coffee and last minute surprise pizza dinners, I could take you to get real dinner?"

"I would love that." Adria's heart was pounding as she sent the text back to Daniel. This was the first time in a long time she had gotten these butterfly feelings, and she was excited about it.

"Great, I'll give you a call when you get back," Daniel's text said.

*****

Nate's voicemail came on and Daniel had to decide quickly whether he wanted to leave a message or not. He decided against it and then hung up.

A few minutes later he thought, *I'll never get answers about Adria if I don't let Nate know why I'm calling.*

He decided to call the number again, and he would leave a message when the voicemail came on this time. But this time, a voice answered after the first ring.

"Hello. This is Nate," he said and looked at his watch, which read five o'clock.

"Hey…uh. Hi. This is Daniel Tanner from high school and a few baseball leagues during college."

Nate was surprised. He hadn't heard from Daniel in months. They had been good friends and always got along so well. Daniel was the pitcher of their baseball team, and they would always go out after each game to grab a beer and talk about the good ole high school days.

"Hi, Daniel. It's been a while," Nate said.

"I met up with your friend, Adria, and we got to talking about how she knew you. I thought, 'I gotta call that guy and catch up.' So here I am," Daniel said to Nate.

"Wow, dude…yeah. I'd love to. I'm out of the country for business, but I can get back at you when I get back," Nate responded, still surprised.

Now that Nate had made the initial "Let's get together," *how do I bring up Adria?* he thought to himself. "Yeah, hit me up… Hey, before I let you off the phone, I was just wondering how you know Adria?" Daniel said, half-embarrassed he had actually had the nerve to ask.

"Uh, well, she is my girlfriend's best friend. They are practically like sisters, so we actually see a lot of her," Nate replied to his question.

"I see," Daniel said.

"You into her, bro?" Nate asked, thinking he already knew the answer.

"We met a few months ago, and I keep seeing her around town. We had dinner together a few nights ago, so I was just curious about her," said Daniel.

"Right on. Hey, I'm heading out to a dinner. I'll catch up with you when I'm back in Idaho," Nate said and hung up the phone.

That was the most awkward conversation Daniel had had in a while. He felt foolish and boyish. He had done this before. He had gone down this road, gotten engaged and married. It was like starting all over again and not knowing anything about how to do it.

He got to thinking that maybe he could call Adria in a few days just to check in and let her know he was thinking of her. She might like that, especially if she was feeling the same way as he was.

Chapter 7

Adria and Carla were getting ready for their dinner reservations, dressing in nicer clothes and fixing up their hair and makeup. It had started raining a bit ago, and Miriam said they could take her car to the restaurant. Carla thought she could handle the drive on the opposite side of the car and road since it wasn't too far away.

When they got there, they found a parking space pretty quickly. They made it to the front door, and a server was there to seat them right away. When they were seated, they decided to order anything and everything that sounded good, starting with a glass of wine and a hummus plate. By the time their meal arrived Adria, was on her third glass of wine. *She won't be driving home,* Carla thought to herself.

Carla ordered the Dried Aged Irish Sirloin Steak and Adria ordered the Beef Lasagne. They each thought their meal pretty good. Carla willingly shared her steak and mushrooms, piling them onto Adria's plate. They talked about their meal, the atmosphere, and how much they adored everyone's accent. By the end of the night, they each ordered another glass of wine, and Adria's conversation turned to slurs.

They were both giddy and laughing at just about everything. Adria leaned over and whispered to Carla that she was a bit dizzy, like it was some funny little secret no one else knew. Carla just laughed back at her friend because she could clearly see Adria was gone.

Sitting at the table for a while longer, they tried to let some of the alcohol wear off. Music was playing in the background, but Carla could just make out the sound of her phone ringing. It was Nate's face that showed on the call screen. She knew she wouldn't be able to hear him if she answered, so she decided she would call him back when they got back to the cottage.

There is nothing more annoying than trying to hold a conversation with him or anyone over a noisy crowd, let alone reveal to him how she shouldn't be driving home. After all, it was only a couple of miles down the road. She would be fine.

"Heyyyy, girlfriend," Adria said to Carla with her eyes glazed over and a huge smile on her face. She was slightly leaning to one side of her chair, about to tip over at any time. "When you ready to get out of here?"

Carla was pretty sure Adria was about to fall right out of her chair, so she raised her hand to flag down the first waiter and ask for their check. Carla paid for both of them and told herself Adria could pick up the next tab. Carla placed their tip on the table and looked up right as Adria slipped out of her seat. *Plop*, she hit the ground pretty hard.

"Down she goes," Carla said.

Carla pushed her chair back quickly and got up to go over and help her friend up, but a tall, cute waiter was there within seconds. He had been standing right behind their table, emptying his tray of drinks to the customers at the larger table. Adria must have bumped into him when she hit the floor.

"Ma'am, are you okay?" he asked as he wrapped his hands under Adria's arms and helped her get back on her chair.

Adria was just laughing silently, her shoulders shaking but not making any noise. "Yes, thank you kindly," she said in a Southern accent. It surprised even her, and she began giggling again.

"My name is Travis. Just let me know if there is anything else I can do to help. Maybe a glass of water?" he said, looking over to Carla.

"That would be great, Travis, thank you," Carla said.

Carla made Adria take a few sips of water before they got up to leave. Adria had her arm over Carla's shoulder, leaning onto her as they made their way from their table and down the aisle toward the front door.

Travis must have noticed that Carla could barely hold Adria up, and he decided to come over and ask if he could help them both out to the car.

"Yes, please, I would really appreciate it," Carla said, clearly needing his muscles.

Travis slid his arm around and under Adria's left shoulder and walked her to the car around the corner from Numero 6. He opened the door for her and let her get in by herself.

"You are very helpful, friend," Adria said to him, holding her right hand out sharply and strongly. Travis shook her hand and laughed.

"I'm so sorry," Carla said from the driver's seat, half-laughing and half-embarrassed.

"Ah, not from around here, are you?" Travis asked, now being able to hear more clearly.

"We're visiting from Idaho. This is our first night," Carla explained.

"Well, it's no problem at all. Have a wonderful evening, ladies," he said as he shut the door to Adria's side of the car.

"Well, that was eventful," Carla said to Adria. "Let's get you home and into bed."

*****

Carla sat Adria down on a kitchen chair while she made up the pull-out couch. Carla helped Adria pull off her pants but left her in the top she was wearing. After pulling the covers up over her, Carla decided now would be as good a time as any to give Nate a call.

She was grateful Adria took the hide-a-bed in the living room. This would give Carla more privacy in the bedroom to discuss anything with Nate.

Carla went to the bathroom first, took off her makeup, and washed her face before heading to her quaint little room. There was a full-sized bed in the middle with a beautiful pink, light blue, and white quilt spread out on the top, an armoire in the corner, and a four-drawer dresser opposite the door. She pulled her suitcase over to the bed and dug through it until she found her pajamas. She couldn't find her phone charger and thought maybe she had left it in her purse in the living room.

Pulling the night shirt over her head, she went to lay down on the bed. She told Siri to "Call Nate" and waited.

He picked up after a few rings. "Hi, it's good to hear from you."

"Hey, what's up?" Carla replied.

"I just wanted to check in with you earlier," said Nate.

"We were at dinner, but I figured it might be a good time to talk now that we are home," she replied. "Adria is in bed already, slightly boozed up." She giggled.

"Ah I see…uh, speaking of Adria, an old friend called me today and asked about her," Nate said.

Carla immediately knew whom he was talking about because it was the burning question she was dying to ask. "Let me guess, Daniel Tanner?"

"How did you know? Have I told you about him?" Nate asked.

"Not that I can remember," she replied, "but he may have been brought up in Adria's conversations lately."

"Ah ha. Is there something going on there that I should know about?" Nate asked.

"I don't think there is anything going on…yet," she replied, "but I think Adria is open to it. They talked earlier, and I think he wants to take her out when we get back."

"Well, that would be cool. Maybe a double date?" Nate said with slight hesitation in his voice.

"Nate, can we not…this is about Adria anyways, not us," Carla responded, getting slightly frustrated.

"Sorry," was all he said.

"Besides, I think she is really into him," Carla told Nate.

"Into who?" Carla shot out of bed as Adria's head peeked in through the bedroom door.

"Gah, you scared the crap out of me," Carla yelled. "It's Nate." She pointed to the phone. "We're talking about Daniel."

Adria closed her eyes slowly and grabbed at her head. She turned to walk back to her bed and said, "Tell me about it in the morning."

"Was that the drunkie?" Nate asked.

"Yes, she is going to be paying for it in the morning too. We're supposed to go antique shopping, so I don't know how useful she'll be," Carla was saying to Nate. "If Daniel calls you again, make sure you say all good things about Adria. She could really use some happiness in her life."

"I think Daniel could too. He's divorced, and I don't think he has dated anyone in a while. Maybe it would be good for both of them," Nate said, thinking how he could help the situation or potential relationship. "He's a good guy," he added.

Carla smiled to herself. "Well, I'm exhausted. I'm going to head to bed and probably sleep in longer than I should. I'll talk to you later, Nate."

"Good night, love."

*****

It was eleven in the morning, and both girls had slept in way later than expected. There was a knock at the door, and they both shot out. Adria was slightly confused of her surroundings and then instantly remembered where she was.

"Good morning," came a chipper voice from the other side of the door.

Adria got up a little too fast and headed to open the door. Miriam was standing there with a tray of food. "I just thought I would bring you some brunch if you are up to it? I prepared waffles with fruit and homemade whip cream. There are also eggs, sausage, and toast," she added.

"Thank you so much, Miriam. You did not have to do that," Carla said, walking out of the bedroom in her sweats and pulling a hoodie over her head.

"It's not a problem," Miriam said, walking into the cottage and over to the small kitchen table.

She set the tray of food onto the table and turned it so it showcased everything she had made. Carla came over, hovering and acknowledging how good everything looked.

"Here are your keys. Thank you again for letting us borrow your car," Carla said.

"Keep them," Miriam said. "I'm sure you have places you'd like to go today, and I have been more of a homebody during my pregnancy."

"We were planning on going to an antique shop today. Do you know of any? Maybe you'd like to come with us. I don't think we're going to be gone too long," Carla said, laughing and nodding toward Adria.

"Oh. I see," Miriam laughed, understanding Carla's meaning. "Had fun last night, huh?"

"She let lose, that's for sure," Carla said.

"Well, the antique store does sound like some fun. Perhaps just for a bit. I will let my husband, Craig, know I'll be out this afternoon. And thank you for the invite," Miriam said.

"We'd love to have you," Adria added as she walked out of the bathroom.

"I'll go get ready," Miriam shut the door to the cottage behind her.

"You look lovely," Carla said to Adria. "Hungry?" She held up the plate of sausage.

"I feel lovely," she said sarcastically but made a face at all the food.

Carla pulled out her laptop and connected to Miriam's Internet. She wanted to look up some nearby antique shops that they could choose from. She also wanted to be true to her word and not be gone long, so she would pick only one today and hit some others up perhaps another day.

"How was your conversation with Nate last night?" Adria interrupted Carla's search.

"You remembered. It was good. Daniel called him. He asked about you," Carla said, raising her eyebrows at Adria.

Adria got instant butterflies in her stomach and was instantly in a better mood. The biggest smile stretched across her face as she realized this just might be the beginning of something. If she felt this way and Daniel was going out of his way to find out about her, then they both had to be feeling the same way. She was so hopeful.

"Nate said he's a good guy," Carla said, trying to give her friend more reassurance.

"Thanks, I didn't doubt that. He's been very friendly and respectful every time I've seen him. At the gym before then the coffee shop and then the pizza place," replied Adria.

"Speaking of which I want to know how you two met," Carla demanded. "I think I missed that part."

"It was the same day I came to work with the cut on my head," Adria said.

"He's *that* guy?" Carla said surprised. "I had no idea. Won't you have yourself quite the 'meet-cute' if this works out?"

"Oh, you mean like yours?" Adria said playfully.

*****

Miriam came back to the cottage door a few minutes later. She was dressed in a different outfit that outlined her baby bump nicely, and her rain jacket matched perfectly. Carla and Adria had their matching rain jackets on, and Miriam couldn't help but laugh. "Well, aren't you two very match-y match-y?"

The two of them looked at each other and started laughing too. "We both found these when we were shopping in different parts of the same store," Adria said.

"They are very stylish, and I love the green," Miriam added. "So here are a few of the antiques shops we can visit." She handed them her cell phone so they could check out the shop names and where they were located. There were three antique stores on the same road and fairly close to each other. Carla would have liked to have gone to all of them, but promised herself she'd only choose one.

"You choose," said Carla. That would make it easier, and she wouldn't be dying to drive a couple more blocks to the next and then the next.

"Oh, I like them all, but let's try Yeats Country Antiques," Miriam suggested. "It's a pretty good one, and I've always enjoyed browsing."

"Sounds good to me," Carla said, and Adria had agreed as well.

Miriam had decided to drive since it was her car and she was the one familiar with the roads and driving around here. Carla didn't hesitate to let her.

It didn't take them long to get there, and Carla was so anxious to start looking. She loved antiques to the point of obsession. It wasn't just the beauty behind the pieces; it was the stories—the stories of history that they told.

Carla could hold a piece in her hand and think about where it came from, who owned it, how old it was, and how it ended up in the shop in the first place. She wanted to know everything. She would purchase a few items and take them home just to look them up on the Internet and see if she could find anything out about them.

A lot of things she had purchased were old photographs. They were mostly of landscapes, and some had small houses or cabins in the background. She would always take the photograph out of the frames to look for old handwriting on the backs. If it wasn't faded and the handwriting was easy to read, then she would be able to put it into Google search. After she was satisfied with what she had found out, she would use the black and white photographs as decor in her own home.

This particular trip, Carla was looking for something specific. She knew that if she was going to find it, she would definitely have to look in more than just one antique shop. She also knew that the likelihood of it being here was very slim, and her chance of finding more than just one of the like item was very high. There were going to be dozens of them.

This trip she would be looking for a key. She would be looking for the key that belonged to Mary Williams Gallagher. The key that would hopefully hold so many answers for Adria but also for Carla to learn.

They entered the store chatting about how excited they were, and there at the register, behind the counter, stood Travis, the waiter from the night before.

Adria didn't recognize him at first.

"Oh my goodness, hi," Carla said. She made a slight head gesture toward him as she turned to Adria. "This is the man that helped me get you into the car last night."

Adria was instantly embarrassed. "Yes, I remember."

"How are you feeling?" he asked Adria. Miriam had just entered the shop behind the two of them. Travis turned to her. "Miriam, I didn't expect to see you out and about today."

"I see you have met my tenants," she said, walking up behind them. "This is my cousin, Travis Hart."

"We met him last night at the restaurant. What a small world," Carla replied.

"Aye, I should have put that together and told you to ask for him," Miriam was saying. "These are the two ladies that are staying in my cottage for the next two weeks."

"That's great," he said, staring at Adria. "And did you sleep well?"

"I did, thanks, and thanks for helping last night," she said sheepishly.

Miriam could tell just by looking at Travis that he wanted to continue the conversation. She gave him a small, suspicious smile and started to walk away, but before he could open his mouth to get the words out, Carla came over and asked, "I'm looking for...we're looking for an old key."

Caught off guard, Travis turned from Adria to Carla. "I've got a box of old keys here to the left of the counter." He waved his hand as he walked that direction, telling them to follow him. He lugged it up on the counter and said, "Go for it."

It was a big, brown crate with dozens—scratch that—hundreds of old keys. Most were rusted, weathered, and worn. Carla knew this would be nearly impossible, but she was determined. She stuck her hands in the crate and started moving them around and pulling them out.

"Have you heard of Castle Creet?" she asked as she was shifting the keys back and forth.

"Aye," he said. "I have." He looked at Miriam. "Are these the two that were asking about the castle?"

"The key belonged to a relative of mine," Adria added to the conversation. "She lived at Castle Creet years and years ago."

"Well, that is probably some story. She must have been a Gallagher?" Travis asked.

"She married my great-great-great-grandfather, who was Henry Gallagher," Adria replied.

"I'm a bit of a history buff. I found your distant grandfather in an article that mentions him," Travis said.

The girls were shocked and surprised and excited. "We'd love to read it if you have it with you," Adria replied to him. "Do you… have it with you?"

"No, but I can get it for you," he said. "I can either drop it by later when I get off or bring it to the restaurant if you fancy yourself another glass of wine."

Adria blushed, and Carla laughed. "You can drop it by the cottage—that would be perfect."

Carla finished digging through the keys and found nothing. They walked through the rest of the store admiring old quilts and furniture. There were little trinkets that looked like children's toys and some beautiful old dishes, but after a while, they decided to wrap it up and head back. Carla could tell Miriam was getting tired and was ready to return.

*****

Miriam let the girls make a quick stop at the store so they could buy stuff to make a quick lunch, and when they got home, Adria whipped up something for all three of them.

"I think Travis was quite taken with you," Miriam said as Adria handed her the plate of food. Adria's cheeks turned bright red, the color of cherries. "He's very handsome."

"And are you taken?" Miriam asked outright.

"I'm...not." She thought of Daniel. But it was true; she and Daniel were not in a committed relationship. She didn't even know what it was really.

"How are we going to get to your grandmother's tomorrow?" Carla asked. "Should we try and take the bus?"

"Nonsense. I'll drive you," said Miriam, answering the question for Adria. "I didn't know you had family that lived here."

"Yes, my dad's mother lives here. She is in an assisted living home called the Four Ferns," Adria replied.

"Why, that's here in Dublin," Miriam said.

"I thought it was near Bray Harbour?" Adria asked.

"It's about twelve minutes north," Miriam was explaining. "What time are you to arrive?"

"I actually need to call the facility and check about visiting hours. I'll go do that right now," she said, and she grabbed her phone and headed to the bedroom.

Miriam had expressed that her body hurt; she was tired and needed to lie down. She thanked Carla for the food and headed back to her own house across the way. "Let me know what time we need to leave tomorrow," Miriam said.

A few moments later, Adria had come back into the living room. "Visiting hours start at ten o'clock a.m. The receptionist was very nice and added that my grandmother is expecting me promptly at that time."

"Okay, I'll text Miriam and let her know."

They had a quiet evening and stayed close to the cottage for the rest of the day. They took a short walk through the gardens and then made their way back to the cottage to find leftover stew on their doorstep. They had only known Miriam for two days, but she was becoming quite a great friend and very helpful. Plus, they weren't expecting her to drive them places or act as a tour guide. Nonetheless, Miriam had made their trip very easy so far.

Carla decided it was time to head to bed, and they both went to brush their teeth and get ready. When Carla was finished, she entered her room, pulled out her journal, and plopped down on the bed.

Dear Journal,

I've made it to Dublin. We checked out our first antique shop, but I couldn't find any key that resembled the one that could have been on the page of the letter. I'm going to try and convince Adria and Miriam to visit another shop tomorrow after our visit with Adria's grandmother. Please, please let us find it! Also we need to go to a library and see if we can find where Castle Creet is located.

—Carla

Carla ended her journal there and reached over, turning off her light. She snuggled down into her covers and closed her eyes, letting the darkness take her to sleep.

That night, Carla had a dream, a dream about Mary Gallagher and all that could have happened to her. She dreamed that Mary committed suicide after the sudden loss of her child and of the devastation Mary must have felt after losing a daughter.

*****

When Carla woke the next morning, she couldn't stop thinking about the dream she had had. It would make sense about the suicide side of the story, but then what about the murder? Were they one and the same? Maybe it was just assumed that Mary had committed suicide when really she had been murdered. So which was true?

Carla rubbed her eyes and pulled the covers back from the bed. She made her way into the bathroom to brush her hair but decided to skip the shower.

Adria came in behind her and started the water to the shower to get it hot before she jumped in. She brought her clothes in and laid them on the counter. Carla grabbed her hairbrush and headed back to her room, getting out of Adria's way and needing to get dressed herself.

When Carla walked back into her room, there was a young girl sitting on her bed. Carla screamed, "Who the hell are you? And how did you get in here?"

Adria ran into the bedroom half-naked and struggling to get the towel around herself. "What what what?"

Carla turned to Adria, white as a ghost, but when Carla turned back to the bed, no one was there. Carla couldn't talk. She had seen it, plain as day, someone sitting on her bed flipping through her journal.

"What is wrong?" Adria said. "You don't scream like that for no reason. Was there a spider?"

Carla was shaking her head and walked out of the bedroom to sit on the couch. "There was a girl in my room. She was sitting on my bed going through my journal."

"What?" Adria said. "You're messing with me."

"I'm not joking, Adria!" Carla pleaded with Adria to believe her.

"Okay, okay, I believe you. You mean it was like a…ghost?" Adria asked. She could hardly make herself say it.

"If it wasn't, I don't know what the hell it was," Carla blurted out. She needed to catch her breath.

Adria went into the kitchen and came back a few minutes later with a glass of water. She was still wrapped in her towel. "Will you be okay if I finish my shower?"

"Yes, I'm going to call Miriam," Carla replied.

Carla dialed Miriam's number just as there was a knock at the door. Hanging up, she tossed her phone on the couch and went to open the door. "Thank goodness," she said, but it wasn't Miriam. It was Travis. "What are you doing here?"

"Sooo Miriam wasn't feeling well and asked if I could drive you to your grandmother's," responded Travis. "May I come in?"

Carla moved back as he stepped inside the cottage and started closing the door. "Leave it open," Carla said. "And it's Adria's grandmother," she corrected him.

"Are you all right?" Travis asked. "You look like you just saw a ghost."

"I'm not so sure I haven't." Carla looked up at Travis.

"What do you mean?" he said, intrigued.

Carla recounted the episode of what happened just moments before he arrived. She knew it sounded ridiculous and she probably seemed like a madwoman, but Travis listened intently.

Adria came out of the bathroom, which opened right into the living room. She was still in her towel and had come out to grab her pants that must have fallen from her hands on her way to the bathroom. She froze and looked at Travis wide-eyed. "Oh hell," she said and jumped back in the bathroom quickly. She was even more embarrassed than she had been just the day before when running into Travis after her tipsy endeavor.

Carla couldn't help but laugh hysterically.

"Well, I'm glad I can make you laugh," Adria shouted from the other side of the bathroom door. "Bring me my pants."

Carla had missed Travis's reaction, but by looking at him now, she could tell he was embarrassed too. "I needed that," she said, still laughing.

Miriam knocked on the open door and showed herself inside. "Hey, I saw that Travis's car was here. I was going to try and make it over before he got here. I hope you don't mind him driving you today?" she asked Carla. "I woke up with a bit of a headache."

"Not at all, I don't, but Adria might." Carla laughed some more.

Miriam smiled. She knew there was some inside joke here. "Should I even ask?"

"Adria just walked out in her towel and didn't know Travis was here," Carla responded. Miriam looked at Travis as his cheeks flushed again and he looked away.

"I'll just wait outside," he said and walked back out to his car.

"Adria, you can come out now," Carla shouted to her friend.

"A little heads up would have been nice," Adria said as she opened the door and peeked out into the cottage living space.

"I literally thought you could hear him," Carla said innocently. "Travis is going to drive us to your grandmother's assisted home today."

"Well, I'm ready. Let's get this over with then." Adria rolled her eyes. Miriam and Carla chuckled as all three of them walked out the front door.

*****

Adria got in the car and rolled her eyes again as she heard Carla call after Miriam. Carla ran over to Miriam before she got into Travis's silver sedan.

Clearing her throat, she said, "Miriam, have you ever had dealings with…ghosts in the cottage? Or maybe had any guests bring it up?"

Miriam's eyes opened wide. "Uh, no. What happened?"

"I will have to tell you when we get back. Just wanted to let you know I think I may have encountered one this morning." Carla was saying.

She turned and walked back to the car and could see that Adria and Travis were talking. *Oh, good,* she thought, *they are getting along again.* Carla decided to make her pace a little slower.

"Shall I pick you up around seven?" Carla heard Travis as she opened the passenger side car door.

"Where are we going?" Carla asked.

"Travis and *I* are going to grab dinner tonight," Adria replied.

Carla looked from Adria to Travis and back to Adria. "Is that right?"

"Uh, you can come if you want." Travis threw the invitation out there.

"No thanks. You two have fun," Carla said, half-joking, half-sarcastically.

Chapter 8

The three pulled up to the assisted care facility, and Carla hopped out first. Adria unbuckled and pulled herself up closer to the driver's seat. She opened her mouth to say something but then closed it again. She moved back toward the door to get out, but then the words just came spilling out.

"Look, this isn't a date or anything… Maybe Carla should come," she said after pausing between sentences.

Travis tried to hide that he was crushed by replying. "I said she could. She is the one who doesn't want to… Look, here's my number. Call me when you are ready for me to pick you up."

Adria wasn't trying to hurt his feelings, but she really didn't want him thinking this was a date. He was sweet when she got into the car after their little mishap at the cottage, and he made her feel comfortable around him. This was just a new friend and a new friendship.

"Thanks for the ride," Adria added as she slid out the door and went to catch up with Carla.

Carla was standing by the front door and had just hung up the phone when Adria walked up to her.

"Who was that?" Adria asked.

"Nate," Carla said.

"Hey, you're not mad, are you? You can come tonight if that is what this is about," Adria was saying, pleading for Carla not to be mad at her.

"I'm not mad. I just thought this trip was for us to hang out. It's fine and I get it… You should go," Carla responded as she started walking inside the two sliding doors.

They walked inside and found the receptionist desk to the right of the entrance. "My name is Adria Layne. I'm here to see my grandmother, Roisina O'Brien."

"Ah, yes. She is expecting you. She is in room 212A." The nice lady pointed toward the hall. "If you follow this hallway, it will take you to the elevator. Her room is on the second floor to the left."

"Thank you," both girls replied.

"I won't go out tonight," Adria said as they walked toward the elevator.

"Yes, you will. This will be good for you. Who knows, Daniel might not turn into anything, and how romantic would it be to be involved with an Irish gent?" Carla was starting to lighten her mood and gave her a mysterious look.

They took a left when they exited the elevator on the second floor. There it was, 212A, with Roisina's name on the door.

"I don't want to knock," Adria whispered. Before she could say anything else, Carla tapped three times on the door. They waited a few seconds, but there was no answer.

"Maybe she can't hear very well," Carla said and knocked three more times, louder this time. Nothing…again three more knocks, a little harder.

"Hold on, hold on." A voice came from the other side of the door. "I heard you the first time…oh, I thought you were Laura," Roisina said as she opened the door. "Well, that explains why you didn't just come in."

"Are you Roisina?" Adria asked.

"Good gracious, you look like your father," Roisina said, staring at Adria.

"I actually get that a lot. May we come in, Roisina?" Adria asked.

"For heaven's sake, call me Grandmother. That's what I am after all," Roisina said to them. Eyeing Carla, she said, "You can call me Grandmother too."

Roisina stepped aside and let the two women pass her, but they stopped just inside the door. Not wanting to intrude, they waited for Roisina to show them the way.

She led them to a little living area with one couch, a rocker, a small television, and a big window that overlooked a river. On the wall hung a beautifully painted picture of a castle with wildflowers billowing from the fields. A small well sat in front, and off to the side, a small child was gathering flowers in her basket.

Adria and Carla thought it was beautiful. "Sit," Roisina said, pointing to the couch.

They both took a seat on each end of the couch and waited for Adria's grandmother to say something. When she didn't, Carla took it as her cue to introduce herself. "My name is Carla Murphey."

"I know who you are. Adria's mother told me she was coming with a friend."

There was an awkward silence before she went on. "I'm glad you are both here. I don't get many visitors, and it's not every day I get to see family."

"We're happy to be here too, Grandmother," Adria said.

"I'm under the impression that you have come seeking answers to some family history… I hope I can give you the information you are looking for," Roisina said.

"That is what we are hoping also. We are curious about Mary Williams Gallagher," Adria replied.

"Oh, quite a ways back then. Well, I have a box of things there." She pointed to the ground next to the couch. "Most everything I have is in there."

"May we look through it?" Adria asked.

"Of course. That's why I got it down," Roisina said. "Mary Gallagher was on your grandfather's side. His great-grandmother, if I remember."

The three sat there talking about this and that as they pulled out some old photographs. There were a couple of Adria's dad, Charles, and a photograph of Roisina and her husband, Charles, whom Adria's dad was named after. There were two old books and an old sketchbook someone had worked on in their spare time. There was a lace handkerchief, a pair of weathered gloves, a few more pictures, and some odds and ends.

"You know, Mary was about your age when she passed away, maybe a little older," Roisina continued. "She had lost a daughter and ended up passing away shortly after."

Carla and Adria stared at each other, eyebrows raised, questions forming in their heads.

"It's one of the things I remember Charles telling me about. Some family story passed down from his family," Roisina said, sitting back in her rocking chair and closing her eyes.

"If you're tiring, we can come back?" Adria spoke.

"Nonsense. You came for this story, did you not? I can see by the looks on your faces," Roisina said. "Now let's see, your grandfather, Charles's mother, was named Claire. Her mother was named Fiona. And Fiona was one of Mary Gallagher's daughters," Roisina had begun.

*****

Daniel was at his morning workout at the gym he shared with Adria. She hadn't been there in several days due to her vacation. Daniel found himself missing their interaction and random conversation. He also found himself looking forward to and counting down the days until she would be back.

When he thought about a date with her, he got excited, nervous, and hopeful. He started planning out in his head what they would do when she returned. He could take her to Barbacoa Grill or Melting Pot. Maybe a drive up to Table Rock to watch the sunset. He could bring a bottle of wine for them to share, and then he would take her home and ask to call on her again. He wondered if Adria was a "kiss on the first date" type of person.

Daniel couldn't get her out of his mind. Why, if he didn't have his daughter, Sophie, this weekend, he would get on a plane and fly over there right now. He would take her on a date in Dublin, and it would be the most romantic moment either of them had ever had.

*****

"Grandmother…start at the beginning. We want to know everything," Adria said.

Roisina took a deep breath and began, "Mary Gallagher grew up the way most young girls did. She had a loving mother and father and many siblings. She married a man named Henry Gallagher when she was seventeen years old, and they moved into the family castle, Castle Creet."

They both knew this but didn't say anything further, waiting to hear everything Roisina had to say. They wanted to know everything there was to know about it, the location, what it was like, size, etc.

"The castle was well-known back then. Everyone knew someone who lived there or someone that worked there. There weren't many things that happened that didn't get talked about…eventually."

"So it was popular?" Adria asked.

"It was," Roisina replied, "so after Henry had brought his new wife to live there, there had been talk about it, taking the two of them many years to conceive a child. So much talk that some would have said they were infertile. Well, Mary was twenty-four when she finally got pregnant and had a daughter. They named her Fiona. She would be your great-great-grandmother if I have that correct."

Carla and Adria sat contently, waiting for Roisina to continue. Their minds traveled back and tried to picture this young woman married, unable to conceive right away, and how happy she had probably been when she found out she was with child.

"After Fiona was born they were blessed with another daughter, Amelia, about a year later. Now as I remember the stories, your great-great-great-grandfather, Henry, was none too happy that they had not had a son. From how the family story goes, Henry began to ignore the child, Amelia, which then only made Mary hold her more dear and close. She was a good mother to both of the girls, but she held a special place for Amelia. She felt more protective over her."

Roisina paused a moment to ask the two if they would like to stay for tea. Carla and Adria agreed. Roisina called Laura to see if she could bring up refreshments for the three of them, and then she continued, "When Amelia was ten years old, there was a horrible accident. She was playing down by a nearby pond and slipped in and drowned..." Roisina paused, waiting to see their reaction.

Both Carla and Adria had raised eyebrows and sad looks on their faces. "How horrible," Carla said.

"The most horrible of it all," Roisina began again, "was that there were monstrous rumors that Henry had caused the so-called accident and that it wasn't an accident after all. It scattered the town, but no one knew what to believe."

They both had so many questions, but it was Adria who spoke first. "So it was, in fact, an accident?" she dared to ask.

Just then Laura knocked on the door and entered to bring the three of them their tea and biscuits that Roisina requested. "I hope I'm not interrupting," she said politely.

Adria tried to hide her annoyance because yes, in fact, she was interrupting. Still being polite, Adria thanked Laura for her kindness. She seemed like a nice lady and had only done what Roisina had asked.

"I'll leave you to it," Laura said and grabbed the door handle to close it behind her.

A few moments after the tea had been passed out and the three of them had got their cream and sugar the way they liked it, Roisina went on. "There was never any evidence to claim that Henry had been a part of his daughter's death, but rumor has it that Mary had believed he did."

"There were also rumors that Mary had gone into a very depressed state and the only thing to help keep her sane was to write. Poetry and letters, I mean... There are a couple letters in the box, I believe."

"Here they are," Carla said, pulling a stack of envelopes out of the box that was still setting on her lap.

"More than just a couple, Grandmother. You have a dozen letters from Mary," Adria said.

The three of them sat there for the next hour going through the letters, reading them and then rereading them out loud. Adria and Carla had been completely entranced with the information her grandmother was giving them. It only peeked their interests and made them want to know more.

"Grandmother," Adria said lightly, "Mother had a letter from Mary in her attic box as well. It looked like there had been an old key of sorts with the letter. It had two circles like the outline of butterfly wings."

Her grandmother was nodding as if she knew exactly what Adria was talking about. "Aye, another part of the story goes on that Amelia had been brought back into a room in the castle and later died there. She didn't actually die in the pond. Someone had retrieved her and she died later, unable to regain consciousness. After she was returned to a castle room, the doors had been locked, and it is said they were never opened again."

"Mary had been so grief-stricken?" Carla asked.

"That's how it goes. She wouldn't let Henry or Fiona go into the room. She had locked the wooden and metal door and sent a piece of the key to her mother."

"A piece? You mean it was only part of the key?" Adria asked.

"Aye. It's in the bottom of the box there," her grandmother said.

Carla sucked in her breath quickly, and both she and Adria began rummaging through the box as quickly as they could. Adria was throwing things aside, and Carla was pulling things out. Both of them froze as they spotted it.

It was small, the size of a dollar piece coin. Adria reached in and picked it up, a piece of history she was holding in her hand. "And the other piece?" she questioned her grandmother.

"The only thing the family could think of was that she sent the other bit in a letter to someone else," Roisina said, shrugging.

"A family member, perhaps?" Carla asked.

"Could be," Roisina replied.

"I wonder where it could be now?" Carla was thinking out loud. "We searched at an antique store yesterday."

"That's a good idea. The other half could be at one of those kinds of shops, but also it could be anywhere," Roisina said. "Even long lost."

"We're going to several more antique shops, and now that we know what to look for, hopefully we can find the attachment," Carla added.

It had been several hours, and the two didn't want to overstay their welcome. They both found out more than they were expecting, and now Adria needed to return to get ready for her dinner with Travis.

Adria went and kneeled next to her grandmother. She grabbed her hands. "Thank you, Grandmother."

"You are welcome, my dear," Roisina said with a smile across her face.

Adria and Roisina both looked over and saw Carla admiring the picture on the wall. Roisina let go of Adria's hand and pointed to the picture. "It's Castle Creet," she said to both of them.

"Castle Creet?" Adria questioned. "*The* Castle Creet?"

Roisina nodded and knew what Adria was thinking. "There is a map in the box." She pointed toward it. "It will show you how to get to Castle Creet. Take it with you. Take the whole box… Let me know what you find," she said. She knew if Adria was anything like her, they would set off to find it as soon as they could.

*****

Nate had been busy that Monday at the event. When he finally got a moment to sit down and breathe, they dismissed everyone into the second conference room for dinner. Nate took a deep breath and followed everyone into the other room. People were congratulating him on this and talking to him about that. His speech had been very good, and everyone wanted to put their two cents on the topics.

Nate grabbed a plate and walked off toward the back of the dinner line when he felt his phone going off in his pocket. He dodged the line of people and placed his plate on the table as he walked to the exit door. His first thought was that it was Carla. He pulled the phone out just as the door was closing behind him. It was Daniel. *What the heck does he want?* Nate thought.

"Hello," Nate said.

"Nate, it's Daniel again. I'm so sorry to bug you, man…"

Nate waited for him to continue. "I did something," Daniel said.

"Daniel, are you in some sort of trouble? Do you need—" Nate began.

"I may or may not be…on my way to Ireland," Daniel interrupted.

"Uh…why?" Nate wasn't sure what else to say.

"I had the crazy idea yesterday, and before I could talk myself out of it…well, here I am on the plane." Daniel was shaking his head and slightly regretting his decision.

"Is this about Adria?" Nate asked cautiously.

There was a pause before Daniel continued. "Yes." He closed his eyes thinking, rubbing them. Had he made a mistake? He was beginning to feel foolish as thoughts kept into his head, *Maybe Adria didn't like surprises.*

"You're smitten, dude… Well, I guess girls like this kind of thing, right?" Nate said. "That is, I mean a man chasing them across the world."

Daniel let out a breath, and Nate could hear it plain as day as if Daniel was standing right there next to him.

"I don't even know where she is, like where she is staying," Daniel said.

"I can get you the address," Nate replied, "and I think there might be a hotel close by. You can see if you can get a room."

"Man, I would really appreciate it," Daniel replied, trying to relax.

"You're crazy, dude…" Nate began. "Hey, I have to head back into my conference, but what time are you arriving? Maybe I can sneak away and pick you up from the airport."

"I should be there around seven o'clock a.m.," Daniel said, "so long as everything goes as planned."

"Okay, I should be able to make that happen before my morning meeting. Call me when your plane lands," Nate said.

"Thanks, buddy," Daniel said.

*****

Carla and Adria walked out to the bench in front of her grandmother's care facility and phoned for Travis to come pick them up. He wasn't far away, and it only took him a matter of a couple minutes to pull up to the front door.

"Can I see the map?" Carla asked. "I want to send a picture of it to Nate. He will think it's interesting too."

The map was an ordinary map of Dublin. It was the kind of map you could get anywhere, especially if you were a tourist. The roads to the castle were outlined in a red marker telling them where to turn, right or left.

Adria handed the map over to Carla and then continued to rifle through a few of the other things in the box her grandmother had given them.

Adria and Carla climbed into the car when Travis pulled up buckling their seat belts as Travis took off toward the main road. They barely made it out of the driveway before the questions started.

"Should we go find the castle? Do you think the room is still locked? Do you think Henry had anything to do with Amelia's death? How will we find the other half of the key?"

The questions went on and on, and Travis sat there listening and giving the occasional laugh. They were almost back to the cottage when he heard the last question and instantly perked up.

"You know working at an antique store, I can tell you. We rarely keep things if they are broken," he said.

"We think the other half of the key got sent to someone with an adjoining letter," Carla mentioned.

"Does this have to do with Castle Creet?" he asked.

"Yes it does. My grandmother was able to give us tons of information and answered more than one question we were curious to know the answers to," Adria said.

Buzz... Carla felt her phone go off in her purse sitting next to her on the back seat. It was Nate.

"Have I got a story to tell you," his text said.

"Call you in a bit," she replied back to Nate.

As she put the phone back in her purse, she overheard Travis saying, "The antique stores sometimes keep old letters and poetry they come across if it's interesting enough. They sell them to historians or people who use them for decoration in older homes and cottages."

"Do you think they would keep stuff about the castle?" Adria asked.

"Possibly," Travis said.

Adria turned from the front seat back to Carla and said, "Maybe we should head back to the antique store in the morning. We can check out a couple different shops too."

Travis was amused. Carla and Adria were talking like they were about to solve an age-old mystery. He liked to see them so animated, and he liked listening to their conversation. He just hadn't mentioned that he knew a few things more about Castle Creet himself. He hadn't mentioned it…yet. He thought it would be a good topic to have under his belt at his dinner date with Adria tonight.

They pulled into the long driveway, and Travis came to a stop in front of the little cottage.

"Thanks for being our chauffeur today, Travis," Carla said, and she hopped out of the car and headed for the door.

"No problem," Travis said, and then he turned to Adria sitting opposite him in the front seat. "What time should I pick you up tonight?"

"What time is dinner?" Adria asked shyly.

"I made a reservation for seven-thirty. It shouldn't take long to get there. Will you be ready by seven?" Travis asked.

"Okay, yes, that will work. Thanks for everything today," Adria replied.

Travis reached over and squeezed her hand just long enough to send crippling shivers down her spine. "I'm glad you two were able to find some answers you were looking for today."

Adria smiled and reached to open the door. "Thanks again," she said and shut the door behind her. She heard the car start up again and drive back down the driveway. She let out a breath and tried to figure out what the heck that was. Were those butterflies she was feeling? Travis was handsome, and she was very much attracted to him, but he was quite a bit younger than her. *This will be an interesting date,* she thought.

She walked in the cottage door and was finally able to sit and truly relax since they left that morning.

*****

Adria had two hours until Travis would be back to pick her up, and her mind started racing. *What am I going to wear? How should I do my hair and makeup?* "Gah, I sound like Carla," she said in a whisper and got up to go see if Carla was in her room.

Adria stood in the entryway. "Are you too terribly mad at me for leaving tonight?"

"No," Carla said. "I'm going to research the castle and phone Nate. I'll probably put on some old movie or something and call it a night."

"He'll be here in a bit. Want to help me get ready?" Adria said.

"I don't really have anything to wear."

"What's the occasion?" Miriam said. "Sorry, I let myself in when no one answered the front door."

"Adria is going on a date with your cousin," Carla said slightly jokingly.

"With Travis? Oh I knew he was sweet on you," Miriam replied with a smile.

"We're just having dinner," Adria said, embarrassed.

"Well, did I hear you say you don't have anything to wear? You're more than welcome to borrow something of mine if you'd like," Miriam said.

"I don't want to inconvenience you. Besides, I'm sure I can find something in this suitcase," Adria replied. "I know I have a black top and black jeans."

"What size shoe are you?" Miriam asked.

"I wear a seven," said Adria.

"Perfect. I'll be right back." Miriam disappeared out the front door.

A few moments later, she returned with three different pairs of black heels. "Take your pick." She set them down next to the bathroom where Adria had already started curling her hair.

"Those are so cute," Adria said. "Thank you so much. I'll try them on when I get changed and see which goes best."

Carla came out of the room and began making small talk with Miriam.

"I just came over to ask about your day with your grandmother," Miriam was saying loud enough for Adria to hear.

The next thirty minutes, Adria and Carla went over what they had learned and all the information Adria's grandmother had been able to give them. Carla told her they were planning on visiting more antique shops tomorrow and, of course, invited Miriam to come along.

"You know, Travis knows a little about Castle Creet. I'm surprised he hasn't said anything to you. Or mentioned it on the car ride," Miriam said.

Adria popped her head out the bathroom door and gave Miriam a one-eyebrow raise. Carla's mouth dropped, and they both stared at Miriam.

"You are kidding?" Adria said. "He hasn't brought it up once."

"Well, tonight will give you the perfect opportunity to talk to him about it. He wrote a paper on it in college." Miriam winked.

"How old is Travis?" Adria asked boldly.

"He'll be twenty-nine at the end of summer," Miriam said. "Think he's too young for you?"

Adria smiled. "I was just curious."

"He's a good guy," Miriam said. "He wears his heart on his sleeve."

Adria popped back in the bathroom and shut the door behind her. Five minutes later, the door opened, and she came back out with her outfit on.

"You look so pretty," Carla said, and Miriam nodded in agreement.

"The shoes make the outfit. Thank you so much for letting me borrow them," Adria said and went to sit at the kitchen table. "Why am I nervous?"

"Because you know it's more than just a dinner…it's a date," Carla said, teasing her.

"You'll be fine. Be yourself and don't let Travis talk your ear off too much," Miriam said as she walked over to the front door. "And have fun," she added and walked out, closing the door behind her.

"What about Daniel?" Carla brought Adria back to earth real fast.

"I…don't know. I don't expect this thing with Travis to turn into anything, and I'm technically not taken. Why can't I go out to dinner?"

"You can and you should," said Carla.

They talked a little longer about their visit with Roisina and the castle.

"Shoot. I forgot I was going to talk to Miriam more about earlier and the…ghost," Carla said. Adria was about to respond when there was a knock at the door.

Chapter 9

Travis pulled up right on time to pick up Adria for their date. Carla opened the door for him and thought he looked very handsome in his jeans, collared shirt, and leather jacket. She let him in just as Adria was walking out of the bathroom. She caught her breath, and she too thought Travis looked smashing. "Let me grab my purse," she said. She grabbed a tiny clutch Miriam had brought over as an afterthought.

"Don't be out too late," Carla said, jokingly with a smile on her face.

"Goodbye, Mom," Adria added as she shut the door behind them.

Carla sat on the couch, finding herself thinking about Nate. Did she miss him? She knew she did miss his company. Now that she was alone in the cottage, she kind of was wishing he was there. She pulled out her phone and typed Nate's name so that his number would come up. She hit Call and waited for him to pick up.

"Hi, honey, hold on a second," was the first thing Nate said when he answered.

Carla didn't really think anything about the way he answered. She waited a few seconds, and then she thought she heard a voice in the background...a female voice. *Was there a woman in Nate's room?* she thought. Her mind was racing and the questions started. *What is he doing with another woman? Why is she in his room? Is he cheating on me? Am I jealous?*

She couldn't help it, her mind races and the questions start flooding her mind. She was getting so worked up her hands began to shake. She didn't know if she wanted to talk to Nate anymore, so she hung up before he could get back on the phone. She picked up the television remote and started scrolling through the movie section, all while trying to calm her nerves.

A few minutes later, Nate was calling her back. She let it ring a long while before she picked it up. "Thought you were too busy."

"I'm not busy now," he replied to Carla, sensing there was tension in her voice. "What's wrong?"

"Oh, nothing," was all she said.

"Okay, Carla, I know you. You would think by now I can tell when something is wrong."

Carla didn't even know if she wanted to have this conversation but she began anyway, "I heard the woman in your room, and apparently, she takes priority even when you girlfriend calls."

"You can't be serious? That is why you are upset?" Nate was saying with a harsh tone. "She is a colleague. And I'm not in my room, and I'm definitely not in my room with her."

"You're just saying that," Carla snapped back.

"Do you understand how ridiculous you sound? Do you honestly think if I was cheating on you that I would have answered my phone in the first place?"

Carla thought about it. *Well, that makes sense.* But how was she going to say that to him now? "Where are you, then?" she asked.

"I'm finishing up a dinner conference," he said, still perplexed that she would accuse him of cheating.

"How come I can't hear anyone else?" she asked, still partially accusing.

"I came outside with a few other colleagues while they took a smoke break. I said I wanted to hang out here while the rest of them went in. She lagged behind to make sure I was feeling okay. And that is all," he said with a very matter-of-fact tone.

Carla knew and recognized his tone at once. She knew he was saying, "This is the end of the conversation."

"Nate, I... I...don't. I'm sorry."

"I should think so," he said.

"I…was calling you back from your text message earlier," she said, treading lightly, not knowing if he would even want to talk to her anymore. She felt really bad about the situation she had just caused but she didn't know what else to say to him about it. She heard him take a deep breath as if to speak, and then he let it out because the words did not come.

Nate took another deep breath. "I was calling because Daniel is on his way to Dublin and I just thought Adria would want to know." The excitement, the surprise, his eagerness to tell Carla earlier was gone.

"What in the actual hell," was all Carla could say. It wasn't a question but an actual statement.

"He called me when he was already on the airplane and said he did something crazy." Nate was explaining the conversation he had had with Daniel earlier. "I guess he wanted to surprise her."

"Well, she will certainly be surprised. Especially since she isn't even here. She's on a date with Miriam's cousin," Carla replied, still in complete shock.

"That's a predicament, isn't it?" Nate questioned. "That happened fast… So she isn't into Daniel anymore?"

"I don't think that's it. I think Adria was thinking she isn't tied down, so why can't she have a little fun?" Carla was trying to explain the situation well enough that it didn't make her friend look bad.

"If she and Daniel aren't exclusive, then I guess she can do as she pleases," said Nate, also defending her. "Should I tell him?"

"No, don't say anything. I'll tell Adria when she gets home tonight and see what she wants to do. She might want to see him. Who knows?"

They continued to talk for a few minutes each about their own days. Carla didn't go into too much detail about the information they got from Adria's grandma. It wasn't really a conversation she wanted to have after just accusing him of what she did. Carla was anxious to get off the phone and said she was going to start a movie and try to go to sleep. They said their goodbyes and good nights and she hung up.

*****

Travis pulled up to a parking spot. "You don't mind walking?" he asked.

"Not at all," Adria said.

Travis came around to open the door for her and offered his hand to help her out of the car. She accepted willingly, twisted her legs, and scooted to the end of the seat. She slid her feet down until they hit the sidewalk and she was standing next to Travis.

"We're going to one of my favorite restaurants called Gallagher's Boxty House. It's a cute little place with traditional Irish foods. I thought maybe you'd like to try a little Irish food and drink," he said, and they started to walk down the road toward it, passing a few different buildings.

Adria's eyes lit up as he said the restaurant name. "Gallagher is an old family name," Adria exclaimed. "My many times great-grandmother was a Gallagher."

"I know," he said shyly.

Adria gave him a look. *How would he know that?* She didn't think she had ever mentioned it to him.

He caught the look and began to explain, "When you were talking about Castle Creet, I put two and two together. Everyone knows that that's a Gallagher castle."

"Oh." She was slightly caught off guard but tried to hide it. "Well, speaking of the castle, Miriam mentioned you knew a thing or two about it."

"I know a few things. I can tell you more," he was saying as they walked up to the door, and he opened it for her. They continued on to the young gal standing behind the counter. He held up two fingers to indicate there were two of them. "I called ahead of time to see about getting a table," he said to the seating host. "The name is Hart."

Travis and Adria were led to a more private table in the far north corner of the restaurant. Adria couldn't help but notice that he had probably called and requested this very table. It was very secluded. "Someone will be with you shortly," the gal said as she placed the menus on the table.

They both scanned the menus, but Travis already knew exactly what he wanted. After a few minutes of quiet, Adria said, "I don't know what to get."

"If you'll let me, I can order for you?" he asked. Adria agreed.

When a server came to their table he asked if they would like anything to drink. They both ordered a glass of wine, and Travis asked if they could order their food too.

"I will take the goat's cheese bonbons to start, and then we'll have an order of turkey and ham Wellington and the Dublin Coddle." Travis handed both the menus back to the waiter and then gave his attention to Adria. "If you don't like it, we can switch. If you still don't like it, we'll just order something else." He laughed.

"I'm sure it will be delicious. I'm starving," she added. She waited a few moments before diving into the conversation again. "So tell me what you know about my family."

She didn't say *castle* because it seemed Travis knew more about her family history than he was letting on. Not just the castle but the actual people of her ancestry.

"I guess I'll start with how I learned what I know. I was in college writing a paper and ran across the name *Castle Creet*. It sounded interesting, so I dove in. There was an old paper in the local library talking about when it was built and by whom. You get the idea," he said.

"And when was it built?" Adria asked.

"It was built in 1799 by a family of Gallaghers. It was passed down through generations," Travis began again. "When the oldest son was old enough to marry, he would bring his wife to live there and take care of the older generation, that kind of thing."

"Well, that makes sense. Mary Gallagher was brought there when she married Henry," Adria said.

"Right," Travis agreed then continued, "so I guess in 1875, there was a death in the castle. The death was defined as an accident of unfortunate circumstance. The name was never given of the deceased, or at least I couldn't find a name."

"That is what the article said of how Mary Gallagher died…of unfortunate circumstances?" Adria quickly added. "It couldn't have been Mary, though. She would have only been five years old at the time. Carla and I found that she lived into her thirties."

Travis went on, "There was rumor of a ghost haunting the castle grounds. Doors opening and closing on their own, the fire going out by itself, and so on. The Gallaghers believed it had been the ghost of that particular death because there hadn't been hauntings before, and then all of a sudden, there was."

Adria got a chill and pulled her jacket back up over her shoulders as she waited for Travis to go on.

"Rumor has it that when your many times great-grandmother moved into the castle, there was death upon death of family members and castle staff," Travis said lightly, not wanting to offend her.

"What do you mean? Mary was a murderer?" Adria asked, very confused but not insulted.

"No, no, I'm not saying that. I'm saying that people had died… There was a series of unusual circumstances." Travis pulled an old wrinkled paper out of his back pocket. "I made a copy of this." He set it on the table and pushed it between them so they could both see.

Adria waited for Travis to continue as she looked at the paper wondering what it was.

"This is a list of the people who had died between the dates of 1906 and 1908," Travis pointed to a name. "It's written by Henry Gallagher."

The title was smudged, and it could not be read.

Conor Smith (d. 1907)
Matthew Ryan (d. 1907)
Belinda Callaghan (d. 1907)
William O'Sullivan (d. 1907)
Clara Walsh (d. 1908)

Coll Kelly (d. 1908)
Grant O'Brien (d. 1908)
Amelia Gallagher (d. 1908)
Mary Gallagher (d. 1908)

"Nine people at the Castle died in the matter of...one or two years. Including Mary Gallagher in 1908." Adria didn't know if her response was a question or more of a statement.

But Travis continued on, so she didn't have time to make up her mind. "It was rumored at the time, it had to do something with the ghost and the connection it had to Mary."

"What connection?" Adria asked.

"That Mary was the only one who could see *it*...and communicate," Travis said. "Many people believed Mary to be kind of *coo coo*. She would be found talking to herself."

"Go on," Adria said.

"There were some other stories told and passed down that Mary had been so devastated by the death of Amelia that Mary locked the door to the room her daughter, Amelia, had passed in and wouldn't let anyone enter. The door was locked by a special key, I presume, the key you've been searching for," he said.

Adria nodded like he was recounting what they mostly already knew. "We are impractically searching for half a key. My grandmother confirmed today that we only have the top half of the key," she reminded him.

After a few seconds of silence, he began again. "Anyways, that's mostly all I know. The last thing I can think of would be that it's also rumored that Mary took her own life after the death of Amelia because Mary was so miserable."

Adria gasped. "Oh no," she said. "The ending to someone's life taken by their own hands... That's it, though? That's what you're ending it on?" Adria sounded disappointed. "You have to know more."

"There isn't a lot more to say," he responded. "Only that when Mary died in 1908, the ghost of the castle was also gone and never seen again."

*****

That Monday night, Carla was snuggled in for the night, watching her movie. She realized she hadn't charged her phone and asked Miriam if she had a charger Carla could borrow. She promised she would return it in the morning.

She sent a quick text to Nate: "Forgot to let you know I can't find my phone charger. Hope my phone doesn't die."

"Go buy one tomorrow," he replied.

And that was the end of their text conversation. Carla was halfway buried up and sunk into the blanket she cuddled up in. She was so cozy and warm. Her eyelids were starting to get heavy, and she knew she was getting tired. If she could just rest her eyes for a minute, maybe she could finish to the end of the movie.

Just has she started to feel herself drift off, she was startled awake to the sound of something large crashing to the ground in the little kitchen. She jumped up and threw the blanket off her to the side of the couch. She grabbed at a vase sitting next to her and was ready for whatever was in the cottage with her. She searched through blurry eyes but couldn't find anyone. She tiptoed through the cottage and peeked into the bathroom, expecting to see someone at every turn.

She walked back to her bedroom and shoved the door open. Again, no one was there. She gave it a thorough search and sat down on the bed. No one was in the house. Had she imagined it? Perhaps it was the beginnings of a dream she was starting to have.

She searched back into her thoughts to try to remember what she had been thinking as she drifted off, but nothing was coming back to her.

Just then, there was another *thud*. Carla jumped up and ran back out into the living room. She found Adria's backpack purse sprawled out on the ground. The partial key that Adria had received from her grandmother had fallen out and was laying on the ground.

"Okay," Carla said out loud as her eyes darted here and there. "I hear you." She felt idiotic talking to thin air but clearly someone or something was trying to get her attention. She tried to take a deep breath in and out to regulate her breathing. Her heart was pounding out of her chest like the drum of a Native American warrior. She felt heavy, aware of how hard it was to move her arms and legs.

"I'm listening. What are you trying to tell me?" Again, she felt silly for talking to no one, supposedly.

She waited a minute. Nothing. No more sounds. No more crashes. Carla went over to the backpack and set it back on the table. She bent down to pick up the key, and instant chills passed down her spine. Goosebumps covered her body, and she was afraid to move.

She sat there in her crouching position to see if anything would happen next. "What do you want from me?" she said again and slowly started to stand up.

A gush of wind caused every window in the house to shudder. The curtains blew madly, roaring up and down and then…nothing. Carla took a deep breath, the first real deep breath she could take since this all started moments ago. The heaviness in her chest had dissipated, and she sensed whatever it was was gone.

She fell to her knees. Water filled her eyes, but she did not want to cry. The tears were more from shock than anything else. A million thoughts were running through her head: *It didn't want to hurt me. It could have done so but chose not to. This definitely has to do with the key, but why me?*

A good ten minutes had passed, and Carla decided now would be a good time to call Miriam and tell her what had happened. Carla pulled herself from the ground and went back to the couch.

She sat down and grabbed her phone from the arm rest.

Miriam answered on the third ring, and she insisted that Carla stay with her and her husband that night. They could check things out more in the morning.

Carla agreed and was grateful to get out of the cottage for the moment. She was feeling the need to calm down and regain her composure. She decided to text Adria after she gathered her things and made her way over to Miriam's. Carla would tell Adria to come stay at Miriam's that night also, but when Carla arrived at Miriam's home, they had got into a conversation of more questions. Carla had all but forgotten to text Adria.

*****

Adria hadn't realized during the conversation that she had begun to tense up, holding her fingers tucked into their palms. She also was unaware at just how many glasses of wine she had had. It had been a while since she had been on a real date, and her nerves were getting the best of her. "Travis," she said and prepared for the next sentence so she wouldn't slur her words, "would you mind taking me to the library tomorrow? I'd like to see if there is anything else I can find out about the castle." The wine was making her a bit dizzy, but she was also becoming very bold in their fascinating discussion.

"I can in the morning," he said, "as long as we're not there too long. I work at the restaurant at eleven-thirty."

"Th-th-that will work," she said and realized she had stuttered. "Oh goodness, this is getting to me." She held up her wine, giggling. It was everything she could do to not start crying. She had done it again, drinking way too much, having way too much fun, and simultaneously, she was going to need Travis's help to get out of here.

Travis could tell she had probably had enough, so he waved down a waiter and paid for their meal. "Would you like to take a walk?" Travis asked and was hopeful she would say yes. He thought the fresh air would do both of them some good.

Adria nodded and began to push back her chair, but before she could stand, Travis was next to her offering his arm. She was grateful for his gentleman-like manners and leaned into him appreciatively, but this also gave way for her stomach to overflow with butterflies like she hadn't felt in years.

Travis knew that out the door to the right of the restaurant was River Liffey. It had a long and narrow sidewalk they could venture to and stroll next to the water. Travis offered his arm again, and Adria took it happily, wrapping her hand around his rather large bicep.

As they continued to walk and make their way around the corner, Travis noticed Adria was staring up at him. She had the faintest smile graced upon her beautiful face. Her face had begun to take the color of a strawberry as the wind in the air was a bit chilly. Travis smiled and began to make small talk, asking about her childhood, where she grew up, and what she did for a living.

Adria answered each of his questions, trying not to sound too boring, She would then reply with a question of her own. She would catch herself missing every other reply as it was hard for her not to pay attention to the strikingly gorgeous sound of Travis's Irish accent.

After walking halfway down the poorly lit street, she stopped abruptly as if something had pulled her to a halt. Pulling her hand down his arm and wrapping her fingers into his hand as he took two more steps, she tugged at him to stop walking. He turned to her curiously and for a moment communicated through locked eyes only. They stood there for a few seconds, their body language intimately connecting them to each other. Adria suddenly pulled him to her and kissed him more passionately than she had intended. It sent even more butterflies through her body, and they deepened their kiss as she remained perfectly balanced on her tippy toes. He backed her up to the side of the building wall, and they both had to come up for air.

They didn't make it to the river, and before she knew it, Adria was standing in Travis's home entry way. He opened the door and walked in behind her to find the light switch in the hallway. She followed him into the living room where the lights were still dark.

"Want a drink?" Travis asked.

She laughed nervously. "Sure." What was she doing? She knew where this led. She turned in circles checking out his place, and before she knew it, Travis was behind her, standing at her back and offering the drink over her shoulder. She took a sip and let out a slight cough as she swallowed. It was a very strong gin and tonic. She took a couple more swigs, trying to work up the courage for what she knew was going to happen.

Travis started kissing the back of her neck, and Adria gave into his warm lips. He took their glasses and reached to set them on the entry table. She pulled her hair off to one side and leaned her head the opposite way to make her neck and collarbone more accessible. He slid his hands down the side of her arms and grabbed at her fingertips. His kisses hit her jaw bone and cheeks and inched closer to her mouth. Still facing away from him, she turned her head until their lips met and their desire connected once again.

She slowly turned around, facing him and sliding her hands up the front of his chest and around his neck. He reached down and picked her up with such ease as she wrapped her legs around his hips and let him lead her to the bedroom. He sat her on the bed and started unbuttoning her top. Adria instinctually began helping him, quickening their momentum. Their want for each other was intensifying, and Adria had lost all self-control.

*****

Carla woke the next morning to the smell of coffee filling her room, and for a moment, she did not remember the night before. She lay in bed for a few minutes, soaking in the warm sunlight that hit the side of her face. She fluttered her eyes open and looked around and realized she was not in the cottage bed she had grown accustomed to the last few nights. It came rushing back to her as fast as the tornado in the movie *The Wizard of Oz* or, better yet, *Twister*.

She was in Miriam's home. There was a ghost last night trying to communicate with her. What the hell was it all about? She thought. She got out of bed and slipped back into her sweats she was wearing the night before. She quietly opened the door to the bedroom Miriam had given her for the night. The waft of coffee hit her face and almost made her melt. She took a quick glance at the clock: 7:00 a.m. *Why does it have to be so early?*

"There are coffee mugs on the table. Help yourself," Miriam offered as Carla walked into the room. "Then come and sit next to me, and let's talk more about the events from last night."

Carla grabbed the pink and purple flower mug and poured a large cup of coffee. Rubbing her eyes with one hand and holding the mug in the other, she made her way over to Miriam. "Where is your husband?"

"He left an hour ago. Early riser," Miriam explained. "And I just can't stay comfortable with this big ole belly, so I've been getting up with him… Now do you think you'll want to find a new Airbnb?"

Carla got to thinking about how, if this "thing" was trying to connect with her, it wouldn't matter where she went. Besides, it had followed her all the way from Boise.

"No, I'll be fine. You do believe me though, don't you?" Carla asked.

"Of course I do. I just don't know what it means," Miriam replied. "We've never had an incident like this before."

Carla sat there a little longer, trying to decide whether or not to add it to the conversation and then just came out with it. "Before we came over, I had two other occurrences with this 'ghost.' I think whatever or whoever it is followed me."

Carla heard Miriam let out a sigh. "I see."

"Is that a good thing?" Carla asked.

"Yes and no. I just can't have a ghost living there while I'm trying to rent it out. Whatever it is trying to tell you, it really wants you to listen." Miriam was going on, sounding sympathetic.

"Oh, shoot," Carla spouted out. "Adria didn't come over last night, did she?"

"No, she isn't in the other room," Miriam said.

"Adria is over there by herself and has no idea what happened. I forgot to text her last night," Carla said. "She probably came home last night and plopped right on the couch, not thinking to look for me in the bedroom. I have got to walk over there and grab her."

"Wait a minute and I'll come with you," Miriam said. She made her way to the door and slid her rubber boots and jacket on. Carla grabbed for the umbrella by the door.

They took off walking at a hurried pace as Carla was anxious to get to Adria and let her know what had happened. Carla hesitantly opened the cottage door, knocking softly so she wouldn't scare her. When she walked in, the couch had not been pulled out or bed made up. *Maybe she slept in the bedroom*, Carla pondered bleakly.

Carla went straight for the bedroom, but Adria was not there either. The small clutch she took with her to dinner was nowhere in sight. In fact, there was no sign that Adria had been there since the evening before.

Carla's shoulder slumped heavily, and she glanced at Miriam. In unison they said, "She didn't come home."

Ding. Carla's text notification went off: "Call me so we can arrange for Daniel to surprise Adria later tonight.—Nate."

Carla had forgot all about Daniel being in Ireland, but for now she had too much to think about. With a suspicious ghost haunting her and a lost friend, she had not been thinking about that bombshell of a surprise.

"Was that her?" Miriam asked hopeful.

"No, my boyfriend," Carla said.

"Let's walk back over to my house. We'll get another cup of coffee and I'll call Travis. I'm sure she is fine," Miriam said.

*****

Adria woke the next morning, topless and hair tousled in every which direction. *This is not the pullout couch,* she thought. She rolled over in bed, grabbing the blankets to her chest; she sat up. She did not recognize any of the furniture or decorations. "Oh Lord, what have I done?" she said out loud.

She looked at the storage bench at the foot of the bed and saw the same leather jacket Travis was wearing the night before. Everything came flooding back to her including the hangover headache she was hoping to sleep off. Alas, she had spent the night with Travis. She laid back down, fighting with her inner thoughts of the night before.

"Can I get you anything to eat?" came a voice from the bedroom doorway.

Adria sat up quickly in surprise, the blood rushing to her head. She was lightheaded and couldn't speak right away.

"Are you okay?" Travis asked.

She put her index finger out as if she was saying "One second," but instead of getting any words to come out, she found herself throwing the covers from the bed and running into the master bathroom. She barely made it to the toilet bowl before spewing everything from the night before.

She cleaned her mouth with a towel nearby and stood to walk to the bathroom sink. She dabbed her hands under the water and softly smacked each side of her cheek. She stuck her lips under the running water to swish and spit any remaining taste left in her mouth.

She embarrassingly covered her body with her hands before walking back into the bedroom, but Travis was gone. She had to talk herself out of getting back in bed and covering her head in shame. She went and sat on the storage bench and slid her arms into her top from the night before. She pulled on her black jeans and grabbed Miriam's heels. She sat there hanging her head in humiliation.

Travis came strutting back into the bedroom with nothing on but his gray sweat bottoms. "Here," he said, and handed her a couple ibuprofen and saltine crackers. "What can I do to help?" He knelt down in front of her and swiped the hair off her forehead.

When Adria looked up to meet his face and see what he was offering, she had tears in her eyes. Travis set the hangover snack on the nightstand and came back to kneel down beside her.

With both his hands, he started rubbing the outer top of her arms, starting from the shoulders and working down to the elbow and back again. "What's wrong, Acushla?"

Sniffling and trying to compose herself, she said, "I've never done anything like this before."

"It's going to be okay." Travis was comforting her the best he could. He came up to sit next to her and put his arms around her, and she leaned into his warmth.

They sat there for a few more minutes, not talking, just embracing each other and hoping they knew how to proceed with the day and whatever it was now that was between them.

"Do you regret it?" Travis asked hesitantly, not knowing if he really wanted to know the answer.

Adria sniffed again, trying to gain strength in her voice. "No," she replied, "and yes." She let out a small whimpering sound. "Oh, Travis, I'm so sorry. I didn't mean for this to happen."

Travis placed his fingers under Adria's chin and lifted until she had no choice but to look at him. "I don't regret any of it, Acushla. And I would do it all over again in a heartbeat."

Silent tears slipped down Adria's cheeks, and she grabbed at her own sleeve to wipe her eyes.

"Here, let me get you a tissue," Travis said as he rolled over to the nightstand and opened the drawer. "A small pack of tissue I bought as an impulse buy years ago. Who knew they would ever come in handy?" He chuckled.

Adria let out a soft chuckle and reached for the never-opened package of Kleenex. "What does *Acushla* mean?"

Travis squeezed his lips together nervously. "It means *my darling*...in Gaelic."

Adria wasn't sure if she liked being called the Gaelic word for darling. She didn't know if she liked being called *darling* at all. She was confused, and nodding was the only thing she could do.

"If you're ready, I can drive you back to the cottage. No doubt Carla will probably be wondering where you are," Travis said tenderly.

As if right on cue, Adria's phone went off. And quite comically, Travis's was ringing from the other room also. Adria picked up her phone to a text from Carla: "Want to explain where the hell you are?"

Travis walked back from the living room and stood just inside the bedroom door. "Yes, she is with me. We're heading that way now." He covered the bottom of the phone and mouthed *Miriam* so Adria would know who he was talking to.

"I'm on my way now." Adria punched out in her reply to Carla. Then she quickly added, "No questions" and hit Send.

*****

"Thank God they are together," Miriam said to Carla.

"Well, thank God they are safe," Carla said.

Carla decided now that they had found Adria, it was time to call Nate. She punched in his phone number, but there was no answer. She tried again. Still no answer. She decided to leave a voicemail message. "It's me, wanted to chat about the crazy last twenty-four hours I've had. Call me back."

"Oh, I almost forgot," began Miriam. "Before your little encounter last night, I was researching Castle Creet and its previous residents. There is the National Archives of Ireland that holds thousands of documents. I think it would be a good place to see about those letters Mary wrote that you had mentioned yesterday. There might be more."

"Why didn't I think of that?" Carla asked inwardly, making herself feel unintelligent.

"Also, I think the castle is in a pretty secluded area. It might be hard to find. Someone should definitely go with you," said Miriam. "Do you know when you are planning to make it over there?"

"I'm not sure yet," Carla replied.

"I'm not sure about the arrangement of last night, so I'm not sure if Travis will want to go, but didn't you say your boyfriend was in Dublin too? Maybe he could go with you," Miriam said.

"I might actually consider that except, well, two things—he has meetings the rest of the week, and we have a surprise visitor," Carla said with a roll of her eyes.

"What does that mean?" Miriam asked just as she saw a car turning down the driveway.

Carla saw the car also. "Before we left," Carla started, "Adria had a 'kind of date' with someone she met a few months ago. They've been talking a little bit here and there, and now…he decided to fly all the way to Dublin to surprise her." She cleared her throat to try to hide her annoyance of the surprise.

Miriam's eyes got wide as she was beginning to understand the predicament. "He's here," she said pointing to the ground, "now? In Dublin?"

"Yep. He's friends with my boyfriend, and Nate is supposed to be picking him up from the airport sometime this morning."

"Your little vacation is turning into quite the soap opera," Miriam replied with sarcasm.

A car rolled up to the cottage and stopped in front of the walk way. Miriam and Carla could see out the little house window and knew right away the car did not belong to Travis.

"I'd better go over and check it out," Miriam said.

Carla pulled on her boots and grabbed the umbrella again, this time waiting for Miriam to finish getting her boots on also. Miriam moaned slightly and grabbed at the side of the table to get her balance. Wrapping one hand around her belly, she bent over at the waist and wailed again.

She hadn't quite got her second boot on when Carla rushed over, "Miriam, are you okay? Is it the baby?"

"Oh, I'm fine," she replied. "These cramps happen every now and then… It will pass in a second." She took a deep breath and tried to calm her breathing.

And so it did after a few seconds. Carla was still worried about Miriam and offered her her arm.

"Okay, I'm fine now." Miriam waved her hands at Carla. Miriam didn't want her to make a fuss over these little cramps.

"As long as you are sure." Carla was saying as she opened the door for Miriam.

Chapter 10

Nate pulled up to the airport pickup area and saw Daniel standing with his one small carry-on. Nate would have recognized Daniel anywhere. "Hey, buddy," Nate yelled out the window when he rolled it down.

Daniel waved when he spotted Nate driving up. "Thanks again for picking me up," Daniel said as he opened the door and hopped into Nate's rental car.

It was about nine in the morning, and Daniel was beginning to feel very jetlagged. He rubbed his eyes with one hand and shook Nate's hand with the other. Daniel buckled into his seat. "I'm sorry it's later than I thought." Daniel's plane had had an unexpected layover and hadn't arrived when he originally had thought.

"I'm just glad it worked out, and I could get away for a bit," Nate said. "What place did you book? I can take you to your hotel."

"I was actually wondering if we could go straight to where Adria is staying? I've worked up so many nerves. I just need to get this surprise over with," he said with a nervous side smile.

Nate couldn't help but laugh at his clever, amusing comrade.

Halfway through the drive, Daniel said, "Man, maybe I should have caught up on some sleep before I showed up unannounced."

"We can turn back if you'd like," Nate suggested. "I text Carla this morning, but I haven't heard back from her yet."

"No use now. We're already on the way... I'll sleep later," Daniel yawned.

They used the rest of the drive to catch up on this and that. Nate asked how Daniel's daughter was, what he had been up to lately and his teaching job. And Daniel returned with his own questions about pediatrics, how Nate ended up coming to Dublin and his relationship with Carla.

"It's complicated," Nate said. He turned into the driveway to the address he punched into maps on his phone.

Daniel took a deep breath about to ask another question, but Nate interrupted him, "We're here."

Daniel took it as a hint and shut his mouth. *The place was beautiful,* he thought. "They got lucky getting such a nice place to stay."

"I'll say. It does look pretty cozy," Nate replied.

"You haven't been here before?" Daniel asked and then instantly regretted it. "Oh you've probably been busy with work." He dodged the uncomfortable look from Nate.

They pulled up in front of the cottage and sat for a moment. Daniel was beginning to regret his decision to surprise Adria, and Nate was beginning to regret showing up unannounced.

Especially since Carla said she didn't want to see him during her trip.

They both got out of the car and walked to the cottage door. Nate leaned forward to the door and knocked three times, but there was no answer. "Maybe they're still asleep," he said out loud, and he leaned in and knocked again.

"Nate! Is that you?"

Nate heard someone shout his name and turned around to see who it was. Carla was walking toward them from what looked like another little house on the edge of the property.

Daniel caught his breath. "No turning back," he said. As the two ladies walked closer, though, Daniel realized that that was not Adria with Carla.

As Carla got closer, she began thinking about why they were here in the morning. Getting closer, she said, "I thought you were coming tonight?" She was thinking about the text Nate had sent her earlier.

"Surprise," Daniel said as Miriam and Carla were almost right in front of them. "Where is Adria?"

Carla leaned in and gave Nate a little hug. It felt familiar and not strained like she was thinking it would. "Adria is on her way back to the cottage," Carla said. "Oh Lord, Adria is on her way back to the cottage." She again remembered where Adria was coming from and with whom she was coming with.

For a moment, there was an awkward pause among all of them. Carla could feel eyes darting and bouncing from one person to another, and she quickly changed the subject. "I'm sorry." She cleared her throat. "This is Miriam. She owns the Airbnb and is friends with Jacob."

The men politely shook hands with her, and Daniel said, "Nice to meet you."

"It's nice to meet you both. Shall we head back to the house and I'll put on another pot of coffee?" Miriam suggested.

They all agreed and started walking back in that direction. Daniel skipped ahead next to Miriam and started asking questions about the cottage and garden. He wanted to let Nate and Carla have a moment to catch up and he wasn't a stranger to making new friends.

"It's good to see you," Nate said to Carla.

"Nate," a more serious Carla started, "Adria…she…she spent the night with someone last night."

Nate looked shocked. His face said it all. "Shit, what are we going to tell Daniel?"

"You may not have to say anything. Adria is on her way back right now. She should be here any second…with Travis," Carla said.

"What the hell was she thinking?" Nate sounded angry.

Carla pulled his arm back and made him stop walking. "You don't get to talk about Adria like that. You don't know what happened. I don't even know what happened." Carla was letting his mood get to her, but she didn't want to be angry too.

"You're right… This is going to fall to…" He let the sentence trail off as he heard another car pulling down the drive and turned to see who it was.

Carla turned and immediately recognized the car as Travis's. She grabbed Nate's arm and started walking faster toward the house.

"Come on," she said. As they got closer to the house, she gave Miriam a look of desperation.

Miriam understood right away. "Let's get inside," Miriam ushered quickly.

When Nate and Carla made it to the door, Miriam whispered in Carla's ear for her to stay outside and greet them. "You can let Adria know what is going on, and I will keep these two occupied with coffee and scones."

*****

"Just drop me off at Miriam's house, would you? I see Carla is over there," Adria told Travis.

Travis pulled in front of the house and also noticed Carla was standing outside the door waiting for them. He thought it was odd. Was he about to get scolded? But then realized she was probably just worried about Adria.

He stopped the car and watched Adria unbuckle and gather her things, but before she could get out, he said, "Adria, last night… doesn't have to be as crazy as you're making it out to be."

Adria wasn't sure what he meant by that, and Travis could tell by the look on her face that she was confused. He continued, "I just mean that I want to see you again."

"I don't know, Travis. This is all so complicated and it's so fast," Adria said, grabbing her face with both hands.

"It doesn't have to be," Travis said.

Adria realized there was absolutely no way he could fully understand…because he didn't know about Daniel. She couldn't say anything. She just looked at him with teary eyes. She was begging for her attention to be pulled elsewhere by anything else. She did enjoy her time with Travis, and she was beginning to understand that she had feelings for him, but with that came more uncertainty.

"Shall I come in for a bit? I'm sure Miriam won't mind. Unless this get-together could be weird after last night," Travis said.

"I think it could be very weird. I'd like to have some time to sort things a bit," Adria said, "if you don't mind."

Carla came over to Adria's side of the car and tapped at the window. She waved at Adria to get out.

Adria opened the door and quietly said in Travis's direction, "I'll let you know."

"Hi, Travis," Carla said, trying not to sound too protective.

He nodded in return, not sure if he should say anything and try to explain about what happened.

Adria got out of the car and turned to look at Travis as she shut the door. "Bye," she whispered. She turned to face Carla and waited for Travis to drive away. When she felt the car was far enough gone, she fell into Carla's arms. They hugged for a moment and embraced with a sisterly hug.

Carla was glad that Adria was safe, and Adria was glad to have a supportive friend. "What are you doing at Miriam's?" Adria finally asked as she let go of their embrace.

"Well, I stayed the night here last night, but that's another story. First," Carla began, "there is something else I need to tell you." She grabbed Adria's shoulders softly and looked up at the sky to prepare herself. Carla dropped her head back down to make eye contact with Adria. "Daniel is inside."

Adria couldn't say anything. She stood there searching Carla's eyes. Adria felt like she was going to have a mental breakdown, and she fell back into Carla's arms and began sobbing.

"I don't know what happened last night with you and Travis…" Carla began.

Adria blurted out, "Exactly what you think happened…"

"And do you regret it?" Carla asked.

Adria pulled back to look at Carla. "No, I don't. It was wonderful. Travis is wonderful."

"Look, this might be something we can joke about later, but for right now, we have to figure out what we are going to tell Daniel," Carla said, being realistic and bringing them both back down to the current situation at hand.

"This couldn't get any worse. Why is he here? Halfway across the world…" Adria pulled her posture upright and took a deep breath. She wiped her tears and told Carla to send Daniel out.

"No, you don't have to do this on your own," Carla said matter-of-factly.

"What do I tell him?" Adria asked as she brought her hands up and rubbed her temples.

A lightbulb went off, and Carla snapped her fingers. "Let's tell him you don't feel well. I can walk you back to the cottage and buy you some time to think about what you want to say. I'll help you." She gave Adria's hand a squeeze.

"I'll walk back myself so you can go in and explain. Carla, I'm sorry to put you in this situation," Adria added.

"You go get some rest. I'll be right over in a few minutes," Carla said. She didn't want to leave Adria in the cottage by herself for too long. Carla watched Adria walk back to the cottage and began thinking about what she was going to say to Daniel.

Adria was back at the cottage and opening the door to the little place that had begun to feel like home for the last few days and still was for the next nine and a half days. She decided not to be out in the open living room while she rested; it was too bright. She shuffled back into Carla's room and flopped down on the bed.

*****

Carla tapped lightly and opened the door to Miriam's home and slipped inside, shutting the door behind her. The smell of sweet coffee graced her senses, and she went and poured another cup for herself before heading to join the others.

"Adria isn't feeling well," Carla said as she entered the living room and sat next to Miriam.

Daniel couldn't hide his disappointment. "Does she know I'm here?"

"Yes, I did mention it. I'm sorry to ruin the surprise," Carla said.

Daniel waited. "So does she not feel good or does she just not want to see me?"

"I'm sure it's not that. She really doesn't hold her alcohol very well." Carla was sure that was not a lie. She didn't mention why Adria was probably drinking last night, but she also didn't want to lie to Daniel.

Daniel stood. "Well, no use waiting while she rests. Maybe I will come see her later tonight."

"Yes, I'm sure that would be better," said Carla. "I can have Adria call you."

Carla couldn't help but notice Daniel looked exhausted himself and added, "Maybe you could use a nap too?"

"Yes, no doubt of that. It's probably what I should have done in the first place." He turned to Miriam. "Thank you for the coffee. Nate would you mind driving me to my hotel?"

"Not at all, buddy," Nate chimed in. He stood and walked toward the front door and politely thanked Miriam as well. Daniel was heading out the front door when Nate asked Carla if everything was okay with Adria.

"She'll be fine. She is embarrassed about last night and shocked at Daniel being in Ireland. I just thinking she is overwhelmed."

"If he asks me to bring him back tonight, would you mind so much if I did? I know you wanted this to be 'Nate-free.'" He spoke of himself.

"At this point...it's fine," was all Carla could muster. "See you later," she added.

Carla walked behind Nate and watched him get into his rental car and drive away. Worn out herself from her own drama of last night, she decided to head back to the cottage. She would check on Adria and then cautiously try to explain what happened in the cottage.

*****

She opened the door to the cottage, and Adria was not on the little hide-a-bed. *This is like déjà vu*, Carla thought walking back to her own room. She found Adria sprawled out and passed out in the bed.

She decided to let Adria sleep a little longer to get better rested. Carla pulled out her computer and typed *handling ghosts* in the search bar. She scrolled through and clicked on a random link. A man's name popped up who claimed to be able to remove them from certain places, and another link explained how to communicate during a seance. *No thank you,* Carla thought.

She scrolled though another page until one headline link stuck out to her: *Why are ghosts haunting you?* She decided to click on it, and she read through the first couple sentences until one popped out at her. "Ghosts haunt people they trust," it read. She had to reread it a couple times. Carla wasn't sure if she believed that, but maybe that was what's going on. Did this *spirit* think that Carla could help it in some way?

She opened a few more articles but got tired of all the same ole, same ole. She shut her computer and set it down on the floor next to the couch. Out of the corner of her eye, she saw Adria walk back into the living room.

"I'm awake and can't go back to sleep. I might as well come out here and talk about it," Adria said.

Carla gave her complete attention to Adria and didn't say a word. She waited for Adria to speak first and watched as she walked toward her to the couch.

Adria folded one leg under her and sat down on the couch next to Carla. "I had a couple glasses of wine," she began and looked up to Carla fully expecting a motherly, scolding look. "But I knew exactly what I was doing…and it wasn't him, it was me. I initiated it."

"No judgment, Adria. If you recall, I've been through this too," Carla responded with tenderness in her voice.

"I know, but you said you regretted every second of it, and I… well, I don't," Adria explained.

"What does that mean, exactly?" Carla asked.

"I'm not entirely sure. This whole situation I've put myself in is very confusing. I like Travis, but I like Daniel too." Adria was trying to explain it the best she could.

Sympathetically, Carla looked at her friend. She knew that Adria was in a bind, and neither Daniel nor Travis knew anything about the situation. "Do you know what you are going to do?" Carla finally asked.

Adria thought for a moment. "I have to be honest with both of them. I'll talk to Daniel tonight. Would you mind giving us the cottage? You and Nate could go out."

Hmmph, Carla thought. "Well, I guess my Nate-free vacation turned into 'Let's figure out what I want to do about my own relationship.' I guess we both have things to think about."

Chapter 11

"Laura, has my granddaughter called?" Roisina asked. She was hoping that Adria would want to visit again, but Roisina would not pressure her granddaughter nor would she give in to be the first one to call. Roisina had talked to Adria's mother after Carla and Adria had left yesterday and told her that she had the most wonderful time visiting with the two of them. Adria had reminded her of Charles, Adria's father, and in turn reminded Roisina of herself too.

Adria's mother was thrilled and said that Roisina and Adria needed to get together at least once more before she returned home. Without asking if Roisina wanted it or not, she gave Roisina Adria's cell phone number.

"No, ma'am, she has not. Would you like me to see if there are any messages downstairs?" Laura asked.

"Don't fuss. They will make their way up here eventually if there are any messages," said Roisina.

"I take it you had a good visit?" Laura asked as she changed the sheets and pillowcases.

"It's always good to talk to someone. It's special when it's family," Roisina replied.

"Did the two of them find what they were after?" Laura asked.

Roisina was confused for a moment; she had not told Laura anything about the conversations or visit. "What do you mean?" she asked coyly.

"The box of family heirlooms," Laura reminded her. "Was it just rubbish, or was there something specific your granddaughter was coming for?"

"Aye, you are a clever lass, aren't you?" Roisina said, smirking. "My granddaughter is interested in learning about Castle Creet. She and her friend came to Ireland to vacation but ended up finding out some family history. They seem to be on a mission to find some answers to long-told family secrets."

"Oh my. I keep forgetting that that is your family's old home," Laura said.

"Well, I never lived there, but yes, years ago it was. On my husband's side," Roisina explained.

"You know, that's where my young Conor went and disappeared from a couple years ago," Laura said with caution. "Oh, he came back a few days later, scared as a dog. I would have kilt him myself if I hadn't been so relieved."

Roisina thought about it a moment. "I didn't know that was your lad."

Laura looked at Roisina. "I don't think it's a safe place," Laura said hesitantly, looking to see if Roisina caught her meaning. "You know…possibly haunted."

"Yes, I've heard the rumors," Roisina said.

"Conor claims he got stuck in one of the old rooms and couldn't get out. Almost like he was tied down to something. I never did get the full story… I think he was too shook up."

Roisina just sat and listened to Laura's story and then began thinking, Did Roisina remember that was Laura's boy? It was surely the talk of the town.

"Would you like for me to give your granddaughter a call?" Laura went on, interrupting Roisina's thoughts. "I can let her know it's dangerous and see if she is still persistent about finding it."

"They already know where it is and may have been up there already…but maybe you should," Roisina said, "and tell her I'd love another visit before she leaves."

"I can do that," Laura said with a smile and turned to leave the room, taking the dirty sheets and garbage bag with her.

Roisina grabbed her cane that was leaning next to her chair and wobbled to stand up. She thought about an article she had saved from the young boy's disappearance. She wanted to read it again, so she shuffled her feet over and opened her top dresser drawer. There was a box sitting just inside. Carved on the top lid was the family name *Gallagher.*

Roisina didn't think much of the castle. It was Charles's family history, and they had never lived there. It was as much of a story to them as it was to anyone, but something had demanded her to go retrieve the small wooden box. It was stained a beautiful deep mahogany color with a gold clasp at the front latch. She pulled it out with both hands and made her way back to where she had been sitting. Slowly she opened the lid and found the article folded up and sitting right on top.

> Conor Smith disappears April 2017—seven years old. Last known whereabouts, near the old grounds of Castle Creet.

Roisina had kept it to remember. She figured she could have someone research or look more into the boy later. Only her age was getting the better of her, and she had completely forgotten.

She set the story aside and began reminiscing about other things in the box. A beautiful brooch handed down through Charles's family. There was an old hairbrush that had belonged to her as a little girl. Her mother's wedding ring was in a small lace cloth tied with beautiful satin ribbon, a couple coins she couldn't remember why she kept, and her brother's old pocket knife.

At the very bottom of the wooden box was an old handkerchief. She didn't recognize it as anything special, and she didn't remembering placing it in the box. She pulled it out and laid it in the palm of her hand. She slowly and steadily unfolded each of the corners and gasped when she saw it. There laying in her hand was the hard and jagged stem of a key. The tip, the peak of the key, was still attached. It had very unique markings all the way up and down the shaft.

There at the other end of the stem was a hook that looked to be broken. As she looked harder, it looked like some part of a puzzle. *How did this get here?* she thought.

"I guess I'm giving in and calling my granddaughter," she said out loud. Roisina was still completely stunned she had the missing piece to the mysterious key the girls had been after. She picked up her landline phone, still shaking her head, and punched in the front desk number.

"Please tell Laura she doesn't need to call Adria. I will make the call myself," she said. "Okay thank you."

*****

"Look, Adria, I know you don't want to hear any other problems right now, but there is something else I need to tell you," Carla said lightly.

Adria sat there, waiting for Carla to continue.

"Well, I had another encounter last night. They seem to be getting bigger and becoming more real... I was in the living room last night, and I heard something fall in the kitchen. I searched the whole house stopping in the bedroom when I couldn't find anything that could have made the noise. When I came back out to check in the kitchen, your backpack was laying on the ground tipped over, and some of the contents had spilled out, including the metal key. There was an eerie feeling, and I instantly felt cold and distant. I went over to pick up your purse and put the key back in the pocket, and that's when I felt instant chills run down my spine."

Carla paused for a second, making sure she was getting the story right and trying to read if Adria was following along.

"It was like something was here or someone... I talked to it like a stupid idiot. I was totally freaked out. Then there was a gust of wind, and everything went silent. I ended up spending the night at Miriam's last night."

Adria sat still, taking it all in. She was in shock for Carla. "Thank God you are all right," she finally said "Has anything happened since?"

"No," Carla replied. "I've been on edge while we've been here today, but I haven't seen or heard anything else... I think if it wanted to hurt me, it would have by now."

Adria thought about it a while. "Do you believe this is the same 'spirit' that was following you around back home?" she asked.

"Yeah, I do, and now I'm starting to believe it has to do with the key, with the castle, and with your ancestry," said Carla.

"Then why would it not haunt me too?" Adria replied, thinking about it. "It's my ancestry."

"I don't know," said Carla. There was a ringing noise in the background, and Carla realized it was her phone going off. She picked it up. "Hello."

It was Nate calling to ask how Adria was feeling.

"She is much better now that she has been able to rest," Carla said. "We've been sitting on the couch talking."

"And has she decided what she is going to do about Daniel?" Nate asked.

"She wants to tell him the truth," Carla replied.

"I think that is a good decision. Shall we come by later then?" Nate asked.

"Yeah, and then you and I will go have dinner somewhere. I told Adria we'd leave them the cottage to sort things out," Carla said. "They have a lot to talk about."

Adria stayed on the couch, while Carla talked to Nate and agreed with everything Carla said. Adria was frightened and anxious, and her stomach was starting to turn into knots. She just wanted to get the evening over with.

She had made her decision to give up Daniel, to end things or not start in the first place. She wasn't really sure what *this* was, but it was the only thing she could think to do that made sense. After what happened last night, there was no way she could date Daniel now. She wouldn't do that to him. *Why had he come all this way?* The thoughts were running through her head.

Adria's phone was going off now, and she picked it up and headed to the back bedroom. She didn't recognize the number and could only think it was a call from somewhere in Ireland, but who would be calling her?

"This is Adria," she answered.

"Adria." A small older voice came on the line. "It's your grandmother, Roisina."

"Grandmother? What can I do for you?" Adria said. "We were planning to come back and visit but had not decided on a day... I was going to call you." She threw the last part in there.

"Don't worry about that. I would love to see you again, and after I tell you the news I have for you, you will probably come sooner than you were planning," Roisina said.

"What is it, Grandmother?" Adria asked curiously.

"I found the missing piece," said Roisina.

Adria was confused at first. What on earth was her grandmother talking about, missing piece to what? And then just then, she sucked in her breath, and it hit her. Her grandmother was talking about the key. "The key, the key. You've found it?" she questioned Roisina, wanting all the information.

"I didn't even know I had it," Roisina said.

Adria started jumping up and down, a slight squeal squeezing through her lips.

Carla had since then hung up the phone with Nate and came to the back room to see what all the ruckus was about. "What is going on?" she asked.

Adria held up her finger to Carla. "Grandmother, would you mind if we came in the morning? Okay, perfect. See you then." And she hung up the phone with her grandmother.

Adria stared at Carla. "She found the missing piece of the key. She has it. Now we have the whole key!" She practically screamed it at Carla.

Carla excitedly joined in with Adria, jumping up and down. They ran to each other, hugging and jumping in circles together. Things, events, the past—it was all beginning to fall into their laps, and they weren't sure how it was possible. The past twenty-four hours had been a bit messy, but now, more information was coming together.

When they had finally settled down, Carla told Adria of the evening she had planned with Nate. "You can order in when Daniel gets here, if you want," she added. "Nate and I will leave and go somewhere so you can have some privacy with Daniel."

"Thank you," Adria said solemnly. "I don't think there will be any gold glitz and glam to this conversation." She was brought back down to the present and pondered the night that lay in front of her.

*****

Nate and Daniel rolled up in the same rental car they had come in earlier. Daniel was still nervous, but now for different reasons. He wasn't sure if Adria had been telling the truth about not feeling well and he didn't really know how this evening was going to go. He did know one thing, when he was ushered inside Miriam's home, he had managed to glance out the front window and saw it was a man dropping Adria off this morning. He tried not to think anything of it, but the spare time he had at his hotel made him overthink the whole situation. He was beginning to regret his stupid decision to fly all the way to Ireland to surprise her.

"They're here," Carla called out as the car drove up the to the front walkway.

Adria tried not to let her nerves get the best of her, but she swore if she didn't sit down, she would vomit up the last thing she ate. She rushed to a kitchen chair and let Carla answer the door.

"Hi, there," Nate said as he looked up. Carla was already standing at the open door, waiting for them. "Are you ready to go?"

"Hi. Yes, let me get my coat," replied Carla.

Both men walked through the front door into the cozy little place. Daniel stepped in behind Nate, glancing around the cottage until his eyes found Adria sitting in the dining area, open to the living room. "Surprise," Daniel said a bit sarcastically, holding out his arms like some dancer doing a famous number on the Broadway stage.

Adria looked up and hesitated but gave an insecure smile in Daniel's direction.

Carla went over to Adria and bent halfway down to give her a hug and whispered in her ear, "Good luck." She headed toward the door and followed Nate as he headed to the car to leave. Adria and Daniel both waited until they heard the car drive away before either of them spoke.

"Daniel, Adria." They both said each other's names at the same time.

Daniel chuckled. "You go first," he said and he came and sat next to her at the table.

Adria took a breath. "I know you meant for this to be a surprise. I'm sorry it got ruined." Adria was being sweet, a sort of sunshine before the storm. She knew what she was going to tell him was going to break his heart, but she didn't want to sugarcoat anything.

Daniel waved it off. "It's not a big deal. I'm just glad to be here with you. I've"—he thought his words out carefully—"missed our time together."

She ignored his last statement. "I didn't order any food. I wanted to talk first and then we could decide…" She trailed off, her lips quivering.

Daniel didn't say anything.

"I went on a date last night," Adria blurted out, like a runner sprinting toward the finish line. The words came out as fast as they could, and she couldn't stop them. She didn't mean to and she immediately put her hand over her mouth. Her eyes were wide, waiting for his reaction.

"Okay, well, that explains the man who brought you home this morning…" Daniel let the words sink in. "This morning." His eyes grew bigger as he stared at Adria. "He brought you home this morning?"

Adria winced as he said it again. "Yes… I stayed the night with him." Tears started to run down her face.

Daniel got up and started to pace the kitchen to the living room and back again. He was rubbing his hands through his hair and covering any expression that might have been present on his face.

"I care for you, Daniel," Adria began again. "I…"

He didn't let her finish. "Not enough though, huh?" Daniel's tone was short.

"We're not exclusive. We're not dating," Adria shot back at him defensively and then caught herself. "I'm sorry. I don't want to yell."

He flipped around to face her. "I just flew all the way to Ireland because I thought we were on the same page. I thought we were going to make something of this..." Daniel said, holding out his arms and feeling bewildered.

There was silence in the little cottage. The sun was going down, and pinks, purples, and oranges were beaming down through the cottage windows. Adria had thought this would have been really romantic if it had been under different circumstances.

When Daniel couldn't take the silence any longer, he said, "There can still be something." His voice was soft. He went back to Adria and knelt down in front of her. Their eyes met, and affectionately he reached up and wiped a tear away from her cheek.

"I can't do this, Daniel," she said, turning her head away from him. "I can't do this to you. What I've already done, I could never forgive myself if I just turned around, went home with you, and acted like it never happened. I care for Travis too."

It was a dagger to his heart; she cared for someone else. The sound of the other man's name made Daniel cringe. He didn't need to know his name, and now it would forever be stuck in his head. "So that's it then? I'm just supposed to turn around and act like there was nothing between us. I'm supposed to give you up?" he questioned her and let out a heavy breath.

"Yes," was all she could answer.

"I don't want to. I wanted you, Adria," he said grievously. If he didn't care about what she thought of him, he would have joined her with tears of his own. "And so now he gets you?"

"I don't know," she replied. She really had to think about what she wanted to do next with Travis, but that was not what she wanted to think about while she was sitting here with Daniel.

Daniel felt defeated. She didn't want him anymore. Maybe she never truly did. Maybe he had read all the signs wrong, and maybe the feelings had never been mutual. So many thoughts were running through his head. "I'll call a cab," he said. "I'll be honest—this is not how I expected the night to go..."

"I know…" Adria tried to console him, but there was honestly nothing she could do that would make this moment better.

"Nate was my ride, and I don't know when he'll be back," Daniel said. "I think it would be better if I leave now."

"Daniel." She said his name softly. "I really am sorry." She watched him walk into the living room and pull out his phone. More tears, more sobs heaved from her shoulders. She hated what she had done to him. She hated how she had made him feel and how she was making herself feel. The guilt was pulling at every corner of her mind.

Daniel ended his phone call. "They will be here in ten minutes," he said. He felt like a moron. He had spent eighteen hours on a flight here just to step on Ireland soil for twenty-four hours and turn around to make the same trip home. "You stupid clown," he said to himself.

He had canceled his plans with his daughter, Sophie, to do this. *Never again,* he thought. He would never be so foolish over a woman. "I'm sorry I came unannounced. I'm sorry I ruined your plans, your trip and this…tomfoolery." He regretted it as soon as the words exited his mouth.

Adria looked at him, searching his face; the tears welled in her eyes, and then she burst into another fit of tears, her shoulders racking as she grabbed a napkin off the table and blew her nose. She was upset already, and he was just adding to the hurt.

"I don't know why I said that. Forgive me?" he said, coming to her side again. He cared for her; why was he being so hard toward her?

"Just go," Adria whispered in between her weeping shortness of breath. She stood up, pushing the chair away from the table, and took off toward the back bedroom.

Daniel didn't say anything else. He just listened as she closed the door to the back bedroom. He didn't go after her; just sat down in the chair and then realized there was no other reason to stay. He gathered his jacket and left the cottage, almost slamming the door behind him. With nowhere to go, he started walking toward the main road. With any luck, he could wave down the cab as it came down the drive. Hopefully he would be able to see it.

*****

Carla and Nate didn't know where they were going to go to dinner. They drove out toward the edge of town and were hoping to stumble upon a little pub they could eat at. The drive was quiet. Not awkward quiet, just a silent peace. The kind where you don't have to talk, the kind that allows you to think and not get your thoughts interrupted. Carla and Nate knew when silence was needed. It was a mutual respect they had learned from one another. And right now they needed the quiet to think about what the conversation ahead of them led to.

"How about this one?" Nate said, pointing at a cute little pub on the corner of a cobblestone road.

"Perfect," she answered.

They drove around to the back of the building and found a small parking lot. It had taken them a few minutes to find a spot, but they squeezed in. Before Carla could open her car door, Nate grabbed her hand. "You're a good friend," he said.

It made her heart soft, and in this moment, she was happy to be with Nate. It was a welcome surprise. "Thank you." Carla smiled. "Adria needs someone who understands, and I guess there is no one better than me."

Nate had to think for a moment what Carla was talking about and then realized what she was referring too. It had been many years ago, before he and Carla got together, but she had also had a one night stand. "She deserves your guidance and understanding," he said.

"Shall we go in?" Carla asked.

He nodded and pulled the handle to open his car door. When he got out of the car, he went over and waited for Carla to shut her door and maneuver her way in between the parked cars. He offered her his arm and she accepted. They walked to the front of the little building and into the little pub where they saw a sign that said, *Seat Yourself.*

They found a charming little side booth, and both slid in, one on each side of the table. Carla knew she had a lot to talk about with Nate—the key and the ghost who visited her last night—but she knew what Nate wanted to talk about—their relationship.

A smaller woman, probably around her forties, came over and offered them water. They both accepted, and Nate also ordered a beer. After a few minutes glancing over the menu, they both knew what they wanted and waited for the woman to return.

She returned a few minutes later and told them the specials. They both declined, and after ordering, Carla began, "I have a couple things to tell you." She paused, wanting Nate's complete attention. "No interruption and no questions until I'm done."

Nate gave her a look but respected her enough to know that what she had to say was important. He set his glass down and folded his hands together and placed them on the table.

Carla began, "Adria's grandmother who lives here in Ireland has the missing piece to the key we've been looking for. She didn't know it until today. We're planning to go over there tomorrow and get it from her…"

Nate raised his eyebrows in a questioning manner as if asking for permission to speak. "Yes, you may talk," she said with a slight giggle.

"That's great news. And you found the castle?" he asked.

"We know where it is, but we have not made the visit yet," she responded. "Now that we have the key, it seems like things are falling into place, though. We just have to get over this little hiccup with Adria and Travis and Daniel."

Treading lightly, Nate said, "Carla, I would love to go with you to the castle?"

"Well, it's not a bad idea to have someone tag along, you know, for safety purposes." She gave him a half-smile. Tomorrow, we will make another visit to Roisina, and then when could you get away to visit the castle with us?"

"Can you wait until Saturday?" he asked. "Then I'll be done with all my work commitments."

Carla thought about it. "I think we can make that work. That will give us time to visit the other places on our itinerary. Plus, I'm sure Adria would love something to take her mind of this present situation."

"Okay, so that was one thing. What's the other thing you want to talk to me about?" Nate said remembering her earlier statement.

Carla had to take a deep breath for this one. It wasn't as if she thought Nate would think she was lying. It was the telling it over and over again that made it start to seem like it hadn't happened in the first place. With more time passing in between the encounter, it made her feel more and more like she was making it all up. She was beginning to have her own doubts... *Did it really happen?* she thought.

"Something happened to me last night. I mean something supernatural." She paused a moment to see if Nate would say anything. She began explaining the events of last night, laying them out in order from the first noise, the heaviness, and the chills she got when she picked up the key.

"Carla, you know this sounds crazy? Of course, I believe you but why would 'it' be haunting you? The history of the key is from Adria's family, not yours. Why wouldn't Adria be the one who is seeing and hearing the ghost?"

"I don't know. I keep asking myself the same question... I slept at Miriam's last night because I was so worked up," Carla added.

"That was probably a good idea. I've heard that when ghosts haunt humans, it's because they have an attachment to them. Can you think of anything that might have attached you to the key or the castle?" Nate asked.

"No, I can't. I've literally been racking my brain, but I can't think of anything," Carla said.

Their food arrived, and Carla hadn't realized how hungry she had been until the first few bites settled in. She remembered she hadn't had anything but coffee that day. They both sat there talking about the ghost, the key, and anything else they could think of to figure this one out.

Carla had a slight epiphany of how safe she felt in that moment. How Nate was making her feel like she could tell him anything with no judgment, the way it used to be. She looked at him adoringly and began feeling tingling butterflies rise in her stomach. He understood her. He knew what made her feel protected, and she was beginning to melt away any shields she had been holding up toward Nate.

She reached across the table and grabbed his hand. He didn't expect it but accepted her touch and gave her a couple squeezes. He smiled at her as if he was seeing her in a new light. Like he was seeing her, see him in a new light. "Carla, I've been thinking a lot."

She knew this was the part of the conversation he was wanting to have. Instead of feeling annoyed or displeased, she felt anxiously excited about what he was going to say and wondered herself how she was going to respond to him.

"I love you, always have," he began. "I know you have questions that you want answered. You have things you need to work out."

Carla sat on the other side, nodding as he continued.

"I know I have things I need to work on, but I don't want those things to get in the way of what we have. Yes, it's been rocky, and what relationship isn't? But I want to continue to be here for you, to work on myself, to prove to you that I can be better. I want to work on us and prove to us that this can be better. I love you, and I will never stop, Carla Murphey."

Carla was unsure of what to say, but in that moment, her feelings were that she needed Nate. He had been her rock, and he was trying to be that again. She wanted to let him, to give into him. "I need your help," she said quietly. "I've built up these walls toward you. To keep myself from getting hurt. I don't know how to break them."

Nate pretended to pick up a make-believe hammer and began hammering around the outside of Carla. "It's my hammer," he said, smiling.

"You're an idiot," she laughed.

Nate got up from his side of the booth and came around to slide in next to her. He reached for her hand and held onto it softly. "Let me help you..." He stared into her eyes and looked at her lips. He inched closer and closer until their noses were touching. "May I kiss you?" he whispered.

Carla could feel herself starting to breathe heavier until she realized she was holding her breath. "Please," was all she could say as she let the air rush out of her lungs. She took another deep breath and waited for Nate's soft, warm lips to press into hers. As his lips pressed into hers, she allowed herself to let go, to shed away a layer to the wall she had built up.

*****

Nate dropped Carla off back at the cottage. He waited in the car for Daniel to come back out so Nate could give him a ride back to his hotel, but it was Carla who came back out instead.

"He's already left. I guess the night didn't end well," she said as she leaned in through the open window. "He left in a cab."

Nate was confused but knew Carla probably didn't know much about it yet either. "I'll call him during my break tomorrow and check on him," Nate said as he reached out for Carla's hand. When she reached her hand through the window, he took it and gave a light kiss across the top. "I'll call you tomorrow too. I love you."

"I love you too," Carla said, and she surprised herself with how easy it was to say those three little words this time.

She waited outside, wrapped up in her coat until Nate's car was out of sight. The taillights disappeared into the nighttime. It had been a long time since she said those words to Nate, and she actually meant them. She decided to let the feeling in and not push it away. After a few silent minutes outside with her own thoughts and the sight of her own breath in the air, she realized she still needed to find out what happened between Adria and Daniel that evening.

She walked back inside and was hoping Adria would be in the mood to talk about it. "How'd the conversation go?" Carla asked as she plopped down on the couch.

"It was horrible," Adria started, "but now he knows. I got to the point pretty quickly to save either of us more humiliation, didn't even order food. He got upset. I got defensive. I told him I couldn't give him what he wanted and that I wouldn't hurt him like that. He called a cab and went back to his hotel." She shrugged.

"Sounds like it went how you would expect a conversation like that to go," Carla said. "I'm sorry." Adria didn't say anything else.

Chapter 12

Adria woke up to a ringing noise that left her confused and dazed. She looked over and saw her phone lit up on the side table next to her. Travis's name was visible in big letters at the top of the screen letting her know he was calling. She waited until the ringing stopped trying to focus on the screen so she could make out the time. Nine-thirty. "Goodness," she said.

"Morning, sleepyhead," Carla said when she saw Adria pop her head out from the blankets. Carla was sitting at the kitchen table drinking the rest of her coffee. "You need to get ready so we can go see your grandmother today."

Adria had almost forgotten about their big plans for the day. "Right." She swung her legs to the side of the pull-out bed and sat there a little longer, silently urging herself to fully wake up. "Any weird encounters last night?"

"Nope, Thank God… As soon as you are ready, I will call an Uber and we can get a ride over to the assisted living place," Carla said.

"I'll be ready in twenty," Adria added groggily. She got up and walked to the bathroom closing the door behind her.

On the ride over to the care facility, Adria decided to send a text message to Travis so he wouldn't think she was ignoring him: "Visiting my grandmother, call you later.—Adria."

A notification popped up on Carla's phone; it was an image from Miriam. Carla enlarged it and found it was an article having do to with Gallaghers.

"Travis found it this morning," Miriam text her.

"Henry Gallagher Leaves Castle Creet. Smallpox Outbreak Leaves Many Dead. Nine Dead Including Mary Williams Gallagher."

Carla handed the phone over to Adria so she could see the article for herself. "Take a look at this," Carla said.

"Oh wow," was all Adria could say, "it's true. This must be how the castle became abandoned—everyone left."

"Adria, you're missing the whole point. Smallpox outbreak killed nine including Mary Gallagher." Carla repeated what the article said. "Smallpox killed Mary Gallagher—she did not kill herself."

"That had to explain the other deaths as well. Mary had nothing to do with it," Adria added. "So Amelia did die of smallpox too?"

"Why would your grandmother not have the correct information about Amelia?" Carla asked.

"I don't know, but her name was listed with the others on the paper Travis gave me," Adria said. "We'll have to ask Grandmother more about it when we get there."

The two of them were thrilled once again that they were getting more and more of their questions answered, but it was also leaving them with more and more questions to figure out.

"Oh, that reminds me," Carla said, "would you mind if we visited Castle Creet on Saturday? I told Nate he could go with us."

"Oh, you did, huh?" Adria said sarcastically, poking fun at her friend and giving her a sideways glance.

"Well, I genuinely had a good time last night and he asked, so I said yes," Carla replied, giving Adria a smile.

"When we are done at Roisina's, you'll have to tell me all about it," said Adria.

*****

They walked down the familiar hall and took the same elevator to the second floor. They came to Roisina's door and found it wide open. Two knocks on the door and they waited for a few moments before entering.

"Come in. Come in. I've been expecting you," said Roisina sitting in her rocking chair, "and who did you bring with you?"

Adria looked over at Carla, confused. "It's Carla," Adria said, bewildered why her grandmother wouldn't remember Carla.

"No, that other younger lassie, behind Carla." She pointed toward the door.

Adria and Carla turned around quickly, but no one was there. They hadn't seen anyone following them, and they didn't see anyone there now. "There is no one else with us, Grandmother," Adria said.

"Aye. Oh well. She is gone now anyways. Little thing probably hiding from her mother," Roisina said.

Carla and Adria looked at each other quizzically. They knew exactly what each other was thinking: *Is it the ghost?* They came in farther and headed toward the familiar couch that they had sat on just days before.

Roisina had the key shaft laying out on the table next to the couch. Before Adria or Carla could say anything about the *ghost*, Roisina said, "There," getting their attention and pointing toward the table.

"Grandmother, I can't believe you had the other piece this whole time," Adria said.

"I have no idea where it came from. I don't remember it—ever," Roisina said. "Of course, this old coo coo can't remember everything these days, but I was in as much surprise as you."

The three of them starting up a conversation discussing how Roisina might have come by it, and eventually, Roisina asked if they had brought the other piece.

Adria nodded and pulled it out of her backpack. She tried to wiggle the two pieces together and got a little discouraged when it would not latch back in place. "It won't fit," Adria said. "It's too rusted and worn. We may have to take it to an antique lock smith to see if they can put it back together."

"We'll get it put together. We have to. We're going to need it for when we go to the castle on Saturday," Carla said.

"Ahh, so you haven't gone?" Roisina asked.

"Not yet. We're waiting for Carla's boyfriend to get off work for the week. He will be our brave protector and knight in shining armor," Adria said as a joke, and they all laughed together.

"Take a look here," Roisina said, holding out a paper as she began telling them about the young boy who went missing a few years ago. "I think the boy probably got trapped somewhere or maybe something more embarrassing happened and he doesn't want to confess. Who knows?"

"That is frightening," Adria said.

They settled into easy conversation with Roisina for the next few hours as they explained everything they had learned so far as well. Adria mentioned everything Travis had told her. She of course, didn't mention anything about the rest of the evening with him. She pulled out the paper Travis had given her with the names of those that had died while at Castle Creet.

Roisina become distraught when she heard about Mary killing herself. "That isn't something I had heard, but if it's true, it breaks my heart. I can't imagine, as a mother, being so distressed. What a horrible incident," she said.

"And then we learned this," Carla said, holding out her cell phone and breaking into Roisina thoughts. "You see it had been rumored that Mary killed herself, but she died around the same time as the others. Her name is on the list of those that she died from the smallpox too?"

Roisina was confused. "Then what of Amelia? Was it really smallpox that took her too?" she asked. "Could the story that's been passed down be wrong?"

"That's what we were wondering also," Carla said.

"It's like a game of telephone. Every time the story got told, something changed or got added to it," Adria said.

Carla noticed Roisina was getting drowsy in her chair, gesturing to Adria that it might be time to leave. She was partly relieved because she herself was feeling strangely tired.

"We're going to go, Grandmother," Adria whispered as she knelt down next to Roisina's chair. "We will try to take the key somewhere tomorrow, and I will call you and let you know if they can attach it back together."

"Bring it back by when you get it together. I'd love to see it whole," her grandmother said. They headed downstairs as Carla pulled out her phone to call another Uber.

*****

"You can't just show up here expecting to see her. She is on vacation. She doesn't just stay in the cottage and knit," Miriam said to Travis when he drove over to her house that morning.

"I just wanted to apologize. Plus, who is to say I didn't just come to see you?" Travis said, very self-assured of his own behavior.

"Apologize for what? What's done is done… You just had to pursue her. You had to take it that far. You had to persist to this," Miriam went on.

"I didn't make her do anything," Travis said.

"Oh I know, but you started it," Miriam said, acting motherly and like she knew all.

"I actually didn't," he began. "All I wanted was a date. She is the one who kissed me."

"Sure," Miriam said, rolling her eyes.

"It's God's honest truth. I would never…"—there was a pause—"on the first date. I'm not even one to try a kiss on a first date." He was pleading with Miriam to believe him.

"So you had no idea that was going to happen?" Miriam asked. "How drunk were you?"

"Well, after the first kiss, I knew what was going to happen, but I wasn't that drunk at all," Travis explained. "When will they be back anyway?"

"And what if you end up with one of these?" Miriam held her stomach with both hands. Clearly she was not done with the subject.

Travis didn't have to look down at her stomach to see she was referring to a baby. "Then I will love it," he said. "Besides, that won't happen. We used protection if you must know."

"And you'll move to America or she'll move here? Do you know where Adria lives? Do you know if she even wants kids?" The questions just kept coming, like fire spitting flames on that old Mario Nintendo game.

"Miriam, I love her!" he said abruptly.

She was taken aback. "How can you love someone you just met, Travis?"

"I don't know. I just do," he said. "I felt it that night at dinner. Like I just knew I did."

"And what about this other guy?" Miriam spat at him. She wasn't exactly angry, but she wanted him to see reason, and it was the only thing she could bring up that might bring him back to earth.

"What guy?" he asked as his eyes grew wide.

Miriam knew as soon as he asked that Adria had not mentioned this friend that had come to visit her. Miriam regretted bringing it up immediately. "Nothing, never mind. I shouldn't have said anything," she said.

"What guy?" Travis asked again with more of a tone. "You can't just shut down now."

"It's not my place to say. You need to call Adria." Miriam got up and left the room, ending the conversation.

*****

The two of them got back in the Uber, and Adria shot Travis another text: "Can I see you tonight? I've got some things to talk to you about." She knew she was going to have to tell Travis about Daniel, and she wanted to get it over with.

"So you can explain the other guy?" Travis asked.

Adria was dumbfounded. How had he heard about Daniel?

"As a matter of fact, that's exactly what I want to talk about." Adria said.

Travis didn't respond, and Adria grew worried that he was truly upset, and why shouldn't he be? He, for all she knew, thought she was in a relationship with this guy. His mind was probably thinking all the worst things. *He probably thinks the worst of me,* Adria thought. *He probably thinks I'm a slutty...* Her words trailed off.

"I get off at seven," he finally texted back.

The uber pulled up to the cottage, Carla and Adria hopped out, paid, and made their way through the front door. "Do you want some coffee?" Carla asked as she set her things on the dining table.

"That would be great," responded Adria. "Should we talk about the third 'lassie' Grandmother saw?"

"She is following me. Everywhere I go," Carla said.

"Yes, but this time, she was present while I was there too… and Grandmother," Adria added, feeling excited the ghost had now shown up in her presence, "she has never shown herself while I was around, so why now?"

"That I could not tell you," Carla said.

*****

That evening, Travis pulled into the drive.

"I shouldn't be long. We're just going for a cupcake or something," Adria said as she grabbed her backpack and coat.

"Just tell him the truth." Carla was trying to give some helpful advice but knew Adria would do the right thing.

"That's exactly what I plan to do. Pray for me," Adria said as she left the cottage and closed the door behind her.

She walked out and opened the door to Travis's car. Sliding one foot in, she said, "Hi." Then the other foot. She buckled up and was seated comfortably before truly looking over at him. She waited for him to drive off, but he just sat there.

"Adria, I need to know," Travis said. "I can't go anywhere until I know what is going on. I've been wracking my brain and driving myself crazy. Did you cheat on this other man with me?"

"Travis, no… I'm not that kind of person," Adria began. "Daniel is someone I met a few months ago, and we saw each other around town a few times. We ran into each other the night before I left, and he asked me to sit and eat my pizza with him. That is the extent of the date I had with him. I liked him, and we had been texting a bit. I had no idea he was going to show up unannounced here."

"He's here? In Ireland?" Travis asked.

"He wanted to surprise me, and it totally caught me off guard." She was trying to explain the whole situation in a way that would make sense to both of them.

"So you're not dating him?" Travis asked.

"No. I'm not. And he isn't here anymore. I told him that it wouldn't work out between us. He left," Adria continued.

"So where does that leave this?" He pointed back and forth between both of them.

Adria placed her hand over the side of Travis's face and made him look her in the eyes. "I don't know, but I'm willing to continue 'this.'" She was hesitant with her words. She didn't want to sound too cliche.

Travis's face lit up as he smiled and reached over to embrace Adria. "You don't know how happy that makes me," he said.

"I like you, Travis. I'm not someone who just runs away when things get difficult," said Adria.

Travis started his car back up but didn't let go of Adria's hand. He took off driving toward the main road. "I've got a small and edgy coffee shop to show you. Since you have your own coffee shop, I thought maybe you could bring a little Dublin inspiration with you when you go back home," he said proudly.

It was Adria's turn to be happy and excited. She was beginning to love the giddy feeling that Travis was bringing her. It had been a long time since she had felt it, probably since… Carter. Adria thought for a few minutes, *There is so much Travis doesn't know about me.*

"Travis, I'm delighted about the coffee shop, and I can't wait to see it, but there is something else I need to tell you." She was trying to sound serious but without scaring him.

Travis turned his head to look at her for a second before turning his eyes back to the road. "This doesn't sound good. Do I need I pull back over?"

"It's nothing bad. It's just something I think you should know," Adria said.

"Okay. Shoot," he said, sounding nonchalant.

"I-I-I've been married before. My late husband died about a year ago, and this trip was supposed to be about me moving on and moving forward." Adria was careful with her words. She didn't want to make it sound like Carter didn't mean anything to her anymore.

"And you've had that clarity already?" Travis asked, confused. "Did you sleep with me to get over the loss of your husband?"

"Again, I'm not that kind of person," she said defensively and hurt that Travis would think that of her. "I loved Carter very much and I miss him tremendously—I do think things happen for a reason, and I think I am here to move on. I also think I'm on my way to getting myself back. The person I was and can be again…without Carter."

Travis reached over and grabbed her hand sympathetically. "I'm sorry. Thank you for telling me. If there is anything you need from me, please let me know."

Adria's mood shifted, and she was amazed at how well Travis took all of her news. It warmed her to her core, and she felt like something was lifted off her shoulders; she could breathe again.

They pulled up to the coffee shop and settled in, talking about how they were going to spend the rest of the vacation. Adria filled him in about her trip to visit her grandmother again and that they found the second half of the key but it needed to be soldered back together.

"I can look at it if you want me to," he said, grinning. "Just got to find some time we can get back together."

Adria smiled and did a little happy dance.

Chapter 13

The next few days passed like clockwork. Carla and Adria got up and visited some more antique shops, this time not looking for anything specifically. They were also able to visit Dublin Castle, taking the guided tour inside the castle; both of them were absolutely in awe with the history.

Travis tagged along with them on that trip and added his two cents when he thought he should. They loved every second of their adventure, and they were all able to ask the tour guide a million questions.

Eventually, Carla and Adria were wanting to treat themselves to something a little more fun, so they went to the Dublin Zoo and this time asked Miriam to tag along too.

She, of course, was thrilled. It had been a long time since she had been to the zoo. She was trying to think. "I don't think I've been there since I was sixteen or seventeen," she said.

They walked around for quite some time and eventually needed to rest their feet from all the exhibits they had seen. Plus, Miriam was exhausted, and her waddling was coming on stronger than ever. They decided now would be a good time as any to grab a yummy treat. They stopped at Nakuru Cafe, and Adria and Miriam grabbed some ice cream while Carla ordered and downed her iced coffee.

"I hope that text I sent you the other day was helpful," Miriam said. "Travis sent it to me and asked if I thought you guys would like it. Apparently, he was doing some more of his own research on the castle."

"It was very helpful. I feel like things are unfolding and we're figuring out how they fit together," Carla said.

"But what are we figuring out exactly?" Adria questioned her.

Carla thought about it for a minute. "We still need to find out the truth of what happened to Amelia. We found out Mary died of smallpox and not suicide. I'm hoping we might find more answers when we visit the castle now."

"Yes and possibly why a ghost keeps haunting you," Adria said.

"Us," she reminded Adria. "The ghost was there while you were present too."

"Ugh, that was creepy, but you're still the only one who can see her," Adria said as she explained to Miriam what happened at her grandmother's.

"It was a child," Roisina said, "but there was no one there when we turned around."

"Why would a child be haunting you?" Miriam sincerely wanted to know. "And you think she has been the one haunting you this whole time? Like even back in the US?"

"Yes, I think she is following me everywhere," Carla said.

Adria got a text from Travis: "Want me to look at that key now?"

Adria texted back right away, "Yes, please. We want to go to the castle tomorrow and I think we'll need it."

She punched out another text: "We're at the zoo, and the key/s are at the cottage. Meet us there?"

His response came quickly: "I can take a look at it there. Miriam's husband probably has the tools I need."

"We're packing up. Should be back in 30," came Adria's text.

In the car ride home, Carla and Adria were asking Miriam questions about the baby: if she knew the gender, if they had picked a name, and what kind of features she was hoping the baby would have from Miriam and her husband.

Adria opened up about her miscarriage and shed a few tears when she mentioned how much she wanted to be a mother.

"Don't give up. It will happen for you one day," Miriam said, hopeful for Adria.

"It's so nice to have found a friend like you, Miriam. I feel like we've known you forever," Adria said.

"I feel the same way," Miriam said, glancing back at both the girls.

*****

The three of them pulled in the driveway just as Travis was turning off his car and opening the door.

Miriam came to a stop in front of her house and excused herself, saying she was going to lie down. Before she opened her front door, she gave Travis that look, using two fingers and rotating her wrist from her eyes to pointing at Travis. The look where a mother would say, "Be on your best behavior."

Travis cleared his throat. "I didn't think I'd beat you. I had to stop and get some petrol before heading this way."

Adria gave him a funny look, and he had to remember they called it something different in America. "Um, gas," he said, giving a bit of a laugh.

"Hmm, okay, weirdo," Carla said jokingly.

"Shall we order some dinner?" Adria asked. "I'm starved." She came over to Travis and leaned into him to give him a hug. He kissed her cheek and sent her blushing. Their actions toward each other were becoming natural, like they had known each other for years.

Carla couldn't help but notice and decided she liked the affection between both of them. Travis may be good for her friend after all.

"I'd love to get food. Do you have any place in mind?" he asked.

"Nope, haven't the slightest," Adria responded, looking up to him, her arms still around his waist.

Travis pulled out his phone and asked if they would be down for a good ole cheeseburger, and they both agreed that that sounded delicious. Carla and Adria headed inside, while Travis remained outside to order the food.

He walked in the cottage a few minutes later. "It should be here in twenty minutes." He shrugged and grabbed his arms, letting out a "brr" sound. "It's getting cold tonight and the rain has started."

"Lovely," Carla said. "Well, let him look at the two pieces and see what he makes of it," she said to Adria.

Adria gathered the two parts of the key, the heavier metal shaft and the two smaller intertwined loops. She brought them over to Travis and placed them in his hands. "What do you think?"

"I can't believe you found these," he said delightfully. "I just can't believe it."

He started to examine them, running his fingers along the sides of the shaft and along the bottom half of the loops. He lifted them closer to his eyes, closing one eye as if to focus closer at a single part of the key. "There seems to be a hitch," he said, "like a connecting lock. I think it's supposed to hook into the bottom half of the loops and then connect like a screw."

"That's what I thought too," Adria said, "but I couldn't seem to make it fit, and there was no way I could twist it."

"It's so old. I wonder if soaking it in some anti-rust dissolver for a bit might get rid of enough residue to allow us to twist it in there," Travis said.

Carla got up. "I'll call Miriam and see if she has some, but I got to pee really quick." She got up and headed toward the bathroom.

"I'll text her," Adria added. It wasn't that she was impatient; she just knew she would be faster.

Miriam let her know she had some at the house, and Travis dashed over there, grabbing it before Carla was out of the bathroom.

*****

Carla sat down on the toilet and checked to see if "Aunt Flo" had appeared yet. She thought maybe she felt her period begin. She knew it was coming, but in that moment, there was no sign of it. In fact, there were no symptoms whatsoever. Her breast were usually tender and swollen, and she would cramp for a few days leading up to it. There was nothing to indicate it was coming. She counted back the days in her head. It had been five weeks since her last period. Officially, she was late.

"Adria," called Carla from the bathroom.

Adria was just returning in the living room with a glass bowl of the rust soak. She set it on the table next to Travis.

"I'm out of toilet paper." It was a lie, but Adria didn't need to know that. Carla just needed her to hurry.

Travis and Adria both looked at each other and laughed. Travis started submerging the key in the liquid slowly, and Adria took off toward the bathroom. They would need to wait a few minutes to see if this would help.

Adria knocked on the door and then slowly opened it fully prepared to just toss the toilet paper to Carla. Instead, she saw Carla sitting with her head between her knees fully dressed and obviously not waiting for toilet paper. "What's going on?" Adria said softly as she slipped inside.

"I'm about to pass out," Carla replied.

"What? Why?" Adria grabbed a washcloth and dabbed it under some cold water from the faucet. She placed the cold cloth on the back of Carla's neck and sat down on the rug next to the sink. Adria's eyes leveled out next to the toilet paper holder and she noticed there was plenty left. So this definitely had nothing to do with that little fib. "What's going on?" she asked again.

"I'm late," Carla said flatly.

"What do you mean you're late? Like late late?" said Adria.

"Yes, I should have started a week ago, but there have been no signs of starting," Carla said, about ready to burst into tears.

"Don't freak out. Maybe you have your days wrong," Adria was trying to sound comforting, but she wasn't exactly sure how to react. Was Carla going to cry because she was excited or because this was not great news? "Do you want Travis and me to run to the store? We can get a test," Adria said, trying to be helpful.

"Gah, I guess I should know. I can go with you." But just as Carla had said the last word, she threw herself around and emptied the insides of her stomach in the toilet.

"You're not going anywhere. The key has to soak anyways," Adria said. "Travis and I can be back in like twenty minutes and then you can take the test. Food will be here by then too."

"Blah. Food," Carla said but didn't argue with Adria. Carla knew the upset stomach was more from shock than any symptoms brought on by a pregnancy. It would be way too early for that. She pulled her hair back behind her head and twisted it up with the hair tie on her wrist. "Will you grab me a 7 Up while you're there?" she asked and sat back down on the toilet.

Adria nodded and slipped back out to the living room.

Carla waited until she heard Adria explain to Travis that Carla wasn't feeling well, and they needed to run out to grab a 7 Up. "Be back in a few," she heard Adria shout as she headed out.

Carla went into her room to find some comfy clothes to throw on. *Could it be true?* she thought. Again, she began counting back the days. When was the last time she and Nate were intimate? Yep, about three weeks ago. How did she let this happen?

The amount of questions, thoughts, and ideas running through her head were making her dizzy, like she was falling from the inside of a dream. She needed to sit down and close her eyes before she passed out altogether. She thought about how she was going to tell Nate and thought about how he would handle it. He would probably be ecstatic and thrilled. He had always wanted to be a dad. Carla always wanted to be a mom too, but this wasn't exactly how she would have planned it.

*****

Travis and Adria ran out to his car, trying not to get too soaked in the heavy rain beating down on them. He drove to the closest market, and Adria hopped out of the car and threw open an umbrella. "Do you want anything?" she said quickly as she leaned halfway back in the door.

"No, I'm good. Thank you, Acushla," he answered and gave her a wink. "Hurry up or you'll ruin your clothes."

In the store, Adria went first to find the 7 Up and then made her way to the pharmacy section. *These are sold over the counter in Ireland, right?* she thought to herself, but she was having a hard time finding the pregnancy tests. Up and down the aisles she walked until she finally found a small section in the bottom right-hand corner of an end cap. It was almost invisible if you didn't know what to search for.

She picked one up and read the title and fine print. She set that one down and picked up another, weighing all her options. This one read *5 days sooner*, but it really wasn't going to matter. They were worked pretty equal.

"What are you doing?" someone behind her asked her in a very curious tone.

Adria jumped and turned around. "Dang, you scared me. What are you doing?" she said to Travis, who was standing over her looking concerned.

"I changed my mind and decided I was thirsty." Travis stared at the small rectangular package she was holding in her hands. "Is there something we need to talk about?"

Adria blushed when she realized what he was referring to and tried to think of something she could say to hide that the pregnancy test was for Carla, but there was no getting out of it. Travis was going to end up knowing. It was way too soon for it to have been her, and the only other person at the cottage *who wasn't feeling well...* was Carla.

She blurted it out, and it came out louder than she imagined. "It's for Carla." She let that sink in for a second and also hoped it would give him some peace of mind. Travis's shoulders relaxed, and she realized he had been tensed up until she gave him the answer he was hoping for.

"I see," he said, not really knowing how to act. He was slightly embarrassed about his first assessment.

"Let's go. She'll be anxiously waiting for us to return," Adria said. She tried not to think anything of it but hoped Carla would not be upset when she found out Travis knew.

*****

Nate called Carla that evening to get the scoop on her day, but Carla could barely bring herself to answer the incoming call. She was worried her nerves and the sound of her voice would give herself away. Nate would know instantly something was wrong. She swallowed a sip of water and clicked the green button on her cell phone. "Hello."

"Hey, babe, I finally got ahold of Daniel. He's back home with his tail dragging between his legs," Nate said.

"I'm glad he made it home, and I'm glad he answered your call," Carla said. "I feel bad for him."

Nate chuckled. "I don't blame him for being embarrassed… I doubt you'll ever see him again. He won't want to see the two of you, so he'll probably do everything in his power to avoid the gym and coffee shop."

"Makes sense," she said.

"I've been thinking about the other night. I enjoyed where we left things… I was wondering if I could take you on that date, Carla Murphey?"

Carla thought about it a while. She was going to have to tell him sooner or later, and she knew if the pregnancy test was positive, it would have to be soon. "I was thinking about a night in?"

"Perfect," he exclaimed happily. "How about tomorrow night after we visit the castle? You can come back to my hotel?" He tried not to sound pushy. "We wouldn't have to share our evening with Adria, and maybe she and Travis could do something too."

"Yeah, I think that would be great," Carla said, her voice a little shaky.

"Are you okay? You don't sound that great," Nate said.

"I'm fine. I think I ate something," she lied. "I was going to go lay down and wait for Adria to get back. She and Travis went to get me a 7 Up."

"Do you want me to come over tonight?" he asked, worrying.

She yawned. "No, nothing to fuss about. I'm going to head to bed as soon as we see if Travis can get the key pieces back together... I'll call you in the morning. I think we are going to leave around eight."

"Okay, sleep well, my love," he said with affection. "Let me know about the key, and hopefully, this storm will pass by morning."

*****

Carla was asleep on the couch when Adria came home, so she went over and gave her a gentle nudge to wake her up. She saw that their food had also been delivered and set on the kitchen table.

"Oh, I can't believe I fell asleep," Carla said, coming to a sitting position.

"Here is what you wanted," Adria said as she handed the little bag over to her. "Do you want me to come in there with you?"

"No, I think I already know the answer...and I think you do too," Carla said more quietly when Travis came in the cottage door.

Adria looked over her shoulder at Travis and then back to Carla. "He knows," she said. Carla gave her a wide-eyed look of frustration. "You told him?"

"No, he found me looking in that section of the store. He put two and two together," said Adria.

"Well, that's just great," Carla said sarcastically.

Carla grabbed the bag from Adria's hand and headed toward the bathroom. Once inside, she put her back to the door and closed it behind her, standing there for a few moments with her eyes closed. *I need to rack up enough courage to just pee on the damn thing,* she thought.

She slid down her pants, sat on the toilet and stuck the pregnancy test between her legs. Letting the stream hit the white tip, she was especially careful it didn't splatter or get on her hands.

When she felt like she had saturated it enough, she replaced the cap and set it on the counter next to her.

The package said to wait three to five minutes. All Carla could think was, this was going to be the longest wait of her life. She pulled up her sweats, washed her hands, and then started counting. One…two…three…

Part 2

Chapter 14

When I was ten years old, I can remember lying in bed, my mother sitting next to me and rubbing my face, up and down my cheeks and around my forehead. She would softly caress my hair, running her fingers all the way down through the ends. Now you may think that for ten years old, I probably wouldn't remember the small details, but I remember…everything.

I was very sleepy, my eyes were heavy, and I just wanted to lie there and dream of something happy. I loved flowers, the soft petals, and the way they smelled. I loved how they came in all different shapes and sizes. I loved when they started budding and were right at the beginning of their bloom. I loved when I could picture them opening to full bloom like they were opening their faces up to the heavens. It's a carefree act, and a flower doesn't know anything different.

I used to always make daisy chains, the ones where you would poke a hole in the stem with a fingernail until it was big enough to string another stem through. I would place them on my head and prance around, pretending like I was a princess. I would make them for my sister, and she would pretend she was the queen. I didn't mind so much her being the queen. Yes, she was bossy at times, but I was just happy she was playing with me.

We used to play by the pond behind our castle. "Stop right there and bow to your queen," she would say. I would happily obey her every command.

It was always so beautiful and peaceful down by the quiet water. We would spend hours down there catching frogs and watching the fish. It was a small pond, but it was perfect and serene.

On the day Mother was stroking my hair, I had been asleep for what felt like a long time. I wish I had been dreaming about that pond, but I remember having the same vivid dream over and over again of those daisy chains. It was hard to wake up like a weight pushing down on me. For some reason, I just couldn't come to consciousness. I was physically not able to open my eyes.

When I was not thinking about those beautiful flowers, flowing in my hair, I let the darkness behind my eyelids encompass me and lay there counting sheep. Mother always told me, "If you have trouble sleeping, you should try counting sheep." And in a backward way, I thought, *Counting sheep just might work to wake me up.*

I lay there for a long time—for hours, even—and one evening, I can remember hearing the sound of weeping. It was the sound of my mother's cry. She was lying over me and sobbing and I couldn't quite figure out why. She kept saying my name, announcing different syllables through her gasping breaths. And it hurt me. It hurt down in my chest.

I couldn't wake myself up, and all I wanted to do was hug her. I wanted to throw my arms around her neck the way I had done so many times before. I wanted to tell her it was going to be all right. I was waiting for her to pick me up and take me to her rocking chair. I thought about how she would always rock me to calm me down, but now, I needed to calm her.

Some time had passed, the crying had ceased, and it became harder to make sense of day and night. I was stuck in the conscious state of being aware but still unable to fully wake. I hovered in this reality until one moment, I felt a heavy pull at my heart. A thunderstorm beating down ferociously, striking and pulling.

There was a gust of wind, and I felt it crawl up my entire body like ants racing to their ant hill during a sudden rainstorm. My fingers and toes began to tingle like they were falling asleep, and it was hard to move. My mind was fighting, pleading for my senses to wake up, but they did not. I finally gave into the heaviness and everything around me went dark.

I woke up the next day alone in my room. I opened my eyes, and for the first time since lying there, my mother and sister were missing. Daddy never stayed around long, so it was no surprise to not see him. The embers were burning low in the fireplace, and it was cold. The door was shut, and there was a small draft coming through the upper window of the castle.

I rolled over and pulled the white sheet from my body. I slid my legs out so that I was sitting and my toes were almost touching the floor. I scooted toward the end and let my feet hit the ground, standing so easily. The heaviness had faded, and I felt like floating clouds. I slowly walked over to the doors of the little room. I wanted to find my mother, but when I pulled at the round door handles, the door would not open. It was locked, but why?

I could heard voices on the other side, so I started shouting and pounding on the door, but no one could hear me. *Why weren't they opening the door for me?* I stood there for a moment, trying to focus on what could be going on. I tried a few more times to get their attention, anyone's attention, but still no one would answer and no one came to the door.

I suddenly felt alone, and I wanted to cry but there were no tears. They simply would not come. I turned back around to face the inside of the room and rested my back against the big wooden doors. Something from the corner of the room caught my eye. It was the small bed from where I had just got up. There was something there, lying under the sheet I had just stepped out of.

An odd feeling filled my head.

Curious as I was, I walked back over to the small, wooden cradle-like bed. I slowly began pulling the sheet back to see what lay beneath. Screaming at the sight that filled my eyes, I gasped and fell to the floor in fear. I cradled my head and lay in a fetal position, trying to feel safe in this moment.

Where was, Mother? Why wasn't she here to protect me from this crazy scene before me? I waited and waited, not sure what the passing time would do or how it would help. It had surely been an hour, two even. There was no movement in the room. No sounds. The fire had gone out in the fireplace, and my eyes had to adjust to see in the new darkness.

Eventually, my bravery got a hold of me, and I solemnly began to bring myself to an upright, standing position. I was going to look at the bed again to try and understand the truth of it. My eyes were closed at first, and I waited a second. I opened my eyelids to look again, and sure enough my eyes had not deceived me. I looked at the little girl who lay in front of me. She was cold and unmoving. Her face was pale and drained. Her chest did not rise with the inhale of breath. She was still, and I knew in that moment…she was dead.

I inched slightly closer, searching for the smallest sign of life. I put my hand on her hand, and she was ice. So cold that her skin felt like the snow on the floor of a meadow forest. I looked to her face and pulled the features from her that I could identify. Her hair was curly and brown. She had beautiful, long eyelashes—just like me. A small round nose and rosebud lips… She looked like me.

Like the wind being knocked from me, I froze where I stood, looking straight ahead at the brick wall. I steadily looked back at the girl, and in the matter of a few seconds, another thing became very clear to me. She was not only dead, but…she was me. I was dead.

I was in such a state of shock, the tears would not come even if I tried to force them. I fell to my knees, and the shooting pain told me instantly it would leave bruises. *Bruises,* I thought. What a funny idea. If I was not alive but I was still here, it could only mean one thing. I was a spirit, a ghost, an apparition. I had heard Mama talking about them before but never really listened to what she had to say. *Bruises?* I thought again. *Can ghosts even get bruises?*

*****

I didn't know what would become of me now. Surely someone would come to remove my earthly body, and then I could be buried and put to rest. Whatever that means exactly. Maybe being buried would take me far, far away from here. To a different land or adventure, or would it be like having a new home?

This can't be any sort of life, to hover around in limbo. Not literally hovering, but I'm not here and I'm not me. How do I carry on? How do I continue with whatever sort of life this is? And what does it all mean?

I waited, still, but no one came. A day passed, a week, and a month behind me. I sat in this room and prayed my mother would come for me. I screamed into the castle, but of course no one could hear me. I pounded at the wooden door, but my hammering was as silent as it was to me. I hit the door as hard as I could, but eventually, my hope began to fade.

One morning, the room began to fill with the sunrise just like it had every day before since I found myself dead. As it filled the room, a strange man appeared to me. He was standing by the fireplace, and he began talking, "Hi, Amelia, I am a friend…a friend of your mother's, and she has been grieving heavily for you."

My mind began to race. *Where is she?* was the first question in my mind. I began talking to him and asking him questions. How did he know who I was?

"My name is William. I am also like you. A spirit, if you will. Your mother can see me and talk to me. And I listen like no one else can," he said. "You see I knew her when I was alive. She was five when I died."

He continued to visit me, and each day, he would explain a little more about himself. I was finally able to relax around him, and soon, our acquaintance became a friendship as well. I imagined it to be something like what his relationship was like with my mother and that brought me some comfort.

One day, William asked if I would allow him to take something from the room where I seemed to have been trapped. He held the small item up in his hand, but I didn't pay much attention to it.

Whatever it was, it wasn't valuable to me, nothing was.

He seemed to struggle to pick up the whole thing from the table, and as I watched him, he said in a whisper, "I can't pick the other half up." His voice was still a quiet whisper but grew louder. "Why did I make this two-piece piece of…?" His voice trailed off. He probably didn't know I could hear him, but I knew what he was going to say. Daddy used to use that phrase all the time, and I felt a giggle bubbling up inside me. It was the first time I had laughed in so very long.

I eventually said yes, he could take whatever he wanted, but I asked for a favor in exchange. I asked if he would tell me more about my mother.

He agreed but warned me it was not all rainbows and butterflies. He would tell me about how sad she had become and that she had stopped eating almost completely. He wouldn't go into too much detail because I think he was afraid of scaring me. But I wanted to know, and I begged, but still he would not talk much more about her.

The information I was able to pry from him was, my mother said I was locked in this room because of the devastation of the loss. She didn't have the heart to part with my body. My mother felt that if I stayed in here she could feel close to me or my body at least.

But that's not working is it? I thought when William shared this information with me. She must have thought that I could become a ghost like this man and maybe communicate with her. But I did become a ghost and still I could not speak to her. I couldn't even get the doors open to leave.

I soon learned after many conversations with William, that he was an old family ancestor. His full name was William Samuel Gallagher, and he helped build the castle in 1799. He helped place the stones, carved the wood, and welded the hinges for the doors and windows. He even welded the key made to open and lock the castle doors. He was fifteen then, but the man that stood before me now was an older man, very much could have been my grandfather or even great-grandfather. My mind would not let me work that out.

He was ninety-one when he died from the earthly world in 1875, and he loved the life he had lived here at the castle. When he died of old age, he couldn't give it up, and he chose to stay behind as a spirit with what family remained. His wife had died many years before him, and must have passed on to a different place. She wasn't here. They had also lost two children due to disease, and they also were not in this spirit world.

He spoke of heaven and all the beautiful things he had heard, but he could not fathom how it could be more wonderful than his beautiful castle. He had lived a full and loving life, but now, he had been a ghost for many years and he decided he was ready to leave. "I've become restless," he would say, but he couldn't find his way to heaven. He was worried it was too late and didn't know what to do to get there.

And neither did I?

For weeks, I welcomed his company. Every morning, it was something I looked forward to. He would appear and we would talk about our lives and the things we remembered. My birthday came and went. Holidays came and went, and we celebrated as much as we knew how. I think he needed my company as much as I had needed his.

I didn't know where he went in the evenings, and I didn't care. Even if I could go into deep thought about it, my brain would not let me track down where I even imagined he went too. It did not matter to me, as long as he returned with the sun, I knew I was going to be okay.

That evening before he disappeared, he looked at me and said, "Your father is about to do something…unimaginable."

Before I could comprehend what he was talking about, before I could ask questions, he was gone. What was he talking about? What would Daddy do? I was bewildered and baffled. I guess I would just have to wait and ask him in the morning, but I had a horrible time with being patient.

The sun set that evening, and I laid down in the makeshift bed I had arranged next to the invisible fire. I could hardly wait for the morning sun to grace my face so I could ask William my questions.

*****

It was a cold morning, the day that William did not return. My room felt more empty, deserted, and alone. I could not understand why he was not there. I tried to continue my day like normal, thinking eventually he would appear, but all I kept thinking about was why he was not there: an answer I thought I'd never receive. I remember that day…it was the day I heard a scream from the other side of my door.

Mother came to my mind, and then she was gone in the blink of an eye. *She was gone.* The words stuck in my head like my feet used to get stuck in the muddy puddles I jumped in with my sister. Mother was gone, and I could feel it. This was the first time in my ghost existence that I felt my mother's presence was no longer part of that worldly side.

I wanted to cry. I wanted to bury my head in my arms and lay down in anguish, but I was not able to grieve physically. It was only something I could try to understand. It was the hardest part of all this… *Maybe, if my mother was gone, she would appear to me like William.* The thought came to mind, but she never did.

I had heard a man's voice and thought perhaps it could be William. It was a voice far away and a voice so familiar all at the same time. It was… Daddy's voice.

I pressed my ear up against the door. "She hung herself in the loft," he was saying.

My intuition had been confirmed, and I knew Mother had indeed died. But something about it didn't feel right, and then I thought back to William's words just the day before. *Could my father…could he have hurt my mother?*

The next day passed and another day and another, and soon, I had completely lost track of time. Still, William did not return. Months flew by, and I knew he was gone too. Had he found his way to heaven? I was hoping he would tell me how to get there. Was my mother his way to heaven? Was my mother's death what gave him his escape?

I was afraid of becoming restless like him. I was afraid of not having a purpose. I was stuck waiting for something to happen…but what? I didn't know.

I waited by the door of my little prison room and glued my ear to it. I pushed hard until my ear was sore from the pressure. Surely, someone would come for me now. They just had to.

Someone would let me out of here.

Chapter 15

Years and years had passed, and I mean it felt like a lifetime. I would guess over a hundred but nothing after that amount of time made sense anymore. I tried to mark time, to keep track, but every day started to blur together like a mirage you see on a distant path. I had no idea of my age. My figurative body remained the tiny form of a ten-year-old girl. With each passing season, I could feel myself getting older but not like a human aged. I did indeed feel myself grow restless, and I needed to find my way out too, just like William. I was tired, and just like him, I was done.

This room had become a dungeon, a prison I could not break free from. One day the old upper window close to the roof popped open and a young boy leaped in. He had on a nice pair of jeans and a button-up shirt, not like the kind I remember; these were different clothes. Newer.

"So this is it," he said to no one...or so he thought. "The famous place where my relatives used to work."

What was he talking about? His relatives worked here? Who was he?

It didn't matter. I ran to him and clung onto his hand, pleading for him to feel my presence. If I could attach myself to him like William did to my mother, maybe I could find my way to heaven the way I think he had. The boy froze for a second, and I thought it worked. When I tried to speak, to show him and tell him I was there, he ignored me, and I knew instantly that it did not. Instead, I think he saw the lifeless form of bones from the bed a few feet away.

The window blew closed and the boy was now shut inside, I thought this was my chance. I grabbed him and pushed him into the nearest chair. It worked. I tied him up with a rope I found close to the old cradle-like bed. *I would make him know I was here!* I thought. If I couldn't get his attention by touching his hand or hugging him, I would capture him until I could get his attentiveness. I had him tied to that chair for one, two, three days maybe. I tried so many different techniques for him to hear me.

I knew he was frightened because he cried out for his mother. He cried to me pleading. I think he knew there was a ghost in this room. What else could he think? There was some supernatural power holding him here, tied to the chair. I looked into his eyes. They were a most beautiful forest green with a slight mustard color branching out from the center pupil. I tried pleading with him to not be afraid, but I don't blame him for being scared. It distressed me that I was the one making him feel this way, but I had to try. I had to know if I could make him see me. This felt like the one and only chance I had to be free.

On day one, I dropped things on the ground. Things I found around the room: candles, a cup. I knocked over a wooden chair. I pulled and dragged blankets around the room. I screamed at him, screamed right up in his face and as close to his ear as I could get.

On day two, I tried more physical things. I slapped him across the face, grabbed his arms, and shook him as hard as I could. I didn't want to hurt him, I didn't want to torture him. I grabbed his face with my hand and using my nails like a cat protracting his claws, I slashed him across the cheek. He didn't scream; he didn't cry. It was like he was frozen. He still didn't feel it. But almost instantly, I saw four scratches appear down the left side of his face, and I knew as soon as he saw himself in a mirror, he would know something had tried to attack him.

On day three, after nothing had worked, and I didn't know what else to try, I decided to let him go. I had to be reasonable. It wasn't working, and I knew he probably had family somewhere who were desperately searching for him. I released him from the bind, and he took off running to the side wall.

"I'm free, I'm free," he yelled over and over up into the thin air. He didn't know I could hear him, but I could, and I knew my decision to let him go was the right one.

Before he turned to climb up and out of the window, his eyes locked onto something sitting near the table, and he took whatever it was and put it in his pocket. It looked like a bolt. I didn't care; he could take whatever he wanted. I was too tired to pay attention. I wouldn't need it anyway.

When he left, he scurried up the wall to the window as fast as he could, and he must have took off running because the window remained open. I waited for him to close it, waited hours and hours it seemed like. He never closed it, and I thought for a long, hard time, *Could this be my escape?* I would find my way out, and then I began to climb.

One foot here, and another there, until I grabbed at the sides of the window frame. I heaved and pulled and pushed until I was tumbling and falling out the window to the other side of the castle ground.

The wind hit my face for the first time in forever. I felt the dirt and the grass beneath my hands for the first time in years. There was a slight taste of freedom in this moment.

The outside was not as I remembered. The castle looked broken down and old, like no one had lived here for a long time. I gathered myself up and dusted off whatever I thought had been on my old dress. I walked to the front of the castle and pushed at the heavy doors, but I could not get in. It was locked. I pounded, but like usual, there was no answer.

I turned to go sit on the steps when I caught a glimpse of something from the corner of my eye. There was a piece of paper nailed to the door. I reached up to smooth it out and see if I could read what was on it. It was a list of names, a list of deaths that had occurred at the castle. On the top read, "Outbreak, Smallpox Notice."

This was a list of people who worked at the castle and had died from smallpox, but it was the wrong date, and my name was on it, and my mother's name was also listed. At the bottom written in ink was my father's name. He had written the notice. Is that how I died?

But was he covering up my mother's death? Why would he say that my mother died from smallpox on the notice. He told whoever it was in the hallway that day that she had hung herself?

Daddy also knew that mother, Fiona, and I went away for a time when the outbreak happened. He was the one that sent for us when he felt it was safe to come home. Why would he lie?

I grabbed at the bottom of the paper until it ripped free from the nail, and I went to sit on the front steps, and I waited. I was so tired of waiting, but that's what I did… No one came and no one went.

I finally decided to walk around and take a look at the castle grounds, but no one was there. No one was working in the gardens that were now overgrown. My sister wasn't playing or making daisy chains. There was no family and no family workers. The hedges surrounding the property were overgrown. The weeds had gone wild. The trees were heavy and dark, and the little well that sat in the front was broken.

I walked to the little fenced corner of the back of our property and pushed open the gate as far as I could. It didn't budge much because the weeds had grown so tall on the other side. It was blocking the natural sway of the hard iron. Oh, how easily it used to open, I remember. I walked around kicking and stomping brush and weeds with my feet and pushing it aside with my hands. I finally found a little gravestone marker that read:

> Mary Williams Gallagher, wife, mother, daughter b. 1870, d. 1908

I sat down right there in the overgrown grass. I wanted to be with her for a while and talk to her like we used to. I closed my eyes and pretended she was sitting next to me stroking my head or braiding my hair. *I will find my way back to her*, I thought.

Now the next step was to have a next step. I gathered up my courage and stood to walk off, back towards the castle. A glimpse out of the corner of my eye let me see the pond had since dried up with only a little puddling remaining. I felt a very burdensome feeling enter my heart and realized it didn't so much feel like my happy place any longer.

I thought of Mother a moment longer as I made up my mind to walk down to where the pond used to be, but before I could get there, I was stopped in my tracks. Something was pulling me back to the castle. I dropped to where I was, and my brain flooded with memories... I had been trying to catch a frog on that day so long ago. I had slipped on the banks of the pond, and my foot had caught in the tangled weeds below the water. I didn't make it back to the surface, and just like that day, many years ago, I lost my breath.

*****

The sun had begun to set and the most beautiful multicolored sky filled the air. I gathered myself up and headed back to the castle—I had nowhere else to go. With little hope, I decided to climb back into the little room that had become my dungeon. Right now, it felt like the only solid thing I knew. I would wait until morning, and then I would try to walk up the gravel road this time. Maybe I would make my way to town.

The morning came quickly, and when I woke, I felt an overwhelming sense of heaviness. I had nowhere to go, no family left, and I felt even more alone than I ever had before. In that moment, I didn't want to leave this room. It had become the only "home" I knew after so many years, and so I stayed put in the little room. I felt broken for staying. I felt cowardly for staying. But I couldn't shake this low, and I stayed anyway.

If I had to guess, many months probably passed before I finally decided to stop being a yellow-bellied sissy. So I finally did as I had rehearsed over and over in my head. I climbed back out my window, the one I had looked up at so many times before. I walked down the gravel path, and I just kept walking. I didn't turn around to see how far I had gone. I didn't want to know. If I did, I might turn back. I didn't want to remember the castle; it seemed sad now. I wanted to run. And so I did; I ran as hard and as fast as my little legs could.

Eventually, I knew I would need to stop and take a break. I would need to gather myself and figure out my surroundings. I would need to take in this new world, one I had never seen before. There were new places and new shops on every corner. There were no horses to be seen, no carriages. Instead, there were automobiles everywhere. I can remember William talking to me about them. They had come to Ireland in 1898, and he was in awe of what they would become.

There were more people than I remember too. *This was going to be wonderful,* I thought. There is no way I wouldn't be able to find someone to attach myself to. There would be someone who could see me and hear me. I would find someone who could help me.

At first, I started walking around and would simply touch someone on the back hoping they would feel it and turn around. When that didn't work, I would hit them over the head as hard as I could, but my tiny force was not much. When that also did not work, I would run as fast as I could and pound into someone as if I was trying to knock them over. Again and again my every attempt failed. How was this ever going to work?

Night after night, I would stay down by a slow flowing stream. There was bridge I could take cover under. I could sit underneath and sleep, dream, or just think about my next steps. I didn't feel the cold, and I'm sure whatever season it was, I wouldn't feel much heat either. Not that it got too hot in Ireland, anyways. During the day, I would walk about to different places and thump, punch, and whack different people over the head, begging for them to feel my presence. No one ever did.

I decided to walk my way down the road to Alexandra Quay, the sign said. There were ships there, massive ships. I had never seen a ship before, only read about them. They had to have been three hundred meters long. I decided to journey on board and check it out. What harm could it be? I wouldn't hurt anything, and no one could see me so I wouldn't be in the way.

This particular ship was filled with passengers. I had always thought of how families would gather on board in search of a new life and new adventures. Would that be me today? *I'm done,* I thought. I was ready, a new adventure awaited, and so I found a little corner seat and sat until I could feel the pressure of the water beneath me pull at the big vessel. I rode the ship and pretended I was riding the actual waves of the sea as it was pulled out of the bay.

*****

Didn't know a ghost could get seasick? Think again. My stomach turned, and my insides heaved. This ocean was not my friend, but I was on my way to a new land, and that had to be a positive. Right? "The Land of the Free" they call it. I would find my person, and I would connect with them, and we, together, would find a way to set my spirit free.

We landed in a place called New York eleven days later. I had never been so happy to exit this beautiful but absolutely horrible ride that had taken me on this new quest. I followed the other passengers as they got off, hoping they knew where they were going because I did not. I stayed close to a younger couple I had eyed sitting just a couple rows in front of me. The woman reminded me of my mother. Of course, I tried to attach to her, to get her attention, but to my disappointment, there was no connection.

I still followed them, even got in an automobile with them—my first ride. It was not like the ship. I was half-expecting to get motion sickness, but I did not. Thankfully. Sitting in the car gave me time to think, *Now that I was here, how was I going to find my person? And now that I'm so far from home, where do I go and what do I do?*

Regrets started flooding my brain. My mind started racing. *Maybe I should have stayed in Ireland.* I had to talk myself into bravery—again. To not chicken out. I had a journey to follow, and that meant taking baby steps to find my way.

A car: a shortened name for automobile. It took me a while to pick up what the young couple meant when they kept saying it, but I soon learned the word. The car pulled up to the biggest, largest building I had ever seen. It took every ounce of me not to be afraid of what I could only imagine was someone's castle.

I continued to follow the couple up to the enormous looking doors. I overheard someone say through the background noise that we were at the Plaza Hotel. I wasn't sure what a hotel was, but I was definitely sure now this was a castle. It was way bigger than Castle Creet back home. *Royalty must live here*, I thought, and I began thinking of the kings and queens that I might possibly see.

Inside the building, there were gobs of people walking this way and that. There were bags upon bags, and there were big rolling wagons with even more bags. There were paintings and artwork everywhere I looked and a magnificent chandelier. There were spectacular ceilings and huge columns built from the roof all the way down to the floor. Yes, this was definitely a palace. I never thought I would see the inside of one of these. If I didn't feel small before, I felt tiny now.

The couple took off in a different direction. They were headed toward a grand stairwell when I felt a tug. No, it wasn't just a tug. It was a pull, or maybe it was a push. Either way, I couldn't keep my feet still, and I was forced off walking as fast as I could in the direction of the front door I had just entered. I looked back over my shoulder and slowly watched the couple disappear up the stairs. I knew I would never see them again.

I wasn't quite running, but I could hardly keep my feet from tripping over each other. There was a sort of wind pushing against my backside. It was almost as if my feet weren't moving at all, just gliding along the glorious carpeted floor. It stopped me abruptly in front of a young woman with our noses almost touching. When the pull had let go over me, I stumbled backward so I wasn't so awkwardly in this woman's face. She had to be late twenties, maybe early thirties. She was beautiful. She had long, flowing hair pulled somewhat away from her face.

But why was I here? The women, only slightly taller than me, turned and looked down at me. I sucked in my breath for a moment and then almost laughed when I realized she couldn't see me. I let out my breath and waited, but she was still staring right at me. Could she see me?

"Hello," I said hesitantly, wondering if she could indeed hear me, but there was no reply.

A little voice in the back of my head was telling me she could be the one. I slowly reached up and touched the front of her right shoulder, and a shiver passed through my arm and down my entire body. It must have passed through hers too because I literally saw her body shake, and I saw tiny little goosebumps rise on the tops of her arm.

She stood there a moment, and I heard someone yell for her. "Carla."

Her name was Carla. Okay, well, that's something. I decided to follow her, and hopefully whatever the heck that was, maybe, just maybe, it would be a connection between me and this Carla.

She turned and started walking toward the big glass doors at the front of the building. Without even taking a step, my body started back at it and I was robotically following her. My steps tuned into her steps, and we were leaving the massive palace together. Without my brain even telling my feet what to do, I knew this had to be it. I think I have just attached to Carla.

Now how did William do it? How had he become friends with my mom? I thought. I had to figure this out. This was my chance to end this restless world I had been living in. *Carla is my only hope, and I will not give up.*

*****

At first, this Carla girl didn't pay any attention to me. I tried talking to her, but she didn't hear me, or she just chose to ignore me. I would try and leave her clues, like holding the belt back in the car when she tried to wrap it around herself and click it in to the holder. I even locked the car door so she couldn't get out. Of course, she just unlocked it herself and stepped out.

My body followed her routinely. I couldn't quite figure out where we were, and then I heard a huge zooming noise over my head. When I looked up, there was an enormous silver contraption in the sky. It was loud and thundering toward the ground. Wheels stuck out at the bottom, one in the front and two more on each side nearing the back.

Carla held on to something rectangular and small. She held it up to her ear and started talking into it and I tried to listen to what she was saying: "Sorry, that was a plane. I'm at the airport."

Plane? That's what that was called? A plane: a flying contraption in the air, wide and big and metal. There were windows on the sides, a hundred tiny windows. I didn't know whether to be frightened or thrilled at seeing all the newness to me. This world was not like the one I remember.

Carla was making her way through different places inside the building we had been dropped off at. There was a place where she had to take off her shoes and slide them through a machine and then grab them on the other side. *How odd a thing*, I remember thinking. We walked down a huge hallway-like path with big, open ceilings made out of hundreds of massive windows. There were little tiny shops and places to grab something to eat, which was also odd to me.

When she finally sat down on a small bench, Carla pulled out a book and began reading. It gave me time to think how strange all of this was. Everything was so different. I sat down next to her and I couldn't help but to cry.

This whole process was going to be so much more difficult than I thought. I got up and began to walk away, but that same tug pulled me back close to Carla. I couldn't leave her even if I wanted to. Was this going to be like another prison? Like being captured in the presence of someone and not knowing what to do or how to escape, but at least this one wouldn't be lonely. How would I get her to notice me? *No,* I thought. I would not let this get me down. *I will have a good mindset. I will be positive.*

It had only been about ten minutes when she got up, walked over to a counter, and merged into a line with twenty or so more people. They were waiting, taking a few steps forward every few seconds. Carla got to the front of the line and handed a young man some papers. He shined a red light over it, and that was it—she began walking again. This time, she walked right into a tunnel, and that meant so did I. It was cold, and I could feel a breeze coming from somewhere. Out a little window, I could see one of those big contraptions, and before I knew it, we were stepping inside of it.

It was huge. I mean it was tiny. It was the biggest, littlest thing I had ever seen. Everything was so compact on the inside. There were three little chairs on each side and an aisle running up the middle.

People frumpily sat down, pushing bags under the chairs in front of them and touching elbow to elbow. Carla made her way down to just past the middle of the seats. She practically crawled over the laps of two people until she was sitting next to the window. It was an interesting sight for sure.

And where was I supposed to go? Yeah, good question. I looked around and just waited right there in the middle of the aisle. More people passed by me, bumping into me. Of course, they didn't know it.

Someone stepped on my foot; another person dropped a suitcase on my head. Goodness gracious, I can imagine that that probably would have hurt. Good thing I was small, otherwise they'd probably be bonking me with more elbows and bags.

After everyone got settled and sat quietly in their seats, the plane roared up, and I felt a swiftness as the contraption started moving. *Oh no,* I thought. *We're going to be in the air flying like I had seen when we first arrived.*

I couldn't unsee it, flying in the air like a bird, a huge bird taking flight. I had no time to be scared. We started moving faster and faster. So fast, I felt gravity hit my cheeks. The top half of the plane began to rise, and I tumbled backward. Grabbing at the first thing I could get my hands on was a man's wrist, and with that, black coffee spilled all down the front of his shirt. I steadied myself and stood again, placing my feet shoulder-width apart. I held on to the arms of each chair on each side of the aisle.

Eventually, after a few minutes, the plane leveled out, and I was able to walk around like normal. There wasn't anywhere to go, but at least I could move about. As long as Carla was in sight, I could go anywhere I wanted in this tiny, big plane.

*****

Carla held her rectangular thing up to her ear again. She was talking into it like it was a person. I soon learned it was called a cell phone, and she was talking to someone on the other side. Something connected it so that she could communicate on it. I guess I would figure out that one later. It made my brain hurt. For now, I just listened.

"I'm catching a cab, and I'll be home shortly, Nate," was all she said, and then she slid it into her pocket.

Who was Nate? What's a cab? Where was home?

I began to fall into a routine, Carla's routine. She would go to the gym and run on this belt that moved in a circular motion around and around the bottom of just another contraption. She would go to a coffee shop and talk to all the people. She would write on papers, sitting at a desk. They looked like they were important papers. She would talk more on that cell phone.

I met her boyfriend, Nate, and her best friend, Adria. They were lovely people. Nate was busy and he was not around much, but he just had one of those personalities that made you like him instantly. I couldn't quite figure out Adria, though. It was like I knew her. I didn't know how, but it was like there was something drawing me to her.

I tried to talk to Adria one time too, but she also could not hear me. Our lives went on and on: gym, coffee, Adria, Nate, eat, bed, morning and then all again the next day. Here and there would be trips to the store or library and so on. I could feel myself getting restless again.

One day, I overheard Carla and Adria talking about a trip. They wanted to go somewhere and couldn't figure out where. They talked of a few places but couldn't decide on one singular spot. Oh, how I wished we could go back to Ireland. Maybe if I was there, home, and with Carla at the same time, I could figure out how to let go of my earthly spirit.

It came to me in the middle of the night. I wasn't really sleeping, but it came to me nevertheless. My body needed to be set free. Not this spiritual body I walked around in. My actual ten-year-old body that lay back at Castle Creet. It was probably old dust and bones that now lay there. Bones of my body. I was never given the proper burial I needed. I was left and forgotten, and when my mother had died, I was definitely unremembered.

I thought to myself that if I could plant ideas here and there with Carla, she would pick up my hints and travel to Ireland. That could be her little vacation. She and Adria were at the coffee shop one afternoon, and I was saying it over and over again: "Take me home. Take me home. Take me back to Ireland."

I remembering thinking that would make a pretty good song. I began humming, coming up with a tune in my head…

It was Adria who caught onto my notion first. I thought she couldn't hear me. How did she know? I couldn't figure it out. But as soon as my little song came to my head, it was gone, and then she said the words "Dublin, Ireland." I didn't hear what she said before that. I only heard the words of a place I was so familiar with. A place I called home for so long and yet had also not felt like home all at the same time. But it would always be my place. I needed to go back. I needed to get these girls there. They would be the ones to take me home and send me *home*.

"Maybe we could go there," Adria said.

And I listened to every word intently after that. They were talking about it. They were talking about visiting Dublin. I needed to get Carla to agree. She said she was going to call her brother. And so the details would be laid out. It wouldn't be long now. Plans were being made, and I needed to be a part of it.

I tried and tried. Now it was even more important for Carla to feel me and hear me. She was my person. I had to make that initial contact.

Chapter 16

One day we were in a strange place and there were lots of people. I think Carla called it a post office. I wasn't aware of what it was, but like always, my feet followed hers, and I was here whether I liked it or not. The connection was getting old like always being told where to go and what to do, but it was this day that I *finally* got through to her. I said it loud and as plainly as I could as she walked out of the building, "You'll have fun in Ireland."

She jumped around really fast. I wasn't trying to scare her, but I definitely did. Her eyes were searching the area, darting in several different directions. She was looking for me. She heard me, though, and that was a start. After standing there for several long seconds, I realized she could not see me. Hopefully, I could change that.

And then, another time she went shopping with Adria, and I wrapped my hand around her wrist. She felt that too. But still, again, she could not see me. *How was I ever going to get her to see me?* There were times it made me start wishing William was here! He would know what to do. I wish my mother was here too. It gets so tiring being alone.

Carla and Adria's plans carried on like normal, a repeat of day-to-day life. Finally, the day for their trip arrived, and I was so looking forward to being back in Ireland! I was looking for the familiarity and comfort of a place I felt like I knew, the land, the weather, the smells. I was not, however, looking forward to the travel again. Would we be traveling by plane or taking a ship? *Oh please, no ships! I don't think my stomach could handle it!*

It was an early morning, a very early morning. Carla didn't usually wake up this early, but there I was, waking up right with her. I guess I should say getting up with her. Sleep does not come easy for me. The two girls started getting ready doing this and that, grabbing bags and suitcases that they set next to the front door. When the car arrived, they loaded their things in and we were off. It didn't take long to get there, and before I knew it, we boarded a plane. *Thank goodness*, I thought. And we were on our way—to Ireland.

Again, I had nowhere to sit. I stood and then kneeled and then sat in the aisle of the plane, trying to find "my spot." I was holding on to the side of the plane seats just like last time. I don't think I will ever get used to the airplane taking off. The full blast pressure in my head and heart was enough to make me feel like I could faint.

As I sat on this leg of the trip, I began to think about how weird it was, the things I could and could not feel physically and emotionally. It was like it came and went with the sun and moon. I would think I would be used to it by now. Some days, I could feel different emotions, and other days, I could feel the temperature. Some days, I could feel different sensations—like taking off in an airplane.

The trip was long. However, if I wanted to compare it to my ten- or eleven-day trip on the ship, over the ocean, it was absolutely perfect and I would not ever complain. Everything had played out just like it had before when I was first on the plane with Carla.

Someone picked us up in a car, and we traveled down the busy road. At first, I didn't recognize it, but I didn't need to. I knew we were in Ireland, and that was good enough for me—right now.

Eventually, that road led to another and then another, and finally, we were on a familiar path. I pointed out to myself, shops I had remembered seeing when I first ventured out just two weeks or so ago. It had been easy to pick up street names and landmarks, and now I was remembering them as we passed. I saw the River Liffey and knew we couldn't be too far from the castle. *Now how do I get Carla to the castle?*

*****

I soon found out Miriam was the name of this new girl that had picked us up from the airport. She seemed nice. She was very pretty, and she was expecting a baby. She had the cutest little bump pushing out her dress, making it more noticeable. I thought she was glowing and lovely, but there was something that seemed familiar to me too. Could it be, maybe, a natural instinct to feel this way towards someone from Ireland? She was a bit of home, and I enjoyed being around her. It was a pleasant surprise to find out the girls were staying nearby by her home. It was nice to know they could visit with Miriam often.

Adria and Carla got settled into their cute little cottage quickly as they ooh'd and aah'd over everything, and rightfully so. They put their stuff away like it was their own home—coats in the closest and clothes in the drawers. They put some small accessories in the bathroom, making themselves comfortable for their two-week stay.

I could hear them talking about a castle, and it was so hard to sit here and listen to their different stories of the past. It made me yearn for my own home. The one I used to have before this crazy mess, and then I heard them mention it, Castle Creet. My castle. My home. This had to be why I connected to Carla. She knows about the castle.

Except as I continued to listen, they were telling it all wrong. I wanted to interrupt them and tell them the truth of it. At least as much as I knew.

One day soon, I would set it straight for them. I did like listening to some of their other stories they told. The ones where they told of their home and their coffee shop. Carla talked a little of Nate and Adria talked of Daniel. Miriam had mentioned her husband, Craig. The three of them were getting on well and it seemed as if they had a lot in common. It was comforting for me to a part of it, something that seemed so familiar and yet so far away. It had been so long, I had craved for company, and even though they couldn't see me, I liked hearing the sound of their voices.

*****

Carla was busy doing this and that when something happened. She walked out of the bedroom she had claimed and headed down the hallway. I knew she had been writing in a book the night before, and I thought since she wasn't here, well, I saw this as an opportunity. I would just take a peek. Besides, she couldn't see me anyways. What would it matter? I began flipping through a few pages, trying to make sense of the words. My eyes scanned up and down trying to catch onto something that would make sense to me. I was flipping through the pages, checking dates and reading quickly when she walked back in and yelled. At me.

She shouted at me loud and clear, "Who the hell are you?"

I was taken aback, but before I could say anything, Adria came running into the bedroom, half-naked and half trying to cover up with her towel. Carla looked at Adria as she entered the room and then back to me at the bed.

"There was a girl…in my room," Carla said, staring at the same location I was still sitting. I couldn't move. I was frozen with fear. "She was sitting on my bed going through my journal."

I realized immediately in that instant Carla could no longer see me. Adria had been a distraction when she ran in the room, and the connection between us was broken, lost.

Adria thought it was a joke at first and began with what seemed like a fake laugh, but when Carla had convinced her it was real, they both looked traumatized.

Great, now they are going to think I'm the 'scary' ghost. This isn't easy, I kept thinking, *but I will have to try again and again until it works.* And so I would.

*****

It was one morning, a few days after we arrived, and there was an older woman we were going to see. I learned it was Adria's grandmother, and I went with them to her home. It was small and quaint. She began telling a story to the girls, and I listened very intently. Like I was listening to a story my mother would tell me, but this one was…*about* my mother…and me.

It was so strange to hear my name, her name, and other names of people I recognized. Why did this woman know so much about my family? And then she said, "Fiona was one of the daughters of Mary Gallagher." It hit me that this woman must be a relative. She had heard of my mother and father and my sister, Fiona. Would she be the one to tell the girls the truth?

And then I also realized; it hit me like a stack of books. If this woman was Adria's grandmother and she was related to me, then I was related to Adria too. I began to think, my mind spinning in all sorts of different directions. I wonder if I would have met Adria first, would I have attached to her? Maybe in a weird, roundabout way, I connected to Carla because Carla knew Adria.

I continued to listen while her grandmother recounted details of my past. I wasn't sure what this woman was to me—in the family relationship. It was just easier still to refer to her as Adria's grandmother.

It began to grow harder to listen to her explain and describe my death. It was even harder when she explained that my mother had thought Daddy had something to do with it. That was outrageous! Daddy would never have hurt me. I knew he loved me. He just had a strange way of showing it. As I sat there longer and listened with them, I began to question it myself. Did Daddy love me?

It was true when they said Mother became distressed and alone. William had told me as much. When they began talking about a specific key, I tuned in, listening more intently. Mother had locked me in? Is that why no one came for me?

A key… William used to talk about a key he made for the castle. Had he given it to my mother? *Had William locked me in that room?* The thought came to me and disappeared in a matter of seconds.

The castle doors were locked when I left, and I knew Carla and Adria would need the key to enter. They would need the key to open the main doors and to open the door where I had been left behind. We had to find the other half of the key Adria's grandmother had just given them. I stared at the key and thought for a moment that I recognized its markings. *Maybe I had seen Mother with it before?* I thought, squinting my eyes as if it would help me see better visions in the past. It was too hard to tell with it only being half the key.

The three of them continued to talk over their tea, and I stopped listening after a while because I knew now that even Roisina did not know the whole truth. I was still going to have to find a way to explain the truth to them myself.

I ventured just outside Roisina's door that was left open. It was about as far away from Carla as I could get without feeling that pull that I needed to get back to her.

As I took in some of the pictures hanging on the walls, I noticed there was a boy. He had to have been ten or eleven years old. He was sitting in the corner of the hallway and playing near a rolling cart full of what looked like cleaning supplies and extra towels and sheets. I said hi, but of course he couldn't hear me. I decided to sit down next to him and listen to his imaginative play. There was something familiar about his voice, but just like so many other things, I couldn't place it.

I noticed there was something in his hand he was playing with. I stooped over to take a closer peek and I saw it looked like a screw or a metal…key. And just then it dawned on me. Could this be the rod, the other half to the key Carla and Adria would be looking for? It looked very old and weathered. The markings looked similar as the smaller two loops I had seen the girls with inside Roisina's room.

Could this be part of the key that the three woman were talking about just moments earlier? I thought.

Just then, a woman walking from down the hallway called out his name, "Conor… Conor Smith. Where are you?"

He looked up to the woman who was now standing behind me. His eyes pierced mine, and I locked my gaze to his. He wasn't looking directly at me, but I couldn't stop staring. There was no way I could forget those big, bold eyes, the same forest-green eyes I had seen one day back at the castle just a few years ago. This was the boy who climbed down into my room, the boy whom I had captured, and the boy who stole something off the table just moments before he climbed back out the window and ran to his freedom.

The boy dropped the metal piece down on the ground and stood attentively before his mother. My gaze faded away as he stood and went directly to what he dropped on the floor. That is when I grabbed it and snuck carefully off, tiptoeing back into the room. Again, I don't know why I tiptoed—no one could see me—but I think it made me feel better, like I was actually alive and able to sneak away. *Fair is fair,* I thought. If he took something from me, I was going to take this from him.

When I got back into the room, I realized I would have to put this somewhere Roisina would find it. I couldn't put it in plain sight. That would be too obvious. *That would be a ghostly thing for sure,* I thought. Out of the corner of my eye, I saw her chest of drawers. She had to get in there often, and so it became the perfect place.

I pulled open the top dresser drawer quietly as to not get any attention from the three in the other room. Inside was a box with the name *Gallagher* engraved across the top. It made it even more so the perfect place to put the metal piece. I folded it in an old handkerchief I kept in my skirt pocket, I tipped the box lid open, and I placed it at the bottom of the wooden box. She would definitely find it here.

I settled myself back in, sitting on the floor, and listening to the conversation just as Carla and Adria decided it was time to head back. They were saying their goodbyes when I found Carla staring at a picture on the wall. It was the most beautiful picture I had ever seen. It was an intimately painted picture of something I held so dear. I would recognize it anywhere. It was the castle, my home. And the young girl sitting next to the well…it was me. I was still wearing the same old, light-blue, faded dress as I did in the picture. I had a daisy chain in my hair, and I was gathering more flowers in my basket. After all, it was my favorite thing to do. That time had been such a carefree time in my life. Oh, how I wish it could be again.

In the bottom right corner written in tiny cursive handwriting was my mother's name: *Mary Williams Gallagher.* She must have painted it before she died. *Oh Lord, I miss her! Please, Jesus, bring us back together,* I prayed silently.

*****

Later that evening, Adria was getting ready to go on a "non" date with a man named Travis. I decided that with Carla alone, maybe I could get her attention again. Maybe she wouldn't be as distracted or as engaged as she was when Adria was around.

Adria had left and Carla was alone. She had been watching the television box when the first thing I did was pick up the pot that had been sitting next to the sink. I dropped it on the ground and let its loud ringing determine what would happen next.

I did indeed get her attention because she shot off that couch as fast as lightning. She went searching around the house, and I began foolishly waving my arms waiting for her to see me.

"Carla, I'm right here," I said over and over again.

Still, she couldn't find me as she ran back into the bedroom, but at least she heard me. I mean she heard the pot. Why had she seen me before when I was sitting on the bed but not now? I picked up Adria's backpack purse and tipped it over the side of the dining room table. All I wanted to do was get her attention again, but as I flipped it over, I saw the top half of the key roll out of her zipper pocket.

It lay on the ground and I looked at it for a few seconds, admiring the handiwork, and thinking how beautiful it had probably once been back when it was first welded. William would have been proud to know his handiwork was still admired.

Carla came back in the room, and I could tell she was terrified by the look on her face. I sincerely didn't mean to frighten her, but after all, I guess strange things happening to her over and over again could be quite startling. I would probably have been scared too.

I decided to see if I could pick up the key. She must have been thinking the same thing too because we both reached down and touched it at the same time. Just at that exact moment, a cold chill of wind flew through the house. The windows shook, and the curtains blew up in disarray as I stumbled backward to reassess the situation.

She had had the key within her fingers, so I had let go. As she stood up, I could tell she felt something too, but just as quickly as it had come, it was gone again. The connection, the wind, everything—it was gone.

Carla was completely shocked, and so that night, we didn't stay in the cottage. I knew she was trying to get away from "the ghost." Little did she know the ghost was me, and I was bound to follow her almost everywhere she went. I stayed in Miriam's house that night too. I listened as Carla partially explained to Miriam what had happened. I listened as I slowly heard the fear had begun to leave her nervous voice. The night became later, and slowly Miriam headed off to bed, lights were turned out, and the fireplace coals were getting low. Carla headed to her room to try to get her own rest.

She was restless and tossed and turned some. The moon shown through her room window, and I couldn't help but take in its majestic shape and different shades of color.

The morning came quickly, and Carla and Miriam were drinking coffee the next day. Carla suddenly remembered Adria was alone in the "scary" cottage last night, and they ran over to check on her, but she was not there. Carla had discovered that Adria was not in any trouble but had spent the night with this guy named Travis. I had known they liked each other right away. It had been clear as day. Now I didn't know she would spend the night with him, but I did think this could go somewhere.

I also found out that same day that Nate was coming for a visit and he was bringing Adria's friend, Daniel. I was so excited to see Nate. He was a good guy, and I think he was the right person for Carla even if she didn't know that right now. I had a feeling she would see it too eventually.

Nate had this protective teddy bear way about him. The times he was around, I noticed it immediately. He knew when to be serious, but he also knew how to be lighthearted and have a good time. It would seem I had taken to him like a little sister would take to a big brother.

Things went on like one would probably think in this situation with Adria. She was embarrassed about the previous night, so she made up an excuse that she didn't feel good. She didn't want to see Nate and Daniel that day they came to the cottage. The two men ended up leaving and went back to…wherever they came from, I guess. And Carla went to check on Adria who had gone to rest.

Adria was asleep in the bedroom when we entered the cottage, and so Carla came back out into the living room and started to look something up on the screen of her computer. I had learned what a computer was when I first met Carla, but I still didn't quite understand it. I just let her do her pounding on the little black buttons and decided this would be a good time for me to rest too.

I sat up when Adria woke up and came out to tell Carla what happened with her and Travis. Carla also told Adria about my little visit to her last night. Carla said something about if I wanted to hurt her, I would have done it by now. Of course I didn't want to hurt her. That would get me nowhere.

I then decided that to truly get Adria on board with setting me free, I needed to try and appear to her as well. It was then that I overheard Adria talking to her grandmother on the phone. Adria was talking about finding the other half of the key, and I knew my plan from earlier was starting to work. I also knew that that meant Roisina had found the second half in the box I placed it in. The girls were planning to visit Roisina again, and I knew this would be the perfect opportunity to appear to them both, maybe even to her grandmother as well.

Chapter 17

It had worked just like I planned. Roisina had seen me. But when Carla and Adria turned around, they did not. So I guess it didn't quite work. This was getting exhausting. How did her grandmother see me now and Carla had seen me just the one time? What was it that allowed them to see me all of the sudden and then not see me? It was like a switch someone kept turning on and off. Sometimes it worked, and sometimes it did not.

I saw the same familiar piece of metal I had hidden in the box just a few days earlier. As the girls looked it over, I could see the excitement in their eyes. Of course, Adria had brought the original piece to the key, and they tried to see if they could get it back together. They found out there was a hook, but they couldn't quite get it linked. I wanted to touch it, to grab it out of their hands to see if I could do it better, but I probably couldn't get hold of it even if I had wanted to.

The three of them sat and ended up talking about the article in the text from Miriam, the same one I found on the castle door. They both asked Roisina if she thought we had all died from smallpox, including Mother. Carla and Adria didn't have the story. They didn't know the truth. I needed them to know, but the unwavering question still remained the same: how?

*****

Later that night, Travis had come over and tried to put the key back together. He didn't think he could get it to hook together but instead thought of a plan to soak it in some anti-rust solution to remove the rust. Brilliant as it had become very rusted and worn. It was a wonderful plan, and I hoped, with everything I had, that it would work.

I noticed Carla had become very fatigued the last few days and I couldn't put my finger on it. Was she sick? That night as the key was soaking, Travis and Adria went to grab Carla something from the store. Medicine, I think, and 7 Up is what they called it. It seemed to be a drink to help settle the stomach. Who knows why it would help, but I guess they knew what helped.

Carla had sat down, and one minute later, someone was knocking on the door to the cottage. *Maybe it was Miriam*, I thought. It was not. It was just someone dropping off the food the three of them had ordered earlier. Carla set the food down and then headed to the couch. She looked worse than she did just a few moments ago. She fell asleep almost instantly, and I let her lie there without distractions. I was quiet, trying not to wake her. Obviously, she needed the rest.

Was she stressed about this whole ordeal? Could that be what was making her so tired?

I sat next to her on the floor and just kept my eyes on the key. Slowly, dirty, rusty particles started floating to the top of the bowl. The once clear water was becoming murky and turned a light reddish-brown color. I wish I had some sort of brush to stick in there and to clear anything else off of it.

I was about to reach in when I heard a car door shut outside. I jumped up to go look out the window and found that Adria and Travis had returned. I knew when they got back, they would take another look at the key and hopefully get it fixed back together. We were getting one step closer.

When they walked through the door—Adria first and then Travis—I noticed Adria slowly waking Carla up and was giving her something. It was not the drink she had asked for; it was a small bag. She pulled the box out as she walked to the bathroom. I was curious, so I inched closer and noticed the word *pregnancy*.

Oh Lord. I knew right then. Carla had been acting so different because she was pregnant. I knew it. I totally knew it, or I should have known. I think that ghost instincts pick up on these things. I just couldn't figure out why I hadn't put it together sooner.

I wasn't sure what the box was or why she needed it. This had to be one of those new age things that I didn't fully understand. On the top, it read "results," so I guessed somehow this tiny box was going to give her the answer I already knew. She would know soon enough too.

She came back out of the bathroom a few minutes later and confirmed to everyone in the room what they had all suspected.

"I'm pregnant if anyone wants to know," she said as she walked over and sat down on the couch.

Adria turned toward her, while Travis remained silent. It was Adria who spoke first, asking if she was okay. The rain began to throw itself at the cottage now, pounding loud like a waterfall rolling over its steep, longing edge. Its roar grew louder and became more ferocious, and the lights began to flicker. I shivered a moment, making me miss the way my mother would comfort me in the middle of a storm.

Carla jumped slightly from the sound of the shrieks, but she turned to the other two and began insisting that she was fine. "Look, it's not how I planned something like this to happen, but it is what it is. Now I just need to think about how to break the news to Nate."

"You want to call him? You can go in the bedroom, or Travis and I can go for another drive for a little bit." Adria was trying to be sympathetic.

"No," Carla said, "I will see him tomorrow and I'd rather tell him in person." Carla was not as happy as I imagined a new mother would be. Babies were supposed to be happy news, a happy occasion, and right now she looked…frightened.

I started walking over to her at the same time Adria did too. Adria knelt down beside Carla and grabbed her hands. "Everything is going to be okay," I overheard her say. "You're going to be the best mother. You and Nate will figure this out, and everything will work out."

"I know. It will be fine, and after the shock, I will accept it and be happy too," Carla said as she patted the top of Adria's hand, trying to hide the tears building in the corners of her eyes. She tried to force a smile on her face.

"Are you sure you don't want to call Nate tonight?" Adria asked one more time.

"Yeah. Let's figure this key thing out, and then I'll tell him in the morning," Carla said as she scooted closer to the table where the key sat.

Travis looked inside, "We might be able to empty this now." He took the bowl and walked back into the kitchen. He dumped out the liquid and placed the key on top of a paper towel. Grabbing a dish towel from one of the drawers, he came back into the living room to sit next to the girls.

He began by drying it off with the paper towel first, and then he started to rub it more intensely with the towel. I feel like I could almost see its original polish, or maybe I just wanted to see it. "I think that worked pretty good," Travis said. "Now let's see if we can hook in and screw the pieces together."

Travis held the two pieces together, and pressing the two ends, he started to twist. He could feel the pieces tightening, but he wasn't sure if it would stay. "We may end up needing to weld it back together," he said.

"Could we try super glue?" Adria asked.

"We could try it but no guarantees," Travis replied.

"I'll get the bottle," said Carla. "I saw it in the kitchen a few days ago."

She got up and made her way into the kitchen as Travis asked for Adria to hold one side of the key, while he held the other and tried to tighten it with his other hand.

"There," he said as Carla walked back in the room. "I think that is as tight as I can make it. Carla, can you dab a little glue on the top and make your way around the sides?"

I was hovering over all three of them, trying to see exactly what they were doing the whole time. I was holding my mouth closed like I was holding my breath; I don't know why. I guess I was willing them to fix it. For a second, I wished it was me that was helping.

I had become somewhat a control freak in all these years. Restlessness had done it to me, and so had being alone. *I can do it, and I can do it better.* I knew it was a horrible way to think, but I couldn't help it.

Carla grabbed the bottom of the key to steady it as she touched the tip of the glue to the hook and worked her way around the edges. "You're going to need more than that," I said out loud to no one in particular, and of course, I didn't expect anyone to hear me. I reached toward the key, trying to see if I could help in some way.

As I touched the key, the three of them were still holding, every head whipped in my direction looking at me with fear, hesitation, alarm, and terror. If there was any other word I could enter here, I would. But I couldn't think of any at the moment as I froze staring back at their gazing eyes.

All eyebrows were raised, and I searched back and forth, looking at all three of them with my own uncertain eyes. In the same instant and before anything else could happen, I felt a jolt out of nowhere, and heard lightning strike so close. My ears started ringing, and my vision started to go black.

Part 3

Chapter 18

Nate was getting his things ready for the next morning. He was excited to be traveling with Carla and Adria to Castle Creet. He pulled up the directions to the castle on his phone locations and saw that it was about an hour away. He checked the weather for tomorrow and saw it would be on the chilly side but not raining. He wanted to lay out some clothes he would be comfortable in, so he pulled out some joggers, a light T-shirt, and a thicker zip up hoodie. He grabbed the tennis shoes he brought with him. They would have to do because he hadn't brought any others besides his nice dress shoes.

He also wanted to pack a few snacks and water in case they ended up staying there through lunch. He knew the girls wanted to leave by eight in the morning, and he didn't think they would be there that long, but you never know.

Nate was beginning to wonder if Travis would end up going with them too. They hadn't met yet and it might be nice to know who Adria had her eye on, and especially now since Daniel was no longer in the picture.

Poor Daniel, he didn't stand a chance, Nate thought. He was going to make a point of it to catch up with Daniel when he got back to the States. It was the least he could do for the poor man.

Nate thought about how Carla didn't feel well but thought she would still be awake. It was only eight-thirty, so he whipped out his phone and walked over to look out the hotel window and text her. The storm was beginning to pick up and pound the outside pavement.

He typed out his text: "Will Travis be joining us in the morning?" He hit Send. While he waited for a response, he got to thinking he really did hope the storm was gone in the morning so it wouldn't make the trip difficult.

He set his phone down and went back to organizing his things. He laid his clothes on the couch next to the queen-sized bed in the hotel and decided to add his heavy coat as well. He put his documents and laptop back in his briefcase and set it on the table out of the way. His convention was over, and now he would have time to explore and adventure in Ireland.

Nate was a very organized person, definitely OCD. He wanted to know where things were, and he wanted them to be easily accessible. He grabbed his water bottle and headed back toward his phone. Picking it up to check if Carla had replied, but it was only his lock screen, a picture of himself, and Carla on the beach stared back at him. No text reply yet. He set it back down and switched on the television.

Flipping through the channels, he couldn't decide on anything to watch. He was beginning to feel anxious about their trip. He didn't know what the next day would hold for him, and he was beginning to wonder how it would be with Carla. He hadn't seen her since the beginning of their makeup sort of date. Things had been going good between them. He also couldn't help but wonder how Carla would be feeling in the morning. Would she change her mind about wanting to go?

His fingers tapped on the side of the couch, and his right leg began to shake up and down. He was beginning to get fidgety and decided to send another text to Carla: "How's it going? Are you feeling any better? Maybe after you got some food in you?"

After a few minutes and he still had not received a reply, he decided to text Adria: "What are you guys up to? I haven't heard from Carla and was wondering how she was feeling. Can you have her text me?"

Nate watched the clock, and when it hit nine-thirty and he still had not heard from either of them, he started to become worried. He knew Adria pretty well and also knew she was a night owl.

There was no way she was in bed by now, and she usually always had her phone on her.

He thought maybe he could shoot a text to Miriam and she could run over and check on them, but he also didn't want to make a pregnant woman go out in the rain. In the end, it would make him feel better to know they were okay so he would word it in a way to see if her husband could run over there.

"Hey Miriam, this is Nate. Carla's boyfriend. I haven't heard from Carla in a while and I was wondering if maybe Craig could run over and check on them?"

"Or maybe they are with you?" He added another text.

Her reply came quickly: "No they aren't. I have not heard from them since the zoo earlier. I think they were planning on staying in tonight."

Another text from Miriam came before Nate could reply: "I can see out the window, Travis's car is over there. I'll text him."

"Thanks. Sorry to be a bother. The storm has me worried." He punched out and hit send.

A few minutes passed as he was anxiously awaiting Miriam's reply. He knew if the power went out, they would still have battery charge—at least until their phone batteries died. *Dammit, has Carla gotten a new charger yet?* he thought to himself.

"Sorry. Travis isn't texting me back either. The lights are still on. I'm sending Craig over to check in on them."

Nate was grateful and felt his shoulders relax slightly. He knew Craig would be going out in the storm, but Nate would feel better if he knew the girls were safe. He would sleep better too. He grabbed the blanket off the foot of the bed and went to sit on the couch, waiting for Miriam to get back to him.

*****

I feel like I was thrown from the sky, spit out, and dropped on my head. I hit the ground hard, and I lay in the same position for a long while. It took me a moment to open my eyes. I slowly peeled them back one at a time, blinking quickly to block the sun glaring back at me. I rolled over and pushed up onto one side of my elbow, trying to get control of the situation and realize where I was.

I came up to a sitting position and noticed I was sitting by a little well. With a quick spin, I found myself gazing at Castle Creet. It was back to its beautiful self, not old or worn but colorful and vibrant. I looked around taking it all in and saw Mother sitting on the steps sewing something she held in her hands. Could this be real? I was in awe and confused all at the same time. This had to be sometime back before 1908.

Was all that had happened before just a dream? Did I just awake from a horrible nightmare? Mother had not died yet. She was still very much alive.

In that instant, it didn't matter. I jumped up to my feet as fast as I could, pushing away the headache that was starting to cloud my memory. I ran over to my mother and wrapped my arms around her and squeezed tightly.

My arms grabbed each other on the other side of her, and I fell forward, hitting my head on the stone from the top step of the porch. I turned around quickly. Mother was still there, a hazy form sitting before me. *Oh no,* I thought. *I'm still a ghost?* It was more a question to myself.

"Mother," I said, calling out her name. "Mother, can you hear me?" I came closer to her ear.

"Mother," again I cried, but there was no acknowledgment. She didn't turn to listen to my every word. She didn't wrap her arms around me and pull me in closer to her.

My mother could not see me. She could not hear me, and the rhythm of this happening on repeat didn't skip a beat. I could see and hear her, but once again, she could not hear or see me. Her appearance was the same as I remember. Her hair was pulled back, but I could not see her whole face. On one side of her ear, she wore a beautiful flower behind her hair. Her ivory skin shown soft in the sunlight. She looked like an angel glowing with radiance as the sun beams filtered down through the clouds.

Off in the distance, I heard a young child pull my focus away from Mother. I searched out the familiar laughter and saw my sister,

Fiona, rolling on the ground with gobs of flowers she sent flying in the air above her head. They were falling down on her with such grace and elegance. It was almost as if I were watching in slow motion.

I looked back at my mother, wanting to admire the happiness she always felt, but this time I noticed a sadness I had not seen before. She had a smile on her face looking on toward Fiona, but her eyes were heavier than I remember. She was still beautiful, but her face was pale, and her emotion seemed forced. I felt heartache. I felt guilt and pain. I could barely stand.

As I turned to walk back down the castle steps, the familiar eyes of Carla, Adria, and Travis were observing my every move as they walked slowly toward the castle steps. They had come together and were huddled in a defensive formation. "What are you looking at?" I said, muffled and teary-eyed. I said it knowing they couldn't hear me and I was about to storm off.

"Wait a second. You're here. I touched the key. You were touching the key. All four of us were touching the key. And now we're here, in front of the castle…together."

I began to rethink, to recount how we got here. And I couldn't remember anything. Just the key—we touched it, and *boom*, here we were. All of us.

"Are you okay?" Travis asked as he took a step toward my direction.

Was he talking to me? I looked behind me. He must be talking to Mother. Travis… Mother… Carla and Adria. At least a hundred years between these people, and they were standing right here where my mother was. How was this possible?

"Who are you talking to?" I said back to him, not knowing if he would respond.

"I'm asking if you are okay," he said again.

Carla and Adria still just stood there a little uneasy. I could tell by their body language. "Can you see me?" I asked.

"Yes, what's your name?" Travis asked another question.

"I'm Amelia."

"I'm Travis," he said back to me.

Oh, holy moly. He is talking to me. He can hear me. He can see me. Is my plan really working? I was able to get Carla and Adria here... back to Ireland...back to the castle. Travis wasn't exactly part of the plan, but no matter, we were here! Not exactly how I had planned at all. How did we time-travel back to 1908?

"Yes, I know your name," was all I could say. *How do I explain all of this to him? To all of them.* "You know who I am? Where are we?" he said wearily and started walking closer to me.

"My name is Amelia Gallagher, and this is my home, Castle Creet. That is my mother, Mary," I said pointing back behind me, "and my sister Fiona, in the distance."

I heard Carla and Adria both gasp in the distance. I looked to them and waited for either of them to say something, but no words came from either of them.

So I continued, "I died when I was ten years old, and I have been trying to figure out how to pass on for what seems like an eternity."

"Okay. So why are we here?" Travis asked, clearly talking about him Carla and Adria.

I continued, "I tried attaching myself to different people to see if they could help me leave this world. I had no luck until I was in New York a few weeks ago and practically got thrown onto Carla." I turned to her as I spoke the next part. "I've been following you ever since." I shrugged, giving her a sly, amused look.

"You...you're the little girl from my bedroom," Carla said. "I recognize you."

"And you're the girl my grandmother saw with us the other day?" Adria questioned.

"Yes, and I've been trying to get your attention ever since. I've tried talking to you, grabbing your wrist, throwing pots on the ground." I began to recount everything I had done to try to get Carla to see me and know that I was there.

"Why are we here?" Travis asked.

"I don't know," I said, turning back around to look at the castle and Mother. I kept taking it all in, looking down to the pond and the road. I turned back to them. "I'm guessing something from the key, when it was put back together, must have transported us and thrown us back in time, here to the castle." I probably couldn't explain it any better than they could, and it was beginning to hurt my brain thinking about how this was all possible.

"Could this have anything to do with you passing on?" Carla asked hesitantly. "You said you've been trying for many, many years?"

"It could, I guess. I've been trying to find my way out of this in between realm, and I thought attaching to you would help get me there," I said, trying to make sense of anything.

"Holy hell," Adria said. "This is the strangest vacation I've ever been on. I didn't even know things like this could happen. We're at the castle, my family castle in...what year is it?"

"I think it has got to be between when I died in 1908 but obviously before Mother died," I said, looking back to her again.

Travis walked over to my mother, who was still sitting on the steps, and waved his hand in front of her face. "Hello." She couldn't see him either.

Just then, Daddy walked up from the side of the castle. Everyone froze, including me. He was shouting at my mother, and I was trying to make out what he was saying. Travis backed up a little until he realized Daddy couldn't see him either.

"Why are you still sulking, woman? Get up and go clean something," Daddy said.

Why does Daddy sound so angry? I thought.

He grabbed Mother by her arm and practically yanked her shoulder out of the socket. He pulled her to her feet and gave her a push inside the castle doors.

Mother grabbed her arm and started crying as she ran further into the castle until I could no longer see her.

I looked back at Carla and Adria as tears filled my eyes. This was not the daddy I remembered. Adria came toward me and, with skeptical arms, wrapped them around me in an embrace. It took my breath away; I could feel her arms. They were warm and comforting. It felt good to feel her close to me and to feel the support she was offering. It was the first time in over a hundred years that someone had hugged me. I returned the hug, wrapping my arms tightly around her as I let the familiarity of a hug return to me.

"I think I know why we are here," Carla said, stepping closer to me and Adria. "We all have questions. We came to Ireland in search of the answers we have been looking for. Now we have the chance to find them."

She was looking right at me.

Chapter 19

The dreaded text came from Miriam a few minutes later: "They aren't there. None of them."

Nate sat up in a slight panic, his heart beginning to race faster. Instead of replying via text, he punched in to call Miriam directly. She answered on the first ring.

"What do you mean they aren't there?" he asked, trying to remain as calm as possible.

"Craig said that no one is over there. All of their things are still there, but they are not," Miriam was explaining.

A few minutes on the telephone and Nate insisted that he was coming over to the cottage. He hung up the phone, grabbed his jacket and keys to his rental car, and was out the door in seconds.

It wasn't a particularly long drive to get there but Nate felt like the minutes were passing like hours. He pulled into the long driveway and turned his car in the direction of the cottage. Miriam was right. Nothing looked out of the ordinary. The lights were on, and Travis's car was sitting out front.

He put his car in park behind Travis's and opened the door while he pulled the keys out of the ignition at the same time. Going up to the cottage, he opened the door without a knock. He was hoping to see Carla and Adria and find out this whole thing was just a big mistake, but Adria's purse was still on the table, and their food was sitting out still untouched.

He walked back to Carla's room, but just as he suspected and had already been told, no one was there. Just then Miriam and Craig walked in, shaking out their umbrellas and leaving them by the doorstep.

"How are they not here? Where could they have gone without a car and in this weather?" Nate asked, bemused. He whipped out his phone. "I'm going to call them again." It seemed like calling them until one of them answered was the most logical thing to do.

"I'll try Travis again, and then I'll call my Aunt Shauna to see if she has heard from him," Miriam said as she took her phone in the back bedroom.

Again, Nate switched back and forth between Carla and Adria's number, but still, there was no answer from either of them. The phone rang until their voicemails came on. "This is Carla. Sorry you missed me. Leave a message if you want." It was a voicemail he had heard so many times before, but at this very minute, he was clinging to it as if it was the last time he would hear Carla.

"They couldn't have just disappeared," he said as Miriam walked back into the room.

"Aunt Shauna hasn't heard from Travis either," Miriam said to both the men.

It was Craig this time who spoke up, "Well, I guess it's time to search outside, around the cottage and property. Maybe the three of them got stuck in this horrendous storm."

He headed toward the door and grabbed his umbrella. Nate and Miriam started to follow him, both agreeing that they could have stopped in the weather.

"Perhaps a neighbor," Miriam suggested as she reached for her umbrella.

"Not you, Miriam. You shouldn't be out in the storm in your condition," Craig said to his wife, being protective and stern at the same time.

Miriam wanted to argue with him, not sure she liked being put into the "You can't do anything while you're pregnant" category, but she knew there were bigger matters going on right now. She didn't say anything but gave him a "fine" sneer. She walked back over to sit on the couch.

"Check the garden," she said as the men walked out. "Carla loves the garden."

Miriam was filled with anxiety while she sat on the little fold-out couch. She had no idea where they would have gone and didn't think anyone would be stupid enough to go out in this storm. Especially Travis, whom she knew quite well.

She decided to put on a pot of tea, hoping it would calm her nerves, and then when Nate and Craig did return with the rest of them, it would warm everyone up. Plus, she liked having something to do.

She walked into the kitchen and grabbed the small kettle sitting on the little stove in the corner. She removed the lid and hovered the pot under the faucet while it filled with water. Turning the stove knob, she waited for the gas lighter to catch. It was then that she felt another pinch of pain in her stomach. No, it wasn't her stomach; it was lower in her abdomen. A sharp pain doubled her over for a couple of seconds, and she gasped and held her breath. It passed with time, and she was able to straighten up. Assuming it was the same cramp she had had before, she tried to relax. She had read about these types of cramps being called Braxton Hicks. They didn't alarm her, so she went back to putting the pot on the stove to boil.

*****

"Okay, what do we know?" Travis began saying. "One, we know that we are at Castle Creet—a very long time ago. Two, we know that no one can see us—except us. Three, we think we are here to find out answers to Amelia and Adria's past."

I guess if it is my family's past, it is Adria's too, I thought. I hadn't quite thought about it fully, but it was true. That would make me a great-great-aunt to her... I think. *Well, I guess that means Adria probably wants to know the truth just as much as I do, so I'm glad we are all on the same team.*

"What are the exact questions we want answers to?" Adria was asking everyone.

Carla started listing off a number of questions. "How did Mary Gallagher really die? There seem to be two possibilities. And I'm assuming you don't know"—she turned to me—"since you died before your mother."

I just shook my head and watched as the others continued making mental notes to themselves.

Carla went on, "Why did Castle Creet become abandoned? What happened to the ghost who died in 1875?"

"The one you heard rumor about," said Adria to Travis.

Carla nodded and went on, "Also, there is still the answer of the murder/suicide mystery we had heard about when we were back in Boise."

They all three looked over at me again as if to question if I knew anything.

I thought to myself, *I do. I do know a little something about the ghost of Castle Creet,* so I began carefully. "I knew a ghost that lived in the castle. His name was William Gallagher."

They all just stared at me, and I felt a shyness overcome me. I wasn't used to this much attention, but as I looked at their faces, I recognized all their encouraging looks, so I went on.

"He helped build the castle back in 1799, but when he died, he decided to remain behind as a spirit because he loved the castle so much. He had become friends with my mother when she was still alive, and she could communicate with him. She was able to tell him things, to confide in him, and no one else could understand her like him."

It seemed like a lot of information I was throwing at them, but they were soaking it all in. It made me feel good that they were hearing a part of the story that I knew and that I knew to be the truth.

"He was also friends with me. He was my companion too up until the day my mother died." And so I began explaining everything I knew about William and everything I knew from my side of history—how I thought my mother's death was William's way to heaven and how he must have been the ghost they were referring to.

"So it's true," Travis said. I nodded in response.

"Well now we know," Carla said. "He was not a bad man like the stories were told and had nothing to do with the deaths of the other people listed on that paper. I think that answers that question pretty well."

"What paper? The notice of smallpox?" I asked, hoping that that was what Carla was talking about.

"Yes," Carla said, "but it was Travis who found it."

"I found a paper that had a list with you and your mother's names on it, claiming you had both died of smallpox," Travis chimed in.

"That's not true. Other workers, yes, there were some that did die of smallpox. We were taken away from the castle in 1906. We went and stayed with my mother's mother. I think we were there for about six months before we were finally were able to return home. Daddy had said everything was safe and that those still contaminated were sent away. I don't know why he would claim that smallpox took both of us." I didn't mention that William had once told me that Daddy might have had something to do with the death of my mother.

We sat there for a while, thinking and pondering. No one was talking until I finally said, "I want to know more about what happened to me. I heard the story your grandmother told of me slipping in the pond and that Mother thought Daddy had something to do with it. I want to know the truth."

"Yes, she did say that." Adria was agreeing with me. "The fact of the matter is, if you are already dead in 'this time,' we still may never find out or see what happened to you."

"Maybe if we investigate, you know, start listening to people that are here working at the castle," I started. "People always talk. The helpers might know something." I knew Adria was right of course. Yes, some people talk, but there were a lot of people with closed lips too.

"Amelia, do you want to show us around?" Adria asked me, trying to change the subject.

"Sure," was all I could say as I tried to let them pull me out of my gloomy mood.

Wanting them to see how beautiful it was, I walked them down to the pond first. They could see all the wildflowers and the magnificent blue crystal waters. I wanted them to know why it was my happy place. I knew that when they returned to their own time, the pond would be dried up and gone. This would be the only time they would truly be able to take in its beauty.

The breeze blew softly, and I could feel it floating swiftly through my hair. I could just pick up the faint scent of grass and hay. As we got closer, I realized it was exactly as I remembered. We sat down for a few moments and I told them a couple of stories why I loved it so much, the memories it brought to me, and the peace I felt when I was nearby.

And then I laid out the story I remember, of slipping in while trying to catch a frog. The last thing I remember was being in the sitting room, unconscious, while my mother smoothed back my hair... I died later that night and woke up to an empty room with my mother nowhere to be found. She had locked me in, and she never came back for me.

"Do you want to show us inside the castle?" Carla asked.

"Yeah, I guess it's time to show you." I didn't know if I would be frightened by the sight of everything again or if it would be a joyous occasion. Either way, I was about to know, and come to find out, we didn't even need the key everyone had been searching for.

*****

Nate and Craig came back in through the cottage door about an hour later. They were shaking off their coats and shaking their heads in disappointment.

"They aren't out there," Craig said to Miriam.

"What on earth," was all she replied as she stood up in distress.

"What do you say we give it until morning to see if they show up? We can stay here at the cottage if you'd like," Craig said.

"No, no, I'm fine. I'll stay here and wait for them to return," Nate said. "I'll call the police in the morning if they haven't returned." He sat down on the couch, rubbing his head.

Craig and Miriam walked out of the cottage, shutting the door behind them. Nate noticed the 7 Up that Adria had gotten for Carla, so he knew that Adria and Travis had returned from the store at some point, but their food was untouched. That was what really confused him. It gave him a bad feeling down in the pit of his stomach. Why wouldn't they at least eat before going out again?

He tried both Carla and Adria again a few more times but still no answer. Walking about the inside of the cottage, he found an old bookshelf filled with a few dozen books. He grabbed one off the shelf and returned to the couch, flipping through a few pages but not really focusing on anything.

A buzzing noise went off coming from the kitchen, and Nate jumped to his feet to find out what it was. He nearly tripped over his own feet as he saw Adria's phone vibrating with an incoming call. The name on the front read "Marcus," whom Nate knew was from the coffee shop. He picked up the phone but decided to let it go to voicemail. Nate had hoped it was Carla or even Travis calling to check in with Adria. Walking back to the couch, he collapsed where he had been sitting just before.

Nate lay there for a few minutes, his eyes searching the ceiling while his mind was deep in thought. Something flickered out of the corner of his eye that caught his attention and looked peculiar. He shuffled himself down off the couch until he was in a kneeling position on the floor, crouching over and looking down under the table nearby. Slipping his hand underneath until he could feel the cold metal under his fingers, he pulled it back out. It was the old key, the one Carla and Adria had been talking about.

He had not seen it before now, but he knew what it was. It had looked like it was just cleaned but it was still worn with old rust. "Well, looks like they got it back together," he said to himself as he pulled himself off the floor and sat back down.

*****

I led the three of them around to the front castle, and they followed closely behind. I walked up the familiar stone steps and placed my hands on the entrance. Holding my breath, I pushed open the big, red castle doors, and we walked a few steps in.

Everything from my past came flooding back to me. It was just as I remembered: the castle, the smell, the sounds. When I first walked in, I was standing in the foyer but also a grand hallway that led all the way to the back of the castle. Off to the right was the small dining room with an entrance into the back kitchen. The walls were brick and stone, and there were three windows leading out to the front view. There was a wooden table with eight hand-carved chairs. Daddy had made it, and I remember thinking about how beautiful his work was. Mother had always admired it.

To the left of the front door when you first walked in was a small winding stone staircase. It led to a few rooms upstairs that the castle helpers occupied. The rooms up there were small and dark, and I didn't go up there very often. For one, I was not allowed, and for two, it was a bit scary… My sister, Fiona, had always said it was haunted by a ghost.

Now that I think of it, it sounded so silly. *It was probably William,* I thought. And then I thought about it some more. It could totally be true. As far as I knew, William could go anywhere. Why wouldn't he take one of the bedrooms upstairs? But then again, did ghosts really have bedrooms?

If you kept walking forward through the entrance, there was a hallway to the left that curved and led to a master door where Mother and Daddy slept. Straight ahead was a massive door made out of glass that would lead you back outside. If you turned to the right, it led down a hallway with three more bedrooms and the sitting room. There was also the kitchen with more stairs that led to a library and a tower of sorts. The kitchen also had a door that led outside to the back. Off of the kitchen was a smaller room where extra food was kept. It was a place for extra storage and items that needed to be kept cold.

My bedroom was to the right of the grand hallway, along with my sister Fiona's room. I led the three of them to my room, admiring how it still looked the same, as if it had not been touched. My favorite doll lay across my pillow, and I had a few paintings of wildflowers hanging on the wall. There was a writing desk and a picture my mother had drawn of Fiona and me. On the far wall was a stone fireplace just big enough to heat the room if needed.

"This was my room," I said. "I didn't sleep in here much. My sister and I would always find ourselves getting cold, and it was always me that snuck into her room. We ended up sharing her bed to stay warm... I would tiptoe back into my room in the morning before Mother could find me." I stared off in the distant past while I thought of those times that didn't seem like that long ago.

"I'm not sure where we are going to stay tonight. Do you think we could sleep in here?" Carla asked, and it startled me back to the present or the past or whatever we were supposed to call this supernatural time.

"Yes, I'm sure that would be fine. They can't see us anyway," I replied, looking at them with a solemn face.

That night, Travis tried to get a fire going, but apparently, traveling back in time didn't allow you to build one. Makes sense—sort of. Travis and Adria scooted up on the bed, lying next to each other... "Travis is the little spoon," Carla joked quietly, explaining to me what it meant, and we both laughed.

Carla and I grabbed a few blankets from the hallway drawers and tried to get cozy. She must have heard my teeth chattering because she scooted closer to me and wrapped her arm around my shoulder. I don't remember being particularly cold, but I was definitely anxious about something. I welcomed the feel of her touch and sensation of instant comfort.

The morning came quickly, and I woke up to the sound of screaming and shouting. It was very, very early and no one was awake, not even the workers doing the morning chores yet. Carla, Adria, and Travis were still sound asleep, so I gathered my blanket up around my shoulders and ventured out to find where the shouting was coming from.

I followed it down the hallway and through to the kitchen. There was no fire lit in the kitchen, and the old castle was feeling drafty. As I got closer to the doors that led into the sitting room, I could hear Mother was screaming at Daddy. I inched closer to take a peak and saw Mother grabbing at his dress shirt and pulling at his arms. When I looked to Daddy, my eyes went searching, wandering down his arms to his hands.

He was standing over the little bed in the corner of the room. He was holding a handkerchief in both hands as he was leaning over, pressing it across the top of a young girl's face, smothering her. It covered her nose and mouth and she didn't make a sound.

In that very moment, I felt shook. I looked at Daddy again and then to Mother and then down to the girl, and I grasped in that minute that the young girl in the bed—was me. It flooded me with emotion as the past began to haunt me, that that was me lying there in the white cotton sheets. I didn't struggle. I was mostly unconscious as I remember—from my own memory of the sleepy incident. I didn't feel it. I wasn't scared in that moment so many years ago. I hadn't been coherent enough to understand death.

But I was scared now. I could not believe what I was looking at. I could not believe Daddy would have hurt me. *Why? Please, please let my eyes be deceiving me.* I could not work out the feelings or reasons Daddy would be doing this. I started to get an ache, a feeling way down deep in my gut. My head was cloudy and fogged over.

A few minutes later, Daddy let go, pulling his hands away from my body. He turned and shoved Mother to the ground—hard. She hit her head on the chair she used to sit on by my bed. I could see her head begin to bleed as Daddy threw the handkerchief down at her.

"She was dying, anyway," he said and stomped off.

Mother lay there on the ground, holding herself for a while before she finally pulled herself to her feet. Her cheeks and nose were red, her face tear-stained. She pressed the handkerchief to her cut to stop the bleeding at her hairline. As she walked back over to my body that lay on the bed, she knelt down closer.

"Goodbye, my love," she said, and the tears began to flow more heavily.

Mother walked toward the sitting room door and pulled a key out of her pocket. As she turned toward the inside of the room, she kept her eyes down to the floor. She paused a minute and then placed the key on the table. Walking over to grab both door handles one hand on each metal loop, she closed them slowly as she left the room. She rested on the other side, still leaning face forward on the outside of the door, her hands and head still on the door.

With a deep breath, she took off running, and I didn't know whether to follow her or leave her be. It was too late when I thought I should have chased her. She wouldn't have been able to see me even if I had been able to follow her, and my tie was still holding me tight to Carla—it kept me near my bedroom where Carla was still asleep.

There was also part of me that wanted to let Mother grieve in peace, and so I did not persist. Instead, I ran back to my bedroom where the three guests were starting to wake. Carla was tidying up the bedroom and picking up the blankets from the floor.

"There you are," she said.

All three of them looked to me in the doorway and knew immediately that something was wrong.

They could easily see the tears streaming down my face. Carla and Adria rushed over to me and threw me into a tight embrace. They didn't ask me any questions, and I was grateful for that. They just held me. And I let them.

Chapter 20

"Do you want to talk about it?" Carla asked after an appropriate amount of time had passed.

I wasn't sure if I was ready yet or not. I had just witnessed my real death—what really happened to me. And it was at the hands of my own daddy. My mother had pleaded and fought for him to stop, but he was stronger, and in the end, he had ended my life.

"I-I…" I tried to talk, but words wouldn't quite come out. I was still sniffling and choked up. My throat was dry and hot. My nose became stuffed up from crying even though I was not sick. I tried again. "I just saw my daddy…suffocate me."

Everyone's eyes widened, and no one really knew what to say. Carla pulled me closer into her arms, and I saw Adria look over to Travis, trying to understand the situation. He too was in complete shock.

"You were still in there." It was more of a statement coming from Adria than a question. "We should have looked. Oh, why didn't we look?"

"It's on me," I said. "I should have thought about it. Daddy said I was dying anyways, but to see it with my own eyes, to see the way it happened… I feel so shattered."

"Did you feel anything? Did you feel physical pain?" Travis asked. "Then or now?"

"No," was all I could say.

"Amelia, we are here for you, and we're going to figure this out. It may be painful to comprehend, but in the end, I think we will all feel better knowing the truth," Carla added.

I sniffled some more and wiped my tears. I thought to myself, *There is nothing to do about it now. My physical body is already dead and has been for years.*

"I say we search about today and see if we can make any sense of what just happened," Travis started saying. "Maybe we can find out the reasons why Henry did this and blamed her death on smallpox."

"Well, of course he said I died from smallpox," I snapped. "No one would believe he murdered his own daughter." I blurted it out in anger. "Everyone else knew I slipped in the pond and was unconscious, so no one would know that Daddy was the one who really caused my death. He could say whatever he wanted about the reasoning behind it."

People respected my father. He came from a well-off family. They knew his father and his father before him. People knew Daddy was a good kind. What they didn't know was that that was actually not true as I had just learned moments ago.

"Why wouldn't he just say you died from the drowning then?" Travis said.

"Probably because Mother knew the truth and she would have said something," I began. Then again, I thought maybe Mother couldn't say anything against my daddy. Maybe she was scared of him.

"Look," Adria said, "I'm still so troubled by this, but Travis is right. We need to keep looking for the answers to this mysterious secret."

*****

Carla and I decided to go searching for my mother, hoping she was still somewhere in the castle. She would be in such disarray, but we had to know what was going through her mind. Travis and Adria decided they would go after Daddy. They wanted to know if they could find out anything about how he could've done what he did.

We found Mother upstairs in the library. She was sitting on a bench that was built into the big window. Gazing outside at only God knew what, she was trembling and shaking, and as I got closer,

I could see her pulse beating through the side of her neck. The pace was quite fast, and I thought for a second that maybe she could be about to pass out.

Was she going to faint? I couldn't tell, but she was awfully pale. I slowly came closer and grabbed her hand; of course she couldn't feel it. I couldn't feel it either. But in some strange way, I felt like I was comforting and aiding her.

Just then, she looked up in the direction of the door I had just entered and said, "Hi."

I thought for a second she was talking to me, and I caught my breath and waited for her to say something else, but she had to have been looking through me. I turned a questioning look toward Carla, and I caught a glimpse of William standing in the doorway just behind her.

Of course. He was mother's friend; he would be here. He probably came to comfort her and let her vent to him. *Could he see me too in this past time?* I wondered. Oh, it was good to see him again.

"William, William, can you hear me?" I said, hoping to get his attention.

He could not hear me. I figured as much, but it was worth a shot. He would be finding me soon in my "dungeon" anyway. Plus, it was 2020 in real time; I wasn't supposed to be thrown back to 1908 to begin with. I didn't even know how I was here in the first place.

"Who is that?" Carla asked curiously as she inched closer to me.

"That is William Gallagher," I explained. "He is the old ancestor who helped build this castle. He handcrafted the key you had been looking for. He became my friend after I died and was locked away in that room. That is the ghost you were told about."

Carla was perplexed but was acknowledging the bizarre introduction—on her end.

I just stared and watched as William interacted with Mother. It was comforting to see him being my mother's friend too. She had needed him.

*****

Nate woke up the next morning to a knock at the cottage door. He jumped up quickly. *Could it be Carla and Adria?* he thought, racing over and twisting the doorknob. When he opened the door, he found Miriam waiting outside.

"I have Craig contacting the Garda," she said peeking inside the door just past Nate's shoulder.

"They aren't here," Nate said as he noticed she was searching the inside for them. "Contacting who?" He stepped aside so she could enter the cottage.

"Sorry, it's the law enforcement here. We call it something different," she was explaining. "Look, I didn't think anything of it until I woke up this morning. Carla probably told you anyways, but I just wanted to mention it. She had spoken to me about a spirit visiting her for a few weeks now."

Nate listened. Carla had told him a few things about the odd occurrences that had been happening to her, but now Nate was trying to figure out what Miriam was getting at.

"I don't know anything about the supernatural or how these 'ghosts' handle themselves, but I can't help but think it could somehow be related," she continued.

"I'm not sure how those things relate to this. Are you saying you think a ghost…took them?" Nate said hesitantly and with a slightly exaggerated tone.

"I don't know. You hear strange stories." Miriam shrugged, wondering if she should have even said something.

"I guess the only thing we can do now is wait and see what the police say," Nate said, more worried than ever.

Just then Craig came over to the cottage. "They are on the way and will be here shortly," he said as he walked in and sat at the table.

Miriam began again, this time explaining the story about how a boy went missing for three days a few years back. "Do you think they went to the castle? Maybe this and that event could be related."

"No, I don't think so. We were supposed to go this morning. I don't think Carla would have gone without me," Nate replied.

*****

"He killed her, William," Mother said quietly. "He placed a cloth over her face and smothered her until she no longer had breath to breathe."

"If I could wrap my arms around you, I would," he said. He had a fatherly tone to him. "But since I can't, I will just sit and listen."

"I hate him," Mother went on. "He is not the man I married. He was upset when Fiona was not a boy, and he was livid when Amelia was not. He is not a kind man to me anymore, and now, after what he has done…" The sentence trailed off, and Mother could not finish her thought.

"And you're stuck with him?" William asked.

"I said my vows and made a promise to that man, but I do not love him," Mother said. "He is not the man I married."

William just nodded, listening to her when she needed. "He's welded the door shut," William began hesitantly.

Mother looked up to him in surprise. "What?"

"It's closed. You won't be able to get in again," William said with soft words.

As if a lightbulb went off in Mother's head, she remembered. "William, I left the key inside the room. I need to get it back."

"I shall retrieve it for you," William said.

"And while you do, I need to write a letter to my Mother." It was the last thing she said before she got up and headed toward the desk for writing material.

"I remember this," I said to Carla, "but I didn't think anything of it at the time. He had wanted something that had been sitting on the table, so I said he could have it. He couldn't quite pick it up and I didn't know if he had taken it with him when he left, but I didn't care."

Just then, I began crying again. "This information about Mother and Daddy is new to me, Carla. I had no idea my parents were angry with each other. I had no idea Mother did not love Daddy. I can't say that I blame her after what I just witnessed, but I'm heartbroken and confused."

"You have every right, Amelia," Carla said. "I think maybe…we should head somewhere and take a rest. It would be good for you to lay down."

"We can go back to my room?" I suggested.

"Do you want me to walk you there?" Carla asked. "I'd like to stay here and sneak a bit more of their conversation."

"I can manage," I said as I started walking toward the door and turned the corner. Just then, the swift, fleeting movement pulled me right back to Carla as I had forgotten that I was connected to her. I couldn't go more than ten or fifteen feet without that pull to be near her again.

"Sorry," I said. "I can't leave without you."

"Right. I keep forgetting. Come on. I'll go with you." And she wrapped her arm around me, and we walked back down to my room together.

*****

Nate wanted to splash some water on his face before the police arrived. Walking into the bathroom, he shut the door behind him, turned the water on to warm, and waited for it to get to the exact right temperature. He wet his hands and lightly patted his face, his cheeks first and then his forehead. He added more water to his hands and gave his eyes a gentle rub.

Reaching over, he leaned against the sink for a towel to dry his face. He dabbed at his face until it was dry enough. Setting the towel down and focusing on the counter, he noticed all of Carla and Adria's stuff was still here. They wouldn't go anywhere without it? His head was beginning to hurt from trying to figure it out.

Nate spotted a tiny white stick setting at the back of the sink. He leaned over closer to it and saw the words *not pregnant* with one line next to it and *pregnant* with two lines. He squinted at the box shown in the middle of the stick and noticed there was one very dark line and another faint line lined up parallel next to it.

He picked it up with one hand while the other one shot up to his head and down the back of his neck. He began running his hands through his hair and pacing back and forth in the tiny bathroom. There was only room for about five steps back and forth, so he didn't get much distance before he turned around and headed back the other way.

"Oh shit, oh shit, oh shit," he said over and over again as he was coming to the realization of what this actually meant. He stopped for a moment and had to take a deep breath. He sat down on the closed toilet lid and put his head between his knees, and then a thought occurred to him. "This could be Adria's, couldn't it?" he said out loud.

Questions started popping up in his head as he tried to figure out who's this was and who was pregnant. Did Adria sleep with Daniel? Could Adria be pregnant from Travis. When was the last time he and Carla were together?

He slowly started ticking off his mental list and answering the questions still residing in his head. *Carla would have told me if Adria and Daniel were sleeping together. Their relationship didn't seem that advanced,* he thought, and he didn't think Adria would be able to know if Travis knocked her up yet. It had been a few weeks since he and Carla were intimate, and he knew the possibility was high.

He set the pregnancy test back down on the counter top and put his head between his hands. *Carla is pregnant. When did she find out? Why didn't she call me? Maybe she didn't have a chance to call me before all this happened to her. Where is she? Oh God, help me find her.*

Nate heard the sound of tires crunching over gravel as a car began driving up the cottage road. He would need to gain his composure before he made his way out of the bathroom. As he stood up and went to the mirror, he became lightheaded. For a second, he stood there trying to regain his composure and lightly slapping himself across the face to get himself back together. He took a deep breath, opened the door back out to the living room, and went to wait for the knock at the door.

*****

"I have a thought," I said to Carla as we were sitting on my bed back in my own room.

"What's that?" she asked.

"I have this theory of why I haven't been able to find my way out of this life," I began, "and I think it's because I was locked away in that room. No one ever came back for me, and I was left there to... wither away."

"And you think because you were locked in, you were never able to find the peace on this side of death?" Carla asked.

"That has to be it, right? I mean, I've been so restless with nowhere to go and no reason to go or do anything," I replied.

Carla's mind wandered off in thought before speaking, "You said that William was your friend after your death right? So what happened to him again?"

"He left me when Mother died. He vanished one day and never returned to my room and that's the last I saw of him. I knew he was gone with mother's death because he was connected to her somehow."

"Well, damn," Carla said. "Sorry, I shouldn't use that language in front of you... But, Amelia, if William passed on when your mother died because he was connected to her. Well, you're connected to me. Maybe you can't pass on until..." Carla could hardly bring herself to say it. "Until I die."

"Oh, Carla, no. There has to be another way," I said intensely. "I have been in this state of illusion, being a ghost for over a hundred years. You are going to grow old, old, old before you die. I just know it, and although I have come to enjoy my time with you, I need to find a different way out. Please, you have to help me find another way."

"We will certainly do everything we can," Carla said and pulled the blanket up and rested it just below my chin.

Carla began walking around the inside of my room, touching and rubbing her belly in a motherly way. I don't think she knew I was watching her, but she had this beautiful presence about her.

She had grace and empathy, and I felt her being maternal, nurturing, and gentle. If not to her unborn child, she was definitely being all those things toward me.

"Carla," I said out loud, "don't be afraid of having a baby. They are meant to be blessings and miracles that fill you with love. This should be a happy occasion for you to celebrate, and I know I am not the only one who is over the moon for you."

She smiled, and her face went soft. I hoped she was beginning to understand the reality of her situation, but as I took a second look, deep into her eyes, I saw a spark of fear. I was nervous to ask. I didn't know if I should say anything else, but maybe she needed to talk about it too.

"Is everything okay? Aren't you excited?" I asked.

"I am excited, and it's all I've been thinking about today," she said. "My mother died when I was young, and I'm afraid I don't know how to be a mother. And…oh, Amelia, I shouldn't be putting this on you."

"I asked. I want you to tell me."

"What if I never see Nate again?" she said. "We've been so worried about finding the answers about Castle Creet and yours and Adria's past I don't think any of us have thought about how we are going to get back to real time. What if I can't get back to him?"

Her eyes started to fill with unshed tears, and her chin quivered. I had never seen her this upset in the three and half weeks I had been with her. She had a point, and I felt horrible I had never thought about it. I was only thinking about myself and finding out what happened to me and Mother.

It was my turn to be brave and encouraging, "You love him, Carla. We will find a way, I promise."

She sniffled and looked up at me through her watery eyes. "Yes," she whispered, "I do love him."

Chapter 21

Henry was working at the well outside. He was replacing the worn-out rope and making sure the bucket didn't have any holes. There was no remorse in his posture or on his face. Adria and Travis were beginning to feel ill, thinking about how he had done this without a second thought.

"How could he do that to his own daughter?" Adria said in a whisper, afraid that he would be able to hear her.

Travis wrapped a comforting arm around her shoulder, and she turned into his embrace. There was so much about Travis she was thankful for since they had been tossed into this "new world." Right now, especially in light of the unraveling events, she was glad to have him next to her. He was extra security for her wandering mind and frightening thoughts.

"I think we should go find Carla and Amelia," Travis said. "I don't think we are going to get many answers from him." Travis grabbed her hand and lead her back up the steps and inside the castle.

They made their way to the back room where Amelia and Carla were still resting. Carla was able to fill them in on William and the thoughts they had come up with about helping Amelia pass on.

"Without me dying, preferably," Carla added.

"This almost feels like it's becoming the impossible mission," Adria added. "Sorry to be the Debbie Downer, but has anyone thought about how we are getting home?" She put her pointer finger up and moved it around, pointing toward herself, Carla and Travis.

"I've been thinking about that too actually," said Carla. "I was thinking that maybe we were brought here for two reasons. Obviously to find the truth and to set Amelia free. We got brought here by the key. So maybe the key will be what takes us home after we do our tasks. Maybe if we all touch the key again like before, maybe it will send us home."

"The key," I said with raised eyebrows, "where is it?"

Everyone looked at each other around the room, but no one said anything reassuring. I guess everyone assumed someone else had it.

"It must be outside," Travis said. "That's where we all 'landed' if you will... I'll go look."

"Well, I guess in the meantime, we need to figure out what happens to Mary. We already figured out the truth of how Amelia died. After we get the details about Mary, we just need to set Amelia free," said Adria.

"Amelia, didn't you say you thought maybe you could pass on if you hadn't been left abandoned and locked in the little room? Maybe if we give you the burial you never had..." Carla said, letting her sentence trail off.

"Yes, but we still have to find out how Mother died, and that could be any time in the next year," I said back to them. The process of a burial made sense to me, but I had to know the truth about what happened to Mother. "Also," I added, "if we have time, maybe we could find out why the castle became abandoned and why Daddy ended up leaving."

*****

"When was the last time you heard from them?" Officer Doyle was asking Nate.

Nate explained that he had spoken to Carla on the phone the night before. "It had to be around eight or nine," he said.

Nate overheard another officer saying that there were no signs of foul play in the cottage. It was true. Nothing had been overturned or thrown and knocked over. The only strange things in the cottage were that Carla and Adria's purses were still there and their food was left untouched.

"And you have no reason to believe she would leave on her own?" Another question came from the officer.

"No, she came for a vacation. She and Adria were here to learn more about Adria's family history. She was having a good time as far as I knew," Nate answered.

"You were here in the country at the same time but not here together?" Doyle asked.

"No, we weren't. I had a work event, and she came with a friend. They just so happened to be during the same time," Nate said. "It was a complete coincidence."

"Okay, so what about this other guy?" Doyle looked down as his notebook to remember his name. "Travis Hart."

"Uh, I can vouch for him," Miriam cut in, standing and coming closer to the two men. "He's my cousin, and as you can tell, he is missing also."

The officer seemed to be thinking for a minute and still writing everything down in his notebook. He didn't immediately ask any further questions at the time, and it became quiet in the cottage. Nate was trying to hide his frustration.

"We'll walk around the area and do a thorough search around the property. We will also walk up the road and talk to some of the surrounding neighbors," the officer said to Nate and Miriam. "Don't go anywhere. We may have more questions."

The Garda left the cottage to continue the investigation outside as Nate, Miriam, and Craig remained inside. They made small talk, and Miriam tried to be reassuring. "We'll find them," she said, looking to Nate.

Miriam noticed an unusual look on his face, and Nate must have noticed her looking at him because he finally opened his mouth to speak...but then closed it again.

Miriam broke the silence when she decided to ask, "Are you feeling okay?" She went over to him and put her hand on the back of his shoulder. She reached her other hand out, offering for him to sit on the couch.

Nate decided sitting for a bit might not be that bad an idea. So he walked over and plopped down. "I found something in the bathroom earlier. It's just been on my mind, and I can't stop thinking about it."

Miriam looked shocked. "Is it something you should have told the Garda about?"

"What was it?" Craig asked.

Nate looked up at both of them. "It was a positive pregnancy test. I think Carla is pregnant," he said. He looked to Miriam, thinking maybe she might know something about it and wanting her to reaffirm his thought.

Miriam waddled over to the other side of the couch and sat down next to him. She patted Nate's knee a couple times but didn't say anything, waiting to see what he would say next.

"So you don't know anything about it?" he asked her.

"No, I am as much surprised as you are," she said.

"Well, do you think this could have anything to do with her disappearing?" Nate asked.

Miriam and Craig thought about it for a bit. "I can't say," Craig began. "I don't know them very well since I have been away at work more than I have been here."

"I don't," Miriam piped in and gave her husband a look. "I don't think that sounds like Carla at all."

"She was working things out," Nate said. "She was working on her feelings, and I felt like we had a break through the other night, but now with this…maybe she couldn't do it."

"Nate," Miriam said slowly. She inhaled a long breath through her nose and let it out through her mouth. "That wouldn't explain why she, Adria, and Travis are all missing together. If Carla couldn't talk about this, Adria surely would have got hold of you, and I would have heard from Travis by now. He is more like a brother to me since I didn't have any of my own siblings."

Nate got up and paced back and forth a couple of times in the small living room. "You're right. She would have told me, and one of them would have gotten hold of me."

*****

Travis came back into Amelia's room where the ladies were making small talk about Amelia's old dog, Lucky, and the chickens that used to chase her and Fiona around the back field.

"The key isn't out there," he said. "I searched high and low, and I can't seem to find it anywhere. It's not in anyone's pockets, is it?"

None of us had it.

"Well then there is only one explanation, we can only assume it was left back at the cottage—in the present time," Carla said. "We must have all taken our hands off it when we were sent whirling through the oblivion, so we just have to figure out a new way home."

The orange pink and yellow sun was beginning to set, and it was evening before we knew it. It reminded me so much of the sunsets back home. It was so remarkable at how there was a century between now and then, but the sunsets remained the same.

Carla, Adria, and Travis were trying to enjoy their dinner, but it was hard after all the sad and devastating news we had been coming up with. Just then, we heard someone from the other room asking if someone had stolen their chicken legs.

"I had six chicken legs sitting here," the cook yelled. "Where are they now?"

I started laughing as Carla and Adria scarfed down the rest of their chicken. "Good thing they can't see us or they would absolutely find us and we'd be whipped." It felt good to laugh. It seemed like so long ago since I had had a real belly laugh.

"Are you sure you aren't hungry?" Travis asked me.

"Ghosts don't really eat, or at least we never feel hungry—or full," I said, reassuring him that I was fine, and then I added, "I was thinking that if I could find him, maybe I could follow William around tomorrow.

"It would give me some insight on where he went during the nighttime, and it would also give me more insight on his relationship with my mother. Maybe I can find out more about my mother's thoughts and what her plans were for processing my death."

"We'll go with you," Adria added.

"Well, Carla has to," I said and let out a little snicker.

I heard another voice shouting out in the hallway, so I made my way to the bedroom door and peaked my head outside. At that same moment, Daddy walked by and stopped just a few feet away from me. I froze where I was, and so did the other three behind me.

"He can't see us," I reminded them in a whisper.

"The hell I can't," Daddy said.

"What!" I said as I let out an exasperated breath and grabbed onto the doorway for support.

"She needs to be buried. You can't leave her in there." It was my mother, this time coming up behind him. "You have to bury her."

I realized Daddy hadn't been talking to me. He was talking to my mother, who was pleading with him to open the locked door and give me the proper burial.

"I do not," Daddy said. "I'll leave her in there for as long as I want. A constant reminder of what you did to her." He practically spat at Mother's feet.

"You cannot be serious!" Mother screamed at him.

"You killed her! You did it!" Daddy said, grabbing onto Mother and shaking her until she became violently sick.

Mother started to dry heave, but nothing would come up. I imagine that she probably had not eaten anything in the last twenty-four hours and she had nothing from her stomach to expel. She dropped to her knees, and Daddy gave her a little nudge so he could get past her and make his way down the castle hall.

"Daddy is manipulating her," I said and turned back to the others. "He wants her to believe she is the one who murdered me. Oh, Lord, help her not to believe it!"

It was William who came to Mother's side. He wanted to wrap his arms under her armpits until she was able to fully stand, but physically he could not. He knelt down until he was eye level with her and waited until she looked up to him. Their eyes connected, and as if understanding, she slowly got up and followed him to her bedroom.

Before they were out of sight, I heard Mother say, "I don't want to stay in here. This is not my room anymore, and I will not share it with him." I saw William redirect her and lead her out the back castle door.

*****

"Jacob, it's Miriam. There has been a situation, and I need to talk to you. Please call me back as soon as you can." Miriam hung up the phone.

"It's time. We have to tell Carla's family. Do you want to call her parents, Nate?" Miriam asked.

Nate looked up at her. "Her mom died when she was young and her dad died a while back. There is only Jacob. Maybe you should call Adria's mom, though," he said.

"Oh, I don't know her number. If I can get it from you, I will make the call," she said sadly.

"I don't have it either," Nate said, giving her a concerned look and not thinking of checking the phone Adria had left in the kitchen.

The police did not return that Saturday afternoon, and the day passed slowly.

It was already the next morning, and Nate was sipping coffee at the cottage dining table. The police had only made a phone call to let Nate know they were still investigating and they would be in touch if something turned up.

Nate decided not to return to his hotel and would be staying at the cottage for the rest of his trip. He also made a call to his boss, who had already flown home from their work event. Nate wanted to let him know of the situation and that he would need time off to find Carla.

Another buzz came from Adria's phone. It was almost dead. This time Marcus left a text: "Just had a couple questions about the coffee shop. Call me when you get a chance."

Eventually, Nate was going to have to call Marcus and let him know what was going on. Now just might be a good time to have that discussion, but just as he was about to type in Marcus's number, he was interrupted by Miriam.

"Is that Adria's phone?" Miriam asked.

Nate nodded hesitantly. "Should I have given it to the police?"

"No, it's not that. If that's Adria's, it will have her mother's phone number in it," Miriam replied.

Nate didn't respond to Miriam's comment but just agreed and handed over the phone to her. He then blurted out his own thought: "I'm going to the castle. I'm not going to sit around and wait for the law enforcement to get back to me when I could be searching on my own."

"I don't think they would have gone without you, Nate. They certainly wouldn't have gone in the middle of a storm," Miriam was saying.

But Nate didn't listen. He was already putting his boots on and searching for his jacket. "I can't just sit here doing nothing."

"I'll go with you, mate," Craig said. "I want to help in any way I can."

Craig offered to drive, and the two of them climbed into his little Volkswagen. Nate pulled up the text of the map Carla sent him after their visit with Adria's grandmother. He put the address in his phone, and they set off to find Castle Creet.

Chapter 22

There it was, hidden behind the draping green willow trees. Ivy had since climbed the sides of the weathered gray brick. There was a small well half standing in the front and shrubs covering any walkway that might have been there long ago. The three glass pane windows were still see-through, old and dusty, rusted and chipping. The nicely placed stones encompassing the outer sides was slightly withering away with age. A closer glance and you could just manage a half hanging sign off to the right of the red wooden door, "Castle Creet."

The sound of birds chirping in the background gave a sense of life upon the area. Wild lilies were growing in the deepness of the woods close by. Somewhere in the distance, the sound of a small stream could be heard. The wind blew softly, and the clean, fresh scent of the open air was pleasant to inhale.

"There it is," Nate said as Craig parked the car. "Let's go check it out."

Nate walked up to the door and tried the handle, but it was locked. It was a good thing he had tucked the key he found at the cottage inside his jeans pant pocket. He pulled it out and inserted it slowly, almost expecting something to happen. He twisted the hand, but it was jammed. For a few seconds, he shook the handle until he felt it loosen. With a few good twists, some shoulder nudges, and a good heavy breeze, the door was sent flying open.

"Where'd you get the key?" Craig asked, curious and astonished.

"It was left at the cottage. I think the girls and Travis got it put back together, but it was left on the ground just like the rest of their things."

"Well, they couldn't have got inside without the key themselves, so I doubt they are in here. I'm going to check out back and around the castle," Craig was saying.

It irritated Nate. He knew the girls also couldn't be in here, but why did Craig have to say it like that? He started searching around the entryway for anything that might look familiar or anything that the girls might have been looking for. He walked down the middle hallway and decided to take a right into the kitchen.

"Not much to see," he thought out loud. Just old abandoned rooms like he assumed. He peeked inside a couple of bedrooms and then walked up to the last one on the right. He popped his head inside, searching highs and lows and around the desks and windows, but again, nothing to see.

Nate decided to walk back out and find Craig. "Did you find anything?" he asked when he found Craig walking back up the hill from the empty pond below.

"Nothing, mate. I don't think they are here," Craig responded.

"I don't either, but it was worth a try," he said. "I'd like to look around a little longer if you don't mind. I haven't checked the upstairs yet. The inside is pretty eerie, but I think there is a lot still to see. There are old pictures on the ground, rugs rolled up, dressers tipped over. It looks like it could have been ransacked when it became abandoned."

"Yeah, could be. I bet from people probably searching for answers just like you. Especially why it became abandoned and forgotten," Craig said.

"Or for valuables and money," Nate added.

*****

"Nate!" Carla shouted. "Nate what are you doing here?" He looked over the room, looking up to the ceiling and over through the windows. He glanced at the writing desk and around the floor, but he did not look at Carla. In fact, he did not make eye contact with anyone.

Nate could not see or hear her.

"Nate?" It was Adria this time trying to get his attention. But still nothing.

He turned to walk back out into the hallway and make his way back toward the front door. Carla shot up and took off after him. He was already out the front door when he started talking to someone, and Carla noticed it was Craig.

"Hey," Carla shouted at them as loud as she could. Tears began to stream down her cheeks as she realized they could not hear her.

The others had shown up behind her. "They can't they hear us?" Adria said.

"I think they are in another dimension. Could it be that they are here, at the castle, in the present time?" Travis threw it out there, not knowing if any of it was true, but it was the only thing that would make sense.

It was me that tuned in this time. "Anything is possible," I said. "I was a ghost living in your time. Now you are…sort of spirits revolving in my time. It would make sense that we can see both worlds."

"I will get his attention," Carla shouted with determination as she picked up a broken stone. She pulled her hand back behind her head like a windup.

Travis grabbed her arm before she could throw it. "It's no use," he said to her.

I watched as Nate and Craig turned and headed back inside the castle. They ended up taking the stairs off the front entrance and headed to the workers' quarters. We walked behind them as they checked out the rooms on the second floor.

"They're just plain, basic rooms. I don't think these rooms could have belonged to any of the Gallaghers," Nate said.

They took off back down the staircase and headed down the hallway.

"We have to get his attention. He could be our way home," Carla was saying to the others as we followed the two men around.

"Carla, we have other answers we have to figure out," Adria said to her, putting a hand on her shoulder and trying to be sympathetic.

"I know, but maybe Nate can help us," Carla replied.

She jumped when Craig's phone started ringing the horrendous theme song to *The Office*. He reached into his pocket and pulled out his cell phone. Carla was trying not to become annoyed.

"It's Miriam," he said to Travis and went to stand on the other side of the hallway.

We watched Nate as he nodded but continued to look around a little more. He picked up a few things and laid them upright on the side of the wall. He picked up a few broken vases and set them on the hallway tables, and then I heard him say, "What is that smell?"

"Well, this place has been closed up for a century or so. It would be a bit musty, wouldn't it? There is probably mold and dead animals under the structure too," Craig said, walking back toward Nate. I stepped aside so he wouldn't run into me even though nothing would have happened. He would have walked right through.

"That was Miriam," Craig mentioned again. "The Garda are coming back to the house in about an hour. She said they want to talk with us again."

"Yeah, okay," Nate said.

"I'll go start the car," Craig replied and took off walking down the stone steps of the castle. Nate lingered a little longer, hoping anything would grab his attention that would lead to the finding of Carla.

I couldn't help but wonder what he was thinking.

*****

"No, no, don't leave," Carla shouted at Nate as if demanding it would change the fact that Nate still could not hear her. She picked up a small picture frame and threw it towards him before anyone could say anything. It didn't quite make it all the way to where he was standing, hitting the wall behind his head. Glass shattered in every which direction and flew to the floor.

Carla saw Nate stop in his tracks. Did he hear the glass break? Carla saw him turn back around and look down at the glass strewn out on the floor behind him. She watched as he bent down and picked up a shard of the glass, inspecting it.

As he was examining the glass, Carla heard him say, "This was not here a second ago."

"That's right, baby," she said, crying and falling to her knees. "Don't go."

Carla started dry heaving and, within seconds, realized she couldn't hold it back. Standing quickly and wrapping her hand around her mouth, she ran to the back door and threw up anything that still remained inside her stomach, which wasn't much.

"Did that really just work?" Adria said, looking over to Carla as she walked back in the room.

They all stood there in amazement as Adria ran to Carla and hugged her. "He heard you, Carla. He heard you."

"Is someone there?" we heard Nate ask.

Carla, Adria, and Travis all started talking to Nate at the same time. Surely he would hear one of us. "Nate, it's us. We're here. We need your help. We're stuck in the past." These were just a few of the jumbled sentences coming out of all of their mouths.

Again he said, "Hello. Is someone there?" He stepped farther back into the castle; his eyes searched for someone or something.

"I don't think he can hear you," I said, standing some ways back behind them. They had all but forgotten about me. "This is all my fault. If it weren't for me, you'd be here exploring the castle in your own time…with Nate by your side, and now he can't hear you because you are stuck trying to help unfold my family secrets."

"They are my family secrets too," Adria said. "We have to be here for a reason."

"It's not anyone's fault," Travis added.

Carla noticed Nate shiver and thought she could see goosebumps raise up on his arms, but she couldn't tell if he was cold or felt the eeriness of the castle. It must have been an odd feeling he was having in his gut.

"I have to come back later," Nate whispered.

Carla and Adria watched as he backed out of the castle.

"He's going to come back," Adria said, encouraging Carla. "He's going to go have his conversations with the police, and then he is going to come back. I just know it."

"Maybe he'll come back alone this time," Carla said.

We all watched as he shut the big wooden door and locked it with the old, peculiar castle key.

*****

"Hi... No, it's about Carla. She has gone missing, and we haven't been able to contact her," Miriam was saying into the phone when Jacob finally called her back.

"Yes, I know. Yes, the police are involved. I figured you would want to head over."

There was silence as she was listening to him on the other line. Miriam could tell he was distraught just like any big brother would be.

"Okay, I'll see you soon. Let me know when your plane lands."

Miriam hung up the phone as Craig and Nate were walking back into the little house. "Did you find anything?" she asked, hopeful.

"No," Craig responded. "Just an old, dusty castle that no one has lived in for over a hundred years. It smelled like decomposing animals mixed with droppings, must, and wet mold."

"I knew they wouldn't go there without you, Nate," she said reassuringly. "We should probably head over to the cottage. The Garda said they would meet us there."

The three of them walked back over to the cottage, not mentioning the mist that had started to graze their cheeks. Craig and Miriam were making small talk, but Nate's mind was elsewhere. He couldn't stop thinking about the sound of breaking glass and the shattered fragments on that ground that had not been there before.

"All I know is that they have a few more questions," Nate overheard Miriam saying as his mind came back to the present.

The Garda arrived a few minutes later and made their way up to the cottage door. They knocked, and Nate thought it was an odd thing to do. Knocking...in the middle of an investigation of the cottage and the three missing people. Did it even matter if you knocked if you are coming in anyway?

"Hello, Mr. Duncan. Mr. and Mrs. Smith," Officer Doyle said, nodding in each direction. "We just have a few more questions we'd like to ask and to update you on the status."

"We'll take anything we can get," Miriam said.

"First, we've been able to locate video surveillance of a man with Nate, and it was believed he was on his way to find Adria. A man by the name of Daniel Tanner. Do you have an insight on the man?"

"He is an old friend of mine," Nate said. "He and Adria were hitting it off before we left Idaho. He came here to surprise her, but Adria had made a new connection with Travis when she arrived here, and so she sent Daniel home."

"Travis? As in the other missing person?" Doyle asked. A moment of thinking passed before he continued. "Was Mr. Tanner angry when he left?"

"No. I don't think so. He was more embarrassed than anything," Nate said.

Officer Doyle turned to Miriam. "Did Travis have any irritated or displeased ex-girlfriends that might be holding a grudge?"

"Not at all. His last girlfriend was like two or three years ago, and their breakup seemed mutual," Miriam replied.

The man jotted down more notes in his little notepad and then asked them again, "And you don't have any reason to believe they would want to run away?"

"Together? All three of them?" Nate raised his voice. "Carla and Adria would never run away. And from what I have learned about Travis, he seems like a pretty decent guy. What I want to know is, what are you doing to find them?"

"Sir, we are checking with locals. We have already asked for video surveillance from several places," Doyle began. "They haven't been seen anywhere in town, and it doesn't look like they booked tickets on any ships or airports. We believe that they are still in the city, and we are doing everything we can to look for them. I assure you."

"You're not very reassuring," Nate said again, trying to calm his voice.

"We've been able to contact Adria's mother, Mrs. Layne. She will be flying over as soon as she can. She is supposed to contact us when she arrives. Do remind her if she forgets," the officer said. "We also have not been able to get hold of any of Ms. Murphey's family."

"It's only her brother and her. He is also on his way over from the States," Miriam said. "He should be here by late tomorrow evening."

"We'll have some questions for him too. Let him know not to go far," Doyle said. "Also Travis's mother, Mrs. Hart, mentioned he had been looking into Castle Creet recently. We wanted to ask if you knew anything about them visiting the premises."

"We were planning to make a trip there this last Saturday morning. It's Adria's old family home from a very long time ago. She was wanting to see it," Nate replied.

"We'll drive up there in the morning to check it out," Officer Doyle said. "We don't want to leave stones unturned, and since that boy went missing up there a few years back, it might be a good place to check out."

Nate and Craig nodded in agreement, not mentioning that they had just returned from that very location.

*****

"What do we do now?" Adria asked. "He obviously heard us. Well, maybe not heard but we were able to get his attention."

"We wait. We wait and see if he comes back," Travis said, "and in the meantime, we keep following Amelia's mother to see if she really did indeed kill herself."

"Can we just call it a night for now?" I said. "Nate won't be coming back tonight, and we don't know when something happens to Mother. We might as well try to rest."

We all headed back to my bedroom, and each got as comfortable as we could scattered here and there in the room. On our way in, Travis and Adria had snuck some more food from the kitchen. We sat down eating our bread and sent a bowl of porridge around among all of us.

"It's such an odd thing to think in this time, Amelia's cold, lifeless body is still laying in that room, and the household is going on like normal, like nothing happened. No one else tried to argue with your father," said Travis.

"I bet people didn't argue with it because, as I am quickly learning, Daddy isn't exactly someone you want to have an argument with," I replied to Travis. "I just don't know how I didn't see it."

"You were a little girl," Carla said. "I don't think as kids we pay much attention to the adult stuff. Daddy and I didn't exactly have a special bond or connection, but I always thought he loved me. No, he didn't let me sit on his lap. He didn't pick me up and throw me in the air. He didn't read me stories of fairy tales of wild beasts. He never played with me or took me out for adventures, but it was always one of those things that I thought I knew. He loved me in a different way.

"I also never remember him doing any of that with Fiona. Wait, I do remember him taking Fiona on adventures. They would come back a few days later with dead rabbits and birds. I did see him talk to her more often. I guess I was just very naive and young. I always thought Daddy would take me out when I was Fiona's age."

My mind had grown weary and distraught, and the more I thought of the things I had learned, the more I wish I didn't have to learn them. I knew, though, if I had any notion of setting myself free, I would have to find out the real truth.

*****

Tuesday morning came, and Nate had picked Jacob up from the airport the night before. They were sitting in the cottage, and Jacob had a thousand questions to ask Nate. They flew in one ear and out the other as Nate was having a hard time keeping up with Jacob. Nate's mind was still back at the castle, recounting everything that happened.

"Listen," Nate said eventually, "I will tell you everything I know."

He began laying out the week's events: the antique stores, the visit with Adria's grandmother, the key, and the castle. Nate told Jacob everything Carla had told him.

"And then one night after texting with Carla, she quit returning my texts," Nate said. "I asked Miriam to check on them and her husband came over to the cottage, but they were gone. We called the police the next morning."

"And what have they said?" Jacob asked.

"That they are doing everything they can," Nate went on. "They think they may still be in the city. No flights or any kind of travel tickets have been found under their names. Plus they left everything at the cottage."

"Do they expect foul play?" Jacob asked.

"No," Nate replied. "Nothing was upturned or thrown over in the cottage. There were no signs of a struggle. They are considering it a missing person's case as of right now," Nate said.

"This is a nightmare. How the hell is this happening right now?" Jacob asked but did not expect an answer.

"The officers know you were on your way over, so they are coming over this afternoon. Adria's mother will be here too," said Nate. "They want to ask you some questions."

Jacob walked outside the little cottage door, letting the midday mist hit his face. Now that it was daylight, he wanted to check out his surroundings and look for any little hints or details the police may have missed. After he took a few steps around the little cottage, he thought, *Who am I kidding? I don't even know what I'm searching for.* So after a few minutes of searching for endless possibilities, he decided to return.

When he walked in, he imagined mostly everything was the same as when the girls left, except Nate had moved out of his hotel and into the cottage himself. Adria's backpack was still sitting on the table where it was left.

Jacob found Carla's suitcase in her room the night before, her journal and purse, and a few other things that belonged to her were still in the room. He made his way into the bathroom where their makeup bags sat on the counter along with toothbrushes and…a pregnancy test. A pink and white stick with two lines in the center window.

He stormed out of the bathroom and approached Nate. "You got my sister pregnant?" he said holding up the little stick so Nate could see exactly what he was talking about.

Nate was thrown off guard. "Yes, I do believe that it's Carla's," Nate said calmly.

"Well, of course you did. Why not? Couldn't get her to stay with you so you just knock her up and leave her with no other option," Jacob said.

"That is not what happened," Nate said standing and squaring himself up to Jacob.

"Of course it is," Jacob went on. "She told me about your relationship. Your troubles. The fact that you're never home and don't pay her the kind of attention a man should show his girlfriend. You were probably cheating on her too. No wonder she ran away. You two should never have gotten together." Jacob was yelling and throwing accusations here and there.

Nate thew a punch that landed square over Jacob's jaw and dropped him to the ground. "I love her, you bastard," Nate said angrily, stepping over Jacob and heading into the kitchen. He grabbed a towel and filled it with crushed ice from the freezer.

"Here." He handed the ice-filled towel to Jacob as he was pulling himself up on the couch. "If you're here to help, then stay and help," Nate said. "If you're here to accuse and throw out dirty shots, you might as well book your own hotel or head back home."

Jacob took the ice and placed it over his jaw. Giving Nate a nasty stare, he kept quiet until the authorities arrived.

*****

"We picked up Mrs. Layne at the airport. I hope you don't mind us using your home as our meeting place," Officer Doyle said to Miriam and Craig.

"Not at all. It's bigger than the cottage," Miriam replied.

"Under the current circumstances, we have come to believe that they went missing on their own. There was no foul play involved," Doyle began. "We did search Castle Creet, but we were not able to get inside. The grounds provided no evidence that they had been there. Everything was seemingly left untouched. The insides have not been opened for years, and the key has never been found. If someone wanted in, they would have axed it down or took a bulldozer to it. There was no damage to anything besides it being old and weathered. We decided to leave the inside alone and not enter." The officer went on and on with their evidence—or lack of.

Nate and Craig stole a glance at each other but remained silent.

"You need to get inside!" Jacob said. "You didn't search the inside, so you just assume they aren't in there? What if they got stuck?"

"There is no proof they had any way to enter," Officer Doyle said. "No doors were left opened, and no windows were broken. We just don't see that it's possible."

Mrs. Layne began crying. She had her head lowered and a tissue to her eyes and nose. She kept quiet and only answered specific questions when they were directed at her.

Officer Doyle took a deep breath. "We *are* still searching for them. Our investigation has become stagnant, though."

"Is there anything we can do to help?" Craig asked.

"Not at this time. Stay close to the premises and don't go far. We don't want something happening to anyone else. We'll be in touch if we find anything out," the officer replied.

He grabbed his hat and placed it on top of his head as he made his way to the door. "I'll be in touch," he said again and took off out the front door.

"Shall I make some tea?" Miriam asked as Craig closed the door behind the officer. She walked over to Mrs. Layne and placed an arm over her shoulder. "It's going to be okay. They will do everything they can, Mrs. Layne."

"Please call me Tracy," she said. "Would you like some help? I need to do something to keep busy."

"Of course. Would you mind putting on some hot water? The kettle is right next to the stove," Miriam replied, and she led the way into the kitchen.

"When is your baby expected to arrive?" Tracy asked, trying to make small talk.

"I have about another month and a half," Miriam answered.

A moment of silence passed between them. "Adria always wanted to be a mother," Tracy said and began crying again.

"She will. I know she will, and she will make an excellent mother," Miriam said, trying to comfort her. She pulled out a chair for Tracy to sit down on. "Would you like to stay here with us? We have an extra room."

"That's very kind," Tracy said, accepting the invitation.

Later that evening, while lying in bed, Miriam reminded Craig to call and cancel the reservations for their next Airbnb visitors. They couldn't have anything else going on right now, and they needed to have the cottage freed up for however long Nate and Jacob planned on staying there.

Craig started asking questions of doubt. "What if they don't find them? What if they don't return?"

"Stop being so negative," she replied angrily.

"I'm not. I'm trying to be realistic," he said. "They have been missing for almost five days now. Now what?"

"Let the officers worry about it. We are here to be supportive and understanding. Now turn out the light so I can go to sleep," Miriam said, and slowly she rolled over to her three pillows. She began tucking blankets between her knees and letting her belly rest on the side of the pregnancy cushion she had bought months ago.

Chapter 23

I wasn't sure what day it was, and just like before, I still was not able to keep the days straight. It seemed like we had been following Mother around for weeks chasing the questions we still had, stealing food from the kitchen, and racking our brains trying to figure out what to do next. Could it really have been that long? I would need to ask one of the others if they could keep better track than I could.

I wasn't able to follow Daddy but only because I didn't know where he took off to during the wee hours of the morning. He would go do his work and then come home ready to eat dinner. After he ate, he would spend time in the library or on the back balcony smoking his pipe.

Sometimes, after dinner, I would catch him scolding my mother for all the things she didn't get done that day. He would yell in her face that she wasn't a good wife, that she wasn't fulfilling her wifely duties. He would talk down to her and cut into her very being with his words. I could hardly stand to listen to it. Of course, he never did any of it when others were within earshot, but it had become a regular occurrence, and it was so hard to watch.

I watched as William visited my mother every day, comforting her and offering her a listening ear. Mother had become much more pale over the last few days, and her figure was becoming more slender. I rarely saw her eat anything. William would try to convince her she needed to eat, but to no avail; she would not. What kind of life was she living?

Fiona spent a lot of time in her room reading books or playing with her dolls. I didn't see her outside playing much anymore. She became secluded and kept to herself. I could only assume this was her way of grieving. Only now and then, she would take a walk outside, but I never saw her down by the pond again, either scared of it or it reminded her of my accident.

As far as I knew, Fiona was told that I died from drowning. She probably never knew the truth, and she would probably never find out. Daddy would never tell her, and Mother wouldn't tell Fiona out of protection for her.

Carla, Adria, and Travis were getting restless with nothing to do, and all I could think was, *Think how I feel.* Carla spent a lot of time asking me questions about my mother, my favorite places in the castle, and what I did all those years being stuck inside the sitting room. We would venture out together, visiting the garden and taking walks in the field.

I answered her questions as best I could, but it was beginning to get hard keeping track of everything; 1908 was so long ago and my body was beginning to tire. Although it did make me wonder if "spirit time" moved at a faster pace than real time.

"I used to sing a lot," I told her. "I would hum tunes I heard from my mother and I would try to dance, but that was never my forte. I would imagine what it would be like to be free again, not chained to forever spirit living. What would my life have been like if all this didn't happen? I wondered what it would be like if I had just been able to talk to someone during those long waiting years."

I was rambling on, and Carla listened quietly and patiently. She had been so sweet to me, and I have to admit, it was indeed very nice to talk to someone. I was very glad I found her as she was becoming more like an older sister. Sometimes, I wondered if this was what it would have been like with Fiona and me if we had had more time.

Adria and Travis used their time to go for long walks, still getting to know each other. They would come back holding hands and giggling together like little kids. There was no use keeping cooped up in the castle, and it was nice to see a blossoming love.

It was something I always thought my mother and daddy had, but I never saw them holding hands or hugging. I never saw them laughing at each other's jokes or silly gestures. I hope Adria and Travis could be different, and I hoped it would last.

I was beginning to wonder if maybe Mother really had done what we all thought she had done to herself. Maybe Daddy didn't have anything to do with it after all. It would be easier to think that.

I was beginning to think of how selfish I was being, making the three of them stay here with me. Especially when deep down, I truly thought they could set me free by just burying my body in the other room. If they thought they knew how to get home, I couldn't keep them here any longer. I needed to let them return to their own time, to their own lives.

And then I thought, *If burying me doesn't work, would I go back to their time with Carla too? Would I be forced to follow her?*

I put the thought aside that night and sat down in my little chair to begin the conversation with them. I knew it would be a hard conversation for me but easy for them. They would be so excited, and that helped ease my mind, knowing I would be giving them some happiness.

"I think it's time," I began. "Who knows what we will find out about Mother, but I can't keep you here forever. If burying my body will set my soul free, I think we should do it, and then you will be free to go home too."

"Oh, Amelia, are you sure that's what you want?" Carla asked. "We still haven't found out all that we have been looking for."

"Yes. You need to be free as much as I do," I said to them.

"The only problem is that I don't think we'll be able to get home without the key, and now we know Nate has it," Travis said.

"How do you know Nate has it?" Carla asked.

"He opened the front door of the castle. He has to have it," Travis said.

"Okay, how do we get Nate to come back to the castle?" Adria asked.

"He will. I'm surprised he hasn't been back since that day that the glass shattered," Carla said. "But I know he will. He had a look in his eye."

*****

The truth is, Nate had been back to the castle. He had gone and he had gone by himself, an unsuspected trip when he was headed back from the store. As his hands gripped the steering wheel, his head and heart said two different things. He turned right and headed out of town toward the castle, but when he got there, the castle key was not in his pocket. He had not been able to enter, and so it left him to only search the surrounding areas. He searched the fields, walking up and down rows of the long, thick grass, hunting for anything that would give him a clue, but there was nothing.

And so as the days passed, he found himself thinking of other ways he could help out the investigation, which left him sitting in the living room of Adria's grandmother.

"Hi, Roisina. My name is Nate Duncan. I'm friends with your granddaughter, Adria."

Nate was going to use all the resources he had, and he knew that if there was any insight about it, Roisina would be the one to ask. She, more than anyone, would know something about the castle.

"Thank you for taking time for a visit with me," he began again. "This is Jacob, Carla's brother." Nate introduced Jacob and pointed over to him.

"Well, it's nice to meet you both," Roisina said.

"We just wanted to ask a couple questions and then we'll be out of your hair," Nate said.

"Well, what is it?" she said. "Have you found my granddaughter?"

"Well no, the local authorities are still looking into it…but we found this key," Nate said, pulling it out of the inside pocket of his jean jacket. "We know it belongs to Castle Creet because I was able to use it to enter inside…so we know it was the one the girls were looking for. But what we are really wanting to know is if there is anything special…" He waited a few seconds before continuing. "Something magical about the key that you might know about?"

"Magical?" she questioned them.

Jacob rolled his eyes. He knew this was a dumb idea. Magic wasn't real, it didn't exist, and they were wasting their time.

"I have asked myself a million times why I think this," Nate said, "but I think… Carla, Adria, and Travis were putting the key back together the night they disappeared. I think the key has something to do with it." He was trying not to sound too crazy.

"For all I know, the key is just a key," Roisina answered nonchalantly. "I have no idea what magic you think it could be."

"I also had the key when I was inside the castle a couple days ago. Glass shattered at my feet as if something or someone was trying to get my attention," he began again. "I know it sounds stupid, but I just can't help but think they got stuck in some…alternate universe that the key possesses."

He waited, not wanting to say anything else. He wanted Roisina to take in all the information he was giving to her. He wanted her to think if maybe she really did know anything that perhaps she wasn't telling them. Maybe she had insight, anything really, that would help him figure out where they could have disappeared to.

"The key is just a key, lad. Your crazy notion is going to get you into trouble," she said.

Nate was exhausted, but this was his last resource. In a few weeks, he would have to leave and fly back to Boise, and he could hardly bear the thought of leaving Carla behind. How could he go on with his life not knowing where she was or what happened to her? How could he leave it all in the hands of the authorities in Ireland?

"Thank you for your time, Roisina. We appreciate it," Nate said and stood to walk to the door.

Jacob nodded toward Roisina and walked past Nate getting to the door first when Roisina called out Nate's name. He paused and turned towards her as Jacob kept walking and was making his way towards the elevator quickly.

"If you think that key is magic, use it. Believe it. Conjure the magic to find them. If you say you think something mysterious happened to you when you were at the castle…go back. Go and get your answers," she said.

He gave her a quizzical look but remained quiet. It was the little bit of hope that Nate needed. "Thank you, Roisina," he said with a small smile.

Finally, he thought. She didn't say she believed him, but she didn't shut him down like Jacob and Tracy Layne were doing. He decided he would return to the castle, and this time, he would go alone, bring the key, and find out what was truly going on.

*****

A scream shrieked from the upper tower of the castle, ringing through the cold stone hallway. It was a scream I had heard before. It was faint from my memory, when I was locked behind those doors, but the same scream nonetheless. Now it was loud and rang in my ears. I knew exactly what it was or, I should say, *who* it was. It was my mother. The day she died.

Today must be that day.

It was the middle of the night, and I woke the other three that had been asleep in my bedroom. Through chattering teeth, I let them know I heard a scream from the tower, and I thought it was my mother. Travis immediately said he would go check it out. He said if this was the answer I wanted, maybe I should go too. Which then meant Carla had to go, and Adria insisted she wasn't staying behind by herself.

As we all climbed the stairs as quickly as we could, I realized what I might anticipate seeing. I also realized that we might be too late to find out what exactly happened. We hurriedly took off, taking two steps at a time until we reached the little wooden door at the top.

It was just then that Daddy came charging out of the door and rushed off down the steps. It was true; I was too late. I didn't see the specific evidence if Daddy had anything to do with it. He just took off as fast as he could running down the stairs. Travis slowly pushed the door back open, and there in the darkness, I could see mother lying on the ground, a rope still tied to her neck.

I ran to her falling to the ground and throwing my arms over her. Of course, I still could not feel anything, and it took everything in me not to scream myself. "Why?" I shouted instead. "Why?"

Carla and Adria pulled me to me feet and wrapped their arms around me. I clung to both of them, shaking with alarm. I was hit with a wave of emotion, and everything spilled out in a fit of tears. We walked over to the stone wall, and I tried to stand by myself, but my knees were shaky. My legs were wavering, and it was becoming hard to remain mindful.

"She may not have hung herself," Travis said. "There is no chair or ladder that she could have climbed to carry it out herself. That I can see...at least."

"I don't think this was a suicide," Adria said.

I knew they were right, but there simply was no way of knowing. I would never know if Daddy had anything to do with it or if, indeed, my mother had taken her own life. All I knew and learned during this horribly long escapade was that Daddy did murder me. He murdered me and then covered it up with the notice saying that I died from smallpox, and he said Mother died of smallpox too.

I didn't see what happened here, but I knew I was too late. I couldn't officially blame my daddy for her death.

"I guess I will never know," I whispered and turned my face back into Carla's shoulder.

It was only a few minutes later when we decided to walk back down the stairs, leaving Mother there lifeless and alone. I knew there was nothing else I could do, but it hurt every ounce of me to walk away. We made our way back down the stairs, through the kitchen, and to my room when we passed the grand hallway, and I overheard, "She hung herself." It was Daddy talking. He was holding a candle and whispering to our handyman, Jack, who was standing there in nothing but his pants.

"She hung herself?" Jack questioned back.

"Yes! You implying something else?" Daddy said with a tone.

"No, of course not, sir," said Jack.

"You want to argue about it or take care of it?" Daddy stated but still kept his sharp tone under a whisper.

"Yes, sir, do you want me to move her?" Jack asked.

"Start digging a hole in the back cemetery. We'll say she had smallpox, same with Amelia. I don't want our name and castle disgraced with this kind of death," Daddy continued.

Jack grabbed a lantern from a small cabinet and lit the candle inside. "Shall I grab someone to help?" Jack asked.

"No, we don't need to tell anybody what happened, and they don't need to see the body," he replied. "Just make sure she is buried by morning."

As Jack was walking away, Daddy called out one last thing: "And send a letter to Mary's mother. She'll need to be informed."

*****

Nate walked in the front castle door the next morning, ready and eager to find just what was going on. It was close to 8:00 a.m., and the sun had already risen through the eastern windows. He began his search again and talked out loud to see if he could get any sort of response.

"Hello. Is anybody here? I come in peace… What a stupid thing to say," he said out loud. "What is that awful smell? Where are all the dead animals this stench is coming from?"

Carla was just waking up when she heard the familiar voice flooding in from the outer hallway. She nudged Adria and Travis. "It's Nate. He's back."

"Carla, are you here?" He asked.

"Oh, thank you, Jesus. Yes. You guys! He knows we are here," Carla said in a still groggy voice.

Nate began searching rooms; he had brought a flashlight with him this time. There was no electricity in the castle, and some rooms were very dark. He began touching objects, pressing books, or pulling them from their bookshelves. Assumably, it appeared that he was searching for a hidden button to press or a secret room. Nothing happened.

When he finally made his way by Amelia's bedroom, the four of us were up and at the door waiting to see what he did next. We each took turns saying something, anything to get his attention. Carla tried to squeeze his hand, but he didn't feel that either. When he was making his way back to the kitchen, something made him stop in front of the doors to a different room.

Adria turned to me quickly. "Nate can unlock the door to Amelia's body."

*****

We all turned around quickly when we heard, "Is it done?" It was Daddy asking Jack in a quiet whisper.

"Yes, sir," he answered. Jack was dirty, sweaty, and tired, but he had finished the job just as the sun was coming up the next morning.

"Gather the household," Daddy said. "I will make an announcement to everyone, but first, I want to talk to Fiona. And clean yourself up quickly," he added and walked off toward Fiona's room.

We looked from Nate to Daddy and back, not sure who we should follow. Eventually, we decided to leave Nate and check on what Daddy had up his sleeve.

Fiona was getting ready in her bedroom. She was sitting at her little table and brushing her hair while looking into the mirror. Daddy had come and knocked lightly before opening up the door that was already slightly cracked.

Fiona looked up as he entered and went to sit on her bed next to her little table. He worked up his best look of dread and began by saying, "I'm sorry you've been through so much in your little life... I'm afraid I have some more news to add. There was an accident last night and...well...your mother is gone."

Carla and Adria both rolled their eyes at the same time, not believing a word that came out of his mouth.

Fiona sat and listened. Her hand shot up to her heart. I assumed it started beating faster with each of Daddy's words. Fiona caught her breath when he said "mother is gone." I could tell she didn't understand his exact meaning and had to ask, "Gone where?"

"She is dead, Fiona," he said.

Fiona's lip started quivering, and she flung herself into Daddy's arms and cried. He didn't let her cry for very long, grabbing her shoulders and placing her back in her chair. He wasn't the type of man to handle sympathetic behavior. He got up and moved to go. "I'll leave you to your feelings. You can visit her grave out back when you are ready."

I could tell Fiona was feeling all the feelings of a young girl who had just lost her little sister and now her mother. She would probably end up staying in her room for hours, crying until there were no more tears left to cry. She was as afraid as a young girl would be.

We decided we needed to get back to Nate, but I also didn't want to leave Fiona alone, and I think Travis could tell. "I'll stay with her," he said.

"But..." I began.

"No, it's fine. Someone needs to watch and see what happens," Travis explained.

We all knew he was right. Carla, Adria, and I walked back to find Nate exactly where we had left him in front of the strange door.

*****

Nate was sitting in a kitchen chair with a puzzled look on his face. We could tell not much had happened since we left him. He was staring at the door he hadn't paid much attention to the other day, but now, curiosity was getting the better of him.

As if a thought had just popped into his head, he stood up and went to the door searching for a key hole. He pulled the castle key from his jacket and slid it inside the opening, but it didn't open. Nate stepped back, looking around the door, when he realized that the lock looked like it was welded together. It was old now, and he wondered if he could find a shovel or something to break it open.

He searched back in the kitchen to find anything he could use on the door. There in the corner was a sledgehammer of sorts. Nate grabbed it and walked back over to the welded door, shoving it a couple times with his shoulders but with no luck. So he took the hammer up over his head and pounded down on the lock as hard as he could.

The door shrieked, and dust flew up from within the cracks. The lock broke free, and the door could now be opened easily. I'm pretty sure everyone was waving their hands in front of their faces at the dust and coughing from anything they had inhaled.

The instant he pushed the door back, he covered his nose quickly. "I've uncovered where the stench is coming from, apparently," he said to himself.

He shined the light this way and that as he started walking around the room, past the table, the mantel and fireplace. There were remnants of a skunk laying in the corner, dead and still decomposing. He stopped when he got to the makeshift bed sitting in the corner. A white sheet lay over the top of what looked like rippled bumps.

"Oh Lord, what is this?" He grabbed at the corner of the white sheet and took a deep breath as he slowly started to pull it away. He kept pulling it back as tiny fragments of miniature bones started to appear from underneath. The dress I had been wearing was old, damp, and barely there. It was like rain had entered from somewhere and soaked the old dress.

My body was gone, unrecognizable, and pretty decomposed. It was as if some of the bones had mineralized and disappeared, but small amounts of the brown and ebony bones remained on the scull and legs. Everything else was hidden under my tattered dress.

Just by looking at the size, it was clear to Nate it was a child. He let out his breath and sucked it in for a minute, holding it as I did too. I could barely look.

"Shit, shit. Oh, shit. What do I do?" he said again and again as he took a few steps backward, thinking.

It was at that moment that I became very aware of the situation and I thought, *Now is my time to be brave*. I walked over to him, standing directly by his side. I stretched up on my tiptoes, as far as I could, to get closer to his ear, and I said, "Bury me."

*****

Travis watched as a castle worker came into Fiona's room to light a fire. "Where did Daddy go?" Fiona asked the young worker.

"He is in the kitchen. I'm afraid it's not a good night to visit him, miss. He has drowned himself in a bottle." She stared at Fiona to see if she understood her meaning.

Travis could tell Fiona understood right away, and all she said was, "Thank you."

The young woman left her room, and a few minutes later, Fiona followed. Deciding to venture out of her room, Travis began to follow her. She was headed in the direction of her daddy's voice.

Travis could only imagine she was just wanting to check on him, to offer him comfort in this upsetting moment.

"Maybe I can offer Daddy some sort of help," Travis heard Fiona say.

She was sneaking down the hallway on tiptoes when she made her way to the kitchen entrance. The closer she got, the more she realized she didn't hear crying or sobs or any kinds of sadness coming from inside. Fiona stopped. Travis realized it too and stopped next to her. She peeked around the corner as she caught a glimpse of her daddy laughing and taking another swig from the bottle he held in his hand.

There was a man sitting next to him who was just as tipsy. They were talking through stutters and giggles, and he was telling Henry he should leave Ireland. "Go to America."

Henry didn't say anything at first, and then Travis thought he heard him say in agreement, "Maybe I will."

Fiona gasped. Travis read the look on her face as complete shock.

"Why is he not mourning?" Fiona said in a whisper. "What is the matter with him?" Fiona was so upset by his demeanor she took off running in the direction of her room. Travis followed and found her in another fit of tears lying on her bed. "He can't leave the castle. He can't leave Mother and Amelia. He can't leave our home," Fiona was saying.

An hour or two had passed, and Travis could no longer hear the distant laughter of the two men down the hall. Fiona had stopped crying also and stood from her bed. Walking over to her chest of drawers, she began pulling out some of her warmer clothes and slipped into them.

Travis followed behind Fiona as she left her room and made her way to the back door of the castle. She quietly closed it behind herself, grabbed a candlelit lantern sitting on the porch, and took off walking toward her mother's grave.

It was a small grassy path they walked until they reached the little gated cemetery. Fiona went and sat next to the newly dug mound of dirt. She pulled a blanket up over her shoulders and touched the freshly dug grave with her hand. She let more tears flow as if to let every little emotion filter through her body.

Chapter 24

With one sudden and swift movement, he jumped toward my direction and had the flashlight shining in the place where I was standing. I had definitely startled him. If he would have been able to touch me, he would have completely knocked me off my feet. He shined the light in every which direction, trying to place where the voice had come from.

"Who's there?" he said in a louder voice. "I know I heard you this time. Loud and clear. Who is it?"

"Amelia, he can hear you," Carla said, excitedly jumping up and down.

I decided to get close to him again and whisper it one more time. "Bury me."

Nate sucked in a breath, and in a very brave, steady tone this time said, "Who are you?"

What do I say? How do I answer him? I can't go into my whole life story. There is too much to explain to a man who can't even see me. All I could think of was to give him his answer. "My name is Amelia."

Carla and Adria came and stood next to me, and they each grabbed one of my hands. It was enough support to keep me standing there long enough to see how he would react.

"I've told him about you," Carla said to me. "Not you as the ghost that followed me 'cause I didn't know that until we were transported here, but I've told him about you as a little girl, as Adria's distant relative."

"Why can't I see you?" he asked hesitantly.

"I'm not exactly…alive," was all I could think to say.

257

In a very long time, there was hope that maybe this wouldn't be so difficult. Maybe he would understand. I was starting to get frightened, though, thinking about this plan we had all worked up in our heads. What if this really did work? What if Nate did bury me and that was the end of this world? The unknown was a bit frightening to me.

"Amelia... Amelia," he said. "I know that name." He was still searching for a figure that would never appear to him. "This castle used to be your home, no?" he said, holding his hands out, referring to the castle.

"Yes," I said. "It was my home, but it is no longer." My voice sounded weird even to myself. It was like a whisper, and no matter how many times I tried to talk louder, it came out in the same monotone hush.

"So you're a spirit?" he asked, shaking his head in disbelief.

"Yes, left behind and forgotten about. I need you to set me free. Those are my bones lying there."

A million different thoughts were going through Nate's head. What was he supposed to do? And now a body was involved. Should he call someone, the authorities maybe? How was he supposed to set her free by himself? He started pacing the room back and forth and remained quiet for a few minutes, thinking about his next step.

It was Amelia who interrupted his thoughts. "There is a small plot...out back. Bury me next to my mother," I said.

After a long pause, Nate took a deep breath and let it out again. "I have to call the authorities. I can't touch the body. I can't bury you. I would be messing with...evidence or something." His words were jumbled, and he was very confused and flustered.

"No," everyone yelled. Of course, the only "no" he could hear was mine, and it was still a whisper.

"Tell him to do it himself," Travis said. "I think it would be better if no one else was involved with our ticket home. Plus, there will be a gazillion questions and protocols the Garda will have to go through. It might ruin your chance at freedom too, Amelia."

"Travis is right," Adria chimed in. "We don't know if that could alter anything." I nodded at the three of them.

"You need to do it yourself. No help," I said to Nate in my eerie, unnaturally hushed voice.

Nate was still unsettled about the matter. And why shouldn't he be? He was talking to a ghost, and he had just found a dead body. I got it, but there was a look in his eye when he heard my plea to him.

"Please...set me free."

*****

"We have not found them," Officer Doyle began saying.

"They didn't vanish into thin air!" Jacob said with a pleading tone of voice.

"We want to be as sensitive to this matter as possible, Mr. Murphey, but it is time." The officer took a moment to think about his next words. "It's time to think they may have left on their own free will. At present, there are a few more cases that have many more leads for us to be investigating right now."

"You're giving up?" Miriam asked.

"No, ma'am," he said defensively. "We are not closing the case, but there are other places that are cause for more direct attention." He tried to choose his words wisely.

"This doesn't seem possible," Jacob said.

"We will let you know if something else turns up," Officer Doyle said, looking at everyone and trying to finish up the conversation. When no one said anything else, he turned to make his exit.

Miriam closed the door behind him as he took his leave, and Mrs. Layne broke down in tears. She almost didn't make it to the closest chair before her knees buckled underneath her.

Through sobs, she said, "I never thought I would be going home without my daughter."

Miriam came over to stand next to her, rubbing her back and shoulders. She was shedding a few tears herself. "We won't give up."

"I'm not giving up either," Jacob said. "I'm going for a walk."

Jacob grabbed his hat and jacket and took off down the driveway. He made his way down toward the garden, in desperate need of getting out of the house. With tears in his eyes, he began a silent prayer. *Jesus, bring her home. Bring her back safely…*

*****

Nate leaned up against the stone wall thinking, rubbing his head and temples. This wasn't exactly what he was expecting to find, and yet this was definitely a crazy find, and now he was standing here talking to a ghost girl. "I'm losing my mind," he said out loud.

"Maybe you are," I reminded him I was still here.

"Okay, I'll do it." Nate had made up his mind. His first move was to wrap what remained of my body. He would need to go back into the castle to search for fresh linens or sheets or something that would make it easier for him to pick the remains up with.

He also decided that if he was going to do this, he needed to do it quickly. The sun had already gone down, and all that remained in the sky was a small sliver of orange. "Nighttime will be the best time to dig a hole and bury a body," he said out loud. *This sounds criminal,* he thought. He found what he needed and headed back to the room to wrap the body.

After he finished wrapping the best he could, he went out back to find some sort of digging tools, hopefully a shovel. We all followed him out the castle doors as he started searching, and that's when we found Travis and Fiona.

Fiona seemed devastated.

"There's one," Carla said, pulling our attention back to the shovel. She was about to mention it to Nate when he saw it himself, leaning right on the gate to the little graveyard. He slowly began searching for Mother's headstone, moving weeds and long grass away until he finally found where she was buried. He took the shovel and shoved it into the dirt next to the little plot. He began to dig the hole, and he dug and dug until he thought it was finally big enough.

"That will work," I whispered to him.

He threw the shovel aside and sat down for a few minutes, trying to catch his breath. He had no idea how long he had been out there, but he knew it was the middle of the night and he was exhausted.

"Come on, let's go," I said, urging him to continue.

He gathered the rest of his energy, and with a snort of a laugh, he got up and made his way back to the little room. We were all still following him, but Travis still remained with Fiona. We watched Nate's every move, and I would guess that if he could see all of us watching him, we surely would be making him nervous.

I could literally see the sweat beads dripping down his forehead as he leaned over and slid his hands under the sheet and what was left of my body. He took a deep breath and carefully picked up my remains with ease. "Oh," he said and relaxed a little more.

"What? I'm too heavy for you?" I said in a joking manner.

"Exactly the opposite. Not what I was expecting at all." he responded as a small smile grew across his face that surprised even him.

All together again, we walked back out of the little room and down the hallway toward the back door of the castle. He stepped outside and began talking to himself. Was it regret? "What am I doing? What will happen if I get caught? I shouldn't be doing this."

Since I was the only one he could hear, I knew it was up to me to encourage him to keep going. I just didn't know what to say. I caught Carla and Adria looking at me, and I think they could tell because as soon as I looked at them, they started encouraging me with the right words.

"Tell him he is doing the right thing," Carla said.

"And that he is helping in more ways than he knows," Adria added.

I said the words to him, but I don't know if he actually heard me. I felt silly repeating what the two of them told me to. He didn't know me, and he couldn't see me. Why would he listen to me anyway?

"Amelia?" I heard my name. "Are you still there?" Nate asked.

"I'm here, Nate," I said back to him. "Don't think I would leave you that easily."

Nate laughed. "I really wish I knew you when you were alive. I think you would have been a spitfire, sassy, strong-willed little girl… I think I would have liked you," he added.

And then I heard him say, "You're the kind of daughter I would like to have one day." He said it more to himself than to me, but then it struck me. Nate was going to be a father. He was going to have a child of his own, and at that moment, I didn't have to think of the right words; they just came to me.

"Nate, you're going to be a great dad," I said. "Your little baby will be the spitting image of you and Carla, and though you may not think it now, you will learn as you go. It will come to you, and you will be able to make an exceptional future for that little girl."

Nate almost tripped and stumbled as he was walking back down the graveyard, and in slight confusion, he asked me, "You know?"

"He knows?" Carla spoke up, shocked.

"Oh, Carla, I wasn't thinking. I shouldn't have said anything," I said as I turned toward her.

"Well, he obviously found out somehow..." said Carla, and I couldn't tell if she was mad or not.

"The pregnancy test. Did you leave it in the cottage bathroom"? Adria asked. "You know they would have searched the cottage up and down."

"Carla, I'm sorry," I said.

"It's okay, Amelia," Carla said sincerely. "I'm glad he knows. While you're at it, you might as well tell him how you know too."

I gave her a questioning look, but she reassured me this was the right thing to do. I turned back to Nate. "Yes, I know. I am Carla's ghost. I've been following her for the last few weeks—I know more than I should," I said and let out a slight laugh of my own.

Nate stopped in his tracks as if realizing something for the first time. "If you're Carla's ghost, you know where she is." It was a statement, not a question.

"Yes," I answered.

Chapter 25

Fiona stayed out by the grave all night, trying not to let the chill or wind bother her. We noticed that she had fallen asleep a couple of times but then would wake suddenly. I could tell she was cold and shivering, and we could all hear her teeth rattle. Fiona sat up and began rubbing her shoulders, trying to get herself warm.

"I wonder why she doesn't go back in the castle," Travis said.

"The castle didn't hold much hope and safety anymore," I replied. "It once had. It must be the last place she wants to go back to."

Just then Fiona began talking. As if Mother was sitting right there, she began telling her all she couldn't hold in any longer.

"How do I go on without you? What do I do about Daddy? I miss you." And she began crying again.

Moments later, wiping more tears from her eyes and when her vision was clear, her eyes started dancing, searching the little cemetery.

"There must be some flowers around here," Fiona said.

There usually were. Fiona must want them to lie on Mother's grave. She got up and walked over to the small gate, and just on the other side was a small bundle of wild flowers. She picked many of them and arranged them into two bouquets. Walking back over to her Mother's grave, she noticed that there was only one newly dug gravesite.

"Where is Amelia's grave?" Fiona said out loud. She turned in a circle to see if there was any sort of headstone close by or any sign that dirt had been loosened for a grave. There was none.

I saw her chest rise and fall faster, and I could almost felt her panic as she realized my grave was not there.

It hit me. "I wasn't buried," I said. "I wasn't buried in 1908. She won't find a gravesite for me. Which means she didn't know my physical body was still in the castle, wasting away."

"Where is Amelia?" We all heard Fiona ask again and again. She was on her knees like a baby, still frantically searching for my grave, and she didn't sound happy.

There was no way for me to tell her, to get the information to her. There was no way for her to know where I was…and through her whole life, she never knew.

"Has Amelia been buried somewhere else? Why would Daddy do that?" Fiona said.

She was beginning to understand that maybe she didn't know the real man that Daddy was. *He seems different now. He's not the same person.*

*****

Nate laid the small bundle down on the grass next to the newly dug hole, and he stepped back. "I wish I could see you," he said. "It would make it so much easier to have a conversation with someone I could see."

"You can find a picture in my room that Mother drew of me. Then you will know what I looked like," I said.

"Amelia, tell me where I can find Carla." he asked.

"Carla will be found when my past has been set free," I said.

"What does that mean?" he asked.

"Set me free from this ghostly journey and the restless road I have been walking. Carla will then be set free also—that is the key to her escape," I said.

"The way to get her freedom is by burying you?" he asked.

"Yes. And you will need the key. Do you have it?" I asked him.

"The castle key? Yes, I have it." Nate responded.

"Place the key somewhere nearby, and then you should head back to the cottage," I explained to him.

Nate rubbed the back of his head and neck. *Is she right?* he thought. *Did Carla, Adria, and Travis need the key to get back all along?*

While Nate was thinking to himself, I turned and started my goodbyes to the other three. If this worked, I should be gone before morning. Carla and Adria hugged me tight. It felt right and comforting just as it had all along, like a piece of home I had been missing all these years. I was a little sad to let them go. They had become like family, and I would miss them dearly. I looked toward Travis and thanked him for helping, but he wasn't letting that slide for a goodbye. He came in and wrapped his arms around all of us.

"Take care, Amelia Gallagher," Travis said.

When they stepped back, there were tears all around. "No tears for me," I said. "I have a feeling I will finally be reunited with my mother."

Smiles appeared on Carla and Adria's face. "You will. I have no doubt," Carla said through quivering lips.

I looked from them back over to Nate and said, "Nate, it's time."

He looked up at the direction my voice would have been coming from. "Okay, let's do this." He picked up the covered bundle and gently placed it inside the hole he had dug. As he stepped back he whispered, "Goodbye, Amelia. May you rest in peace and find all your dreams—let that be your freedom key," he added.

He grabbed the shovel and began piling the dirt back over the white sheet in the hole. I stayed standing next to them all and watched. I became quiet then. Taking it all in, I closed my eyes and tried to imagine a happier time when I was with my mother and my sister.

As Nate kept shoveling, I was starting to feel lighter and lighter. Were my words even coming out of my mouth?

"Where is she?"

Quickly and abruptly, we all turned around looking to where the voice came from.

Carla and Adria's eyes grew wide as they realized. "We're still here trapped in 1908. Fiona's life at the castle is still going on," Adria said.

"This time, right now, is still real time for her," I said. "That's why she can't find my grave."

"Fiona can't find your grave because there was no grave in 1908," Carla said.

"She'll know soon enough." I looked back to everyone feeling more like I was fading. "Find out what happened to the castle," I said as loud as I could. "And don't forget me—I won't forget you."

"We won't," Adria said.

"We promise," said Carla, tears slipping down the sides of her cheeks.

There was a swift, mini jolt, and Carla, Adria, and Travis grabbed each other in a small bear hug. I closed my eyes and began humming a sweet lullaby my mother used to sing to me.

*****

"She's gone," Travis said as he started to unwrap his arms from around the two of the women. The three of them looked up. The grave sites in front of them were covered with grass and weeds, overgrown and not looked after in many years. One was marked Mary Gallagher; the other was not marked. Mysterious as it seemed, it was not to them. They knew it was the resting place of dearest Amelia Gallagher.

"Carla!" Nate shouted.

She flinched and turned in surprise. Nate was on his knees next to the shovel and on the other side of Amelia's grave.

"Nate, Nate. It's you. You can see me? We're back!" Carla screamed.

She ran to him and threw herself in his arms. She snuggled into his chest and let his comfort surround her.

Through their hug he could see Travis and Adria hugging as well.

"We made it back," Travis said. "We didn't need the castle key like I thought."

Nate grabbed Carla by the shoulders and held her out so he could search her face. "Where were you?" he asked.

"We were with Amelia…in 1908. I guess there were questions that only we could find the answers to. The key transported us back to her time."

"We need to get you home and let the others know you are safe," Nate said.

"You can't go back looking like that," Travis said to Nate. "You're covered in dirt and filth, and there will be questions."

Nate looked over the castle property until his eyes landed on the small pond. "I'll go clean up. There are still a few puddles down there," he said, nodding toward the pond.

Nate started walking in that direction and fully expected Carla to follow. When she didn't, he turned back to her. "Are you coming?" he asked.

"I'll be right there," she said.

Carla went back to where they knew Amelia had just been buried and kneeled down next to Amelia's gravesite. "We need to get a tombstone," she said to Adria and Travis.

"Agreed," Adria said.

"We can look into it when we get things settled," Travis said. "We won't forget, and now anyone visiting this insane place will not forget either. They will know of Amelia Gallagher."

"It would be nice if we could clean up this little cemetery too," Adria added.

The three of them headed off toward the castle when they saw Nate had finished up and was heading back up that way too.

Reconvening on the stone steps, they began talking about what they were going to tell everyone. No one would believe the three of them were teleported back in time.

"I think we need to tell Miriam the truth. She knew about the ghost following me," Carla said.

"Fine. And what about Mrs. Layne and Jacob?" Nate asked.

"They are here? My mother is here?" Adria asked.

"Yes. You've been missing a long while. We couldn't not tell them. We got the police involved and called family," Nate was explaining.

"Shit, I don't know what we will tell the police," Carla said.

"They wouldn't look inside the castle for you," Nate said. "They didn't have the key, and they said there was no way you could have gotten in there. That is exactly what we say. You got trapped and couldn't get out."

They all agreed, and on the way back home, they would work out the details. They needed to make sure their stories lined up and that they had the details right.

Carla sat in the front seat; Nate reached over and grabbed her hand and gave it a squeeze. He then pulled it over and kissed the top of her fingers. He reached down and placed his hand gently on top of her stomach.

"Nate, I was going to tell you," Carla said.

"I know, but I think being transported back a hundred years had your mind elsewhere," he said affectionately. "Amelia said it was a girl," he said with a smile and soft, tender eyes.

"I know. I heard her." Carla's eyes were gleaming and joyful. Amelia was right. A baby was a happy occasion, and Carla was going to soak it all in.

*****

When the car pulled up to Miriam's house, Nate turned to them all, questioning to make sure they all had the right story. They hopped out when they noticed Craig was outside starting his own car and hurrying to load a few bags into the back seat.

Craig was too busy to notice the car that had just drove up the gravel path, but when he saw everyone get out of the car, his jaw fell to the floor. "Where have you been?" He was talking to everyone, but it was more directed at Travis.

"It's a long story," Travis said as Craig pulled him into a brotherly hug. "Can we go inside and talk with everyone?"

"Uh, It's not exactly the best time," Craig said, looking around at everyone.

Miriam came rushing out of their house with a bag at her side and a blanket and pillow. "It's baby time."

When Miriam saw the three of them, she burst into tears. "Praise the Lord. You're home." Travis ran over to her to hug and give her support.

She wrapped her arm around his neck. When she pulled back, she hit him in the chest. "I will never forgive you for this, Travis Hart." She doubled over, holding her stomach, and hummed through a contraction.

Travis held onto her, his arms under her shoulders for support. Craig came rushing over to offer his aid as well. "Let's get her to the car," Craig said.

Carla and Adria were standing nearby and came to the car door when Miriam was safely seated. "It's too early," Adria said.

"I started having some cramps this morning. My doctor said to time the contractions, and if they got worse, I should come in. They didn't just get worse—my water broke about ten minutes ago."

"It'll be okay," Carla said encouragingly. "You got this."

"Oh, please don't leave," Miriam said. "Stay in the cottage for a while longer so you can meet the baby. We…" She couldn't finish her sentence as another contraction started and she tensed up from the pain.

"We'll keep everyone updated," Craig finished her sentence and came over to shut her door.

"And we'll have a story for you," Travis said.

Adria's mother came rushing out the door when she realized she recognized the voices she heard. Jacob followed, and soon everyone was embracing with tears streaming down their faces. It was a reunion they didn't know if they would ever get to have.

After Craig and Miriam took off, they all went inside and began telling the story they had anxiously rehearsed. After a few hours of reuniting, hugging and all the questions, Jacob phoned the police, and Officer Doyle said he would be out shortly to ask some questions.

Doyle arrived a half an hour later with one other officer and his pen and notepad. Again, they all recounted the story to the officer just how they had rehearsed it in the car on the way over.

"That castle has been closed off for years," Doyle said, baffled. "I would ask what you were doing up there, but I've already gathered it has meaning to Adria's family."

Jacob really wanted to say some snide remark for not checking inside in the first place, but he decided to keep his mouth shut. They were home now, and there was no use causing a scene.

"It was closed down and locked up when Henry Gallagher went to jail for the death of his wife, Mary Gallagher. How did you get in?" Officer Doyle continued.

Carla and Adria looked at each other with astonishment. Their eyebrows were raised and mouths wide open.

"Through a window," Travis answered.

"If I may ask," Adria said to the officer, "how do you know Henry Gallagher killed his wife?"

"A public record at the station," he said. "Everyone knows about Castle Creet. An eyewitness had come forward after a few weeks of Mr. Gallagher's incoherent demeanor and the accusation of an abandoned child."

"Oh, wow," Carla said.

"He was found packing his bags to leave for America and was arrested immediately and taken into custody," Doyle continued. "He died in jail years later, and the castle became abandoned. When the workers and servants were no longer being paid, they all began to leave, I'm sure to find other means of work."

Both of the girls were in shock. Had they really just found the last piece to the puzzle? An overwhelming peace came over them that neither of them could explain. The puzzle was whole. They had finally found all the answers.

"It's my family castle, you see," Adria began. "You have no idea how much help this information has provided." She wrapped her arm around her mother again.

Chapter 26

Dear Journal,

What a wild ride it has been. Sometimes I don't quite know how I made it through this interesting adventure, and then I think of Amelia and what she went through. She was all alone for a hundred years. Oh, how lonely she must have been. I didn't know Amelia for long but not having her with me anymore has been strange, like someone is constantly missing. I miss Ireland since we've been back home. It seems a part of me was left in the heart of that castle. And I gave a part of my heart to Amelia when I promised we would never forget her, and we never will!

—Carla

One year later

"Miriam, he is so beautiful," Carla said as she watched Miriam bounce a one year old up and down on her knee. "Thank you again for inviting us back. I'm so glad I get to see this little dude again."

"We are so glad you made if over for another visit," Miriam said.

"After you brought him home from the hospital, I didn't think he could get any cuter, but I was wrong." Carla leaned over and tickled the little one's belly.

"He is almost walking. He's pulling up on everything. I just can't believe how fast the first year has gone by. And look at your little one," Miriam said.

"She was an unexpected surprise right when we needed her," Carla said. "Nate has been the best father. He's definitely a natural, but I guess working with kids all day does that to you."

"I so wish we could have made the wedding. How did everything go?" Miriam asked. "Obviously I've seen pictures, but tell me more about it."

"It was small but very beautiful. We had all our closest friends and family. Jacob ended up officiating the wedding, and he did such a good job. It's definitely a day no one forgets, you know? We were lucky there were no mishaps and everything pretty much went as planned."

"Travis did say Jacob did an excellent job. Little bit funny but all practical. How was Travis's speech?" Miriam asked.

"As you would except, goofy as always," Carla replied. "But he had everyone laughing, and I guess that's what one expects from a best man speech."

"I'm glad he was able to make it," Miriam said.

"He sure has been a good friend to Nate," said Carla.

"Travis enjoys Nate's friendship too," Miriam said. "I'm glad they have connected the way they have."

"I think he has most of his things packed up, right? He's leaving next week for Boise?" Carla asked.

"Yes, grown up and moving to a different country," said Miriam, giggling with a fake cry.

"He truly has made Adria so happy. It was hard when she lost Carter," began Carla. "Travis has brought a sense of belonging back to Adria. She needed that."

"I am happy for them. I don't think I've ever seen him like this. He would give up everything for her," Miriam was saying. "Has Adria gotten to visit her grandmother yet?"

"She is there now. Otherwise, she would be here with us. She and her grandmother have had a good relationship too since everything happened last year, and I think it was good we told her the truth too. I think in her own way, she knew and believed all of what we went through like maybe she had heard it before. I'm not sure how to explain it."

"It's a crazy story for sure. One I had a hard time believing at first too, but you guys came here to figure it out, and you did. It was a puzzle with a bunch of missing pieces, and now it's whole," said Miriam.

"It seems like just yesterday we were sitting in that cottage, barely knowing each other, when all this happened," Carla said. "You haven't had any trouble renting it out, have you?"

"Nope, people are just as eager for their little getaways as they were before." Miriam was saying. "We had a few weeks where we kept it pretty quiet, but after that, we haven't had any problems."

"Good, there wasn't a lot that happened that would make people be suspicious of the cottage anyways," Carla said as Miriam's baby boy started to make some fuss.

"He is starting to get tired. It's about nap time," Miriam said. "I'm going to take him in his room and nurse him. Make yourself at home."

Miriam got up with Samuel and turned him to her shoulder. Rubbing his back, she made her way down the hall to his room, humming a familiar lullaby.

When Carla was left alone, she decided it would be a good time to put her little one down for a nap too. Maybe she would even sneak in a nap as well. Wanting to be in more comfortable clothes anyway, she peeked into the baby's room and whispered to Miriam that she was headed back over to the cottage.

Carla walked the distance between the house and the cottage with her own little one in her arms. When she got to the little door, she turned around and took in her surroundings, letting the cool air hit her face and listening to the songs of the chirping birds. It was nice to be back.

Ireland had become such a part of her life.

She opened the door, and Nate was sitting on the couch reading a book. "I think it's time for her nap," Carla said.

"A nap or *a nap*?" Nate winked at her.

"Stop it, you!" Carla said sarcastically.

"Okay, seriously, do you want me to lay her down?" Nate asked.

"I'll do it. You can help if you'd like. Will you grab the little blanket behind your head?" They headed to the back bedroom where her little bassinet was. Carla set her down and lay the blanket across her perfect little body as she nestled into the warmth and comfort.

Nate leaned in and gave the baby a little kiss before heading back out to the living room. Carla began talking to the sweet baby girl and humming the same lullaby Miriam had been just a few minutes earlier.

"You've changed my life forever, little one." She rubbed the back of her hand down the side of the baby's face. She tucked the baby in and made her cozy.

"Sweet dreams…my beautiful Amelia."

About the Author

Meagan Hollingsworth moved to southern Idaho a little over two years ago with her husband and two small boys, ages seven and three. She has a background in dance and has coached competitive teams for thirteen years back in her hometown, Lebanon, Oregon. Activities she enjoys include reading, traveling, and outdoor adventures with her family.

Printed in the USA
CPSIA information can be obtained
at www.ICGtesting.com
LVHW091929170524
780600LV00001B/73